BLACK HEART

FIVE

FROM *USA TODAY* BESTSELLING AUTHORS

SARA CATE

RACHEL LEIGH

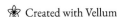

Trigger Warning

Five is a Dark Reverse Harem Romance that contains explicit sexual content, graphic language, and situations that some readers may find uncomfortable, such as murder, torture, and abuse. The Black family men aren't the only rough, controlling, crazy ones anymore. Enjoy!

One

Iris

"Don't leave my sight for a second," Baron whispers with his lips next to my ear. I can feel his hand resting at the small of my back, and I breathe in the familiar scent of his cologne as he opens the door for me.

Entering the seedy strip club, I wait to let my eyes adjust to the darkness, but the pleasant smell of the man standing next to me is overpowered by the very unpleasant stench of cheap air freshener and cigarette smoke.

The moment we're inside, I feel the eyes of every man in the building on me, and the hand that was touching my back is now protectively clutching my waist.

"Not for a second," he growls.

"Yes, babe. I heard you the first time."

He's so possessive, which is odd for a guy who has to share his girlfriend with his dad and brother.

We walk together toward the bar and squeeze into a narrow opening between men staring slack-jawed at the woman dancing naked on stage. Baron leans over the bar, acting casual as he gets the attention of the red-headed bartender with big fake tits and caked-on makeup.

Just as she spots him, her head perks up, and she smiles, sauntering over with interest in her eyes.

"What can I get for you, baby?" she asks, and I clench my jaw.

"Where's Gino?" he shouts over the music, ignoring her question.

She presses her tits together and leans toward him, completely oblivious to the scowling woman on his arm. "You don't want a drink? On the house."

Stern-faced Baron flares his nostrils and shakes his head.

"Gino."

A look of disappointment washes over her face as her shoulders slump and she backs away. "His office is upstairs. Want me to show you?" The way this woman is eye-fucking my boyfriend like he's a hot meal she can eat up is really starting to piss me off. I mean, I get it. With those warm brown eyes, tall built frame, and expensive taste, any woman would throw herself at Baron Black, but he's *mine*, and I've never been one to share.

And no, the irony is not lost on me.

"I think we got it," I snap, grabbing his arm and yanking him toward the stairs. He sneaks a sideways glance at me as we walk, and before we reach the other side of the dark room, he draws me close and presses his mouth to my ear.

"Iris Black, are you jealous?"

"More like murderous," I reply in frustration, as my blood continues to boil. I ignore his taunts and continue toward the second floor.

"Well, I hate to break it to you, but the bartender is not the person we're here to kill." His hand cups my ass halfway up the stairs, giving it a firm squeeze that makes me yelp, and I turn to swat him away.

He holds his hands up with a look of shock on his face. "Why are you mad at me? What did I do?"

"She was flirting with you right in front of me and you know it."

"But I didn't do anything. I didn't even smile at her."

As we reach the top, I spin on him, pressing my hands onto my hips. "Fine. I'll go down there and ask any one of those guys for directions, and let's see how you react."

He snatches my waist, pulling me against him. "Not funny."

"Exactly." Shoving my hands against his chest, I try to push away, but he won't let me budge. "I don't like to see women drooling over you. It makes me angry."

"You know it's fucking hypocritical to be jealous when other women talk to me...all things considered." When he lifts his brow at me, tightening his grip around my waist, I know he's right. It's not fair, but I don't care.

"I never agreed to share you, and don't even act like that's the same thing," I say with a roll of my eyes, managing to slide out of his grip. "Let's just get this over with. It smells in here."

Just as I lift my hand to knock on the office door, he grabs me again. "Oh, so you can sleep with my dad and my brother, but I can't fuck other women—"

I slam my hand against his mouth. Something violent comes over me just at the mere mention of another woman touching him. "Don't you even fucking say that, Baron, or I swear..."

Tearing my hand away, he lifts me up and presses me

against the wall, attacking my mouth with his. I am over-whelmed with desire as he slips his tongue past my teeth and steals every thought from my head. This is what Baron does—he inundates my senses until he is all I see, all I feel, all I know.

"You're so hot when you're angry," he mumbles against my lips.

"And you make me angry all the time."

"Now you know why."

His hands lift my dress, and he grinds against me with my back pressed flat against the wall. My body lights up in excitement as his hard length slides roughly against my hip, and I glance around. It's dark enough in this empty hallway that we could get away with this right here. Not the weirdest or most public place we've done it.

Just as his fingers start to fumble with his zipper, we hear a cry coming from the other side of the door. Baron and I both freeze.

Another scream.

Then it sounds as if furniture is flipped over and some-thing lands hard on the floor. It's definitely the sound of someone getting their ass handed to them in the office behind the door, and since we are here to discreetly take care of the sleazy owner, we can't afford any complications.

In a rush, we burst through the door. The two people in the room both stare up at us in shock. A young woman, who appears to be a dancer, is lying on the floor in nothing but pasties and a thong, her makeup tear-streaked down her face. The man standing on the other side is old and fat with thick, greasy black hair combed over his head. His small dick hangs out of his unzipped pants.

"You must be Gino," Baron says to him, moving to retrieve his gun from the holster at his back.

"Who the fuck are you?" Gino snarls at us.

Quickly, I help the girl up and notice the red, swollen welts all over her face. Memories of Donny Wright and the way he punched me in that seedy motel room two years ago make my blood boil all over again.

After ushering her out the door, I put a hand on Baron's chest and shoot him a silent, pleading expression. He returns his gun to his back and clenches his jaw. If I was with Silas or Gabriel, they would easily let me deal with this asshole, but Baron is a little more resistant. Maybe he's still harboring guilt over the way things went down at the Inferno, but he's always trying to protect me and never wants to let me get my hands dirty.

Except for when our jobs involve slimy abusers like this asshole.

"Get the fuck out of my office!" the man shouts as he charges toward us.

I slam my fist hard against his fat face, feeling the flesh of his cheek split with the impact. He barely has time to react before I crash my knee into his gut, and when he barrels over in pain, I drive the pointed tip of my high heel into his junk.

Gabriel would have loved to watch me do that, and I'm sure he'd really love to watch me torture this piece of shit, but that's not what we're here to do. We're here to make this guy dead as a doornail and to make it look like natural causes. The client paid extra for that. I'm assuming because he has a motive and doesn't want the cops on his back, but that's not really my problem at this point.

While Gino is still writhing on the ground, I give him a few more swift kicks to his rib cage, feeling them crack against my shoe. He cries out in pain, sniveling against the stained carpet.

"It's a shame you have to be so rough with your girls, Mr. Azira. You can't handle so much action. You know... because of your heart condition."

"What the fuck are you talking about, you bitch?" He groans, and from the corner of my eye, I see Baron move toward him, but I put a hand up to stop him. Holding my palm open, I wait for Baron to retrieve the syringe from the inner pocket of his jacket and place it in my hand. Popping the cap, I kneel down next to Gino. He's struggling to stand up, his flaccid dick still hanging from his pants.

"What the hell is that? Who the fuck are you?"

I don't bother answering his questions. He won't have any more in a moment. "You're a real piece of shit," I say as I plunge the syringe into his chest and empty the contents into his bloodstream. It's a solution of Gabriel's own design, a formula of epinephrine and aconitine that stops the heart in seconds. Gino swats at me, and I crack my knuckles hard against his face again, sending him backward where he lands with a gurgled moan.

Putting the cap back on the syringe, I stand up and hide it in my bra, so we can discard it at home. Then, I let out a short, winded cry, shaking my right hand where the knuckles are starting to ache. I kick him again because it feels good.

"Asshole!" I shriek at the gross, lifeless heap of wasted skin on the carpet.

Two arms wrap swiftly around my midsection and lift me off the floor, spinning me until I'm facing the window. I let out a yelp when Baron's lips press against my neck.

"I told you you're hot when you're angry, and fuck... that was so hot."

He nibbles hungrily on my neck and the lobe of my ear, sending chills all over my body.

"I'm glad you enjoyed that. My hand hurts like hell."

"Let me distract you," he says, and I have to hold on to the windowsill as he hikes my dress up above my hips. My body reacts eagerly, the adrenaline from the kill turning from excitement to a ravenous hunger.

"We have to be fast," I gasp when I hear him pulling down his zipper.

Without a word, he yanks my hips back and lines up the head of his cock, sliding in swiftly and knocking the air from my lungs. The music from downstairs echoes through the dim space as he grunts with each brutal thrust.

"Wet for me already," he says in a raspy tone. "Is it from the kill? Baby, you were made for this job."

I can't answer between my moans from being pounded from behind, but he's wrong. It wasn't killing Gino that turned me on. It was him—it's always him.

When his hand snakes around to my throat, he pulls me upright, so my back is flush against him, and I smile as my body reacts with pleasure. I feel Baron everywhere, consuming and owning my body. And I love it.

"Look what you did," he growls into my ear before turning my face, so I can see the man lying lifeless on the floor. "Look at what my girl did."

"He deserved it," I reply breathlessly.

"You're fucking right he did." He bites hard on the flesh of my neck as he fucks me until we're both clutching for something to hold on to as we come, a quick but intense orgasm that leaves us hot and panting.

His forehead rests between my shoulder blades as we try to catch our breaths. "I think you were made for me, Iris. Made for us." His lips press against the skin of my back, and I can't help but smile because this is the same guy who I thought would either hate me forever or kill me.

Now he's the first one to tell me how much he loves me every day.

Once we've both recovered enough to stand up on our own, I pull my dress down and clean up the mess he made between my legs, before we make our way to the door.

And just like that, we waltz right out the front door of the club, leaving Gino Azira's ugly dead body in his office. We don't worry about cameras or witnesses because, as I have learned after two years with these guys, the Blacks are ghosts. We don't exist. Public records have been erased, and there are no traces of our existence.

Silas has had to remind me of this many times since I came here. He hates to see me worry, but how could I not? They are my world, and as I clutch Baron's hand across the center console of the car, my heart feeling like it might explode, I realize that I couldn't bear to lose them. Not even one.

Two

ris

Bent over the sink, I brush vigorously at my teeth. Rinse, spit, repeat. When I stand upright, I grab a towel beside me then gasp at the reflection in the mirror when I realize I'm not alone. "Gabriel! I didn't even know you came in here." My heart rate steadies and warmth radiates through me when he wraps his arms around my waist from behind.

"Since when do you startle so easily?" His chin rests on my shoulder as we watch each other in the mirror. Most women would panic if they found this man in their bathroom—with his lip piercing, tattoos, and crow black hair that matches his pupils. Not me. I love every inch of my crazy man. Fresh wounds, scars, and all.

My head rests back, nuzzling between the nape of his neck and his shoulder. "I didn't sleep well. I guess I'm just a little on edge this morning."

"Of course you are. It was what...like one o'clock in the

morning when you came in last night?" His tone is a mocking one.

My head lifts, and I look at him again through the mirror. "I had a job. You knew that."

His expression is bleak. I'm well aware of Gabriel's jealous side. Even if he is on board with my relationships with Silas and Baron, I don't think he'll ever stop wanting me all to himself.

"I know. Just didn't expect you to be out that late." Gabriel sweeps my hair to the side and presses his lips on my collarbone. My neck slants instinctively, and my eyes close as I chase the feelings he's bringing upon me. "Where did you sleep last night?" he asks through kisses on my damp skin.

My eyes open and I straighten my neck to look at him again. "My bed. You know that I need my space after jobs like that." It's true. I've become really damn good at what I do, but it never gets any easier. Watching a life end is hard. Being the reason that life ends is harrowing. I've learned a lot in two years. I don't vomit at the sight of a dead body anymore. I don't hesitate when my finger is on the trigger—blade, rope, or whatever I use that day. Most importantly, I don't empathize with the hit. They are not victims. These targets are ruthless people who have done far worse than I could ever do.

"And Baron? Where'd he sleep?"

Pulling back, I spin around to face Gabriel. "Hey. What's with you?" My voice is calm and comforting. I know that's what Gabriel needs right now. He's needy, to say the least. I place a hand on his cheek, needing him to feel me and know that in this moment, right now, I am his.

"Last night was my night. You begged for that fucking job, and because of it, I slept alone...again."

Shit. I completely forgot I promised Gabriel we would lie in bed together all night and sleep in this morning. He looks forward to those nights. Part of me thinks he longs for the attention because he's missed a lifetime of it.

"I'm so sorry. It slipped my mind."

Gabriel slithers out from my reach and goes to leave through the open bathroom door. "Wait." I grab his arm. He looks over his shoulder, smoldering—a look that's not thrown at me often. I untuck the corner of my towel, letting it fall to the floor. Creeping up behind him, I wrap my arms around his waist. "We've still got today."

He turns slowly, taking a step back and drinking in my naked body, starting at my parted legs and bare pussy, then to my perky breasts and skating up to my eyes. I bite the corner of my lip, knowing he likes what he sees. "Oh yeah? What do you have in mind?"

I eat up the space he left between us and slide my hands up his black T-shirt, feeling the warmth of his skin beneath my fingertips. "You've been wanting to blindfold me. Maybe I'll let you."

His eyes widen. "You said the idea of being blindfolded was terrifying."

My fingers rim the waistband of his pants, and I lick my lips. "I messed up. I owe you."

"My room. Five minutes." He smacks my ass, really fucking hard.

What the hell did I just agree to? Fortunately, I trust Gabriel. I trust him with my body and my heart. I know he won't hurt me, even if enforcing pain is his second language. I'm the only girl Gabriel has ever been with, and I like to think I taught him everything he knows, but the truth is, Gabriel teaches me. Sex is never dull with him. It's rough, yet passionate. Heart-pounding and so fucking satisfying.

~

The music coming from Gabriel's room is so loud I can feel it echoing through my body as I make my way down the hall. I grip my robe tightly around my waist as I pass by Baron's bedroom, knowing that he's probably still sound asleep after our late night. There's a part of me that wants to peek into his room, just to catch a glimpse of his peacefulness, but the other part knows he'll wake up and ask me to join him.

It took some time for all of us to get into a routine, but I think we're all handling it quite well. Even Gabriel. He has his moments, much like today, but it's easy to make it up to him. Gabriel is much different than Baron and Silas. While they are more passive, Gabriel is possessive.

When I reach his room, I don't bother knocking. I turn the handle and push the door open. He's in the corner, messing with something on his shelf that displays his most prized possessions—his weapons of choice. The room is dark, aside from a dim red light coming from a lamp on his desk. It gives the space a very gothic feel, which is a vibe I've become accustomed to with Gabriel, and one that I've grown to like.

With each of these men, I'm able to be a different version of myself. With Baron, I'm driven and focused. He pushes me to be the best, teaches me to be independent and strong. With Silas, I melt into a puddle of mush. His touch alone sets my soul on fire. He's a man of few words, but the way our bodies react to one another speaks volumes. Gabriel is my wild one. He brings out a nurturing side of me I didn't know I had. He's always full of surprises, but he's also one of the gentlest men I've ever known. Which no one would believe if they saw the way he treats others. He's only like that with me. It makes me feel special—all my guys make me feel special.

"Lie down. Make yourself comfortable," Gabriel says, without even lifting his head from whatever he's doing over there. The room smells of sandalwood incense mixed with a stench of leather. I go to untie my silk robe from around my waist, but Gabriel stops me with a glance over his shoulder. "Leave that on." He reaches out and turns the volume of his speaker down a tad, though it's still loud enough to send a rumble of vibration through the room.

"Um, okay." I say it as more of a statement than a question. Since when are clothes wanted during sex? I'm not sure if I even want to know what he has planned. I toss a few of the extra pillows off the bed and drop down on my back. "What are you doing over there?" I ask, crossing my ankles and tucking my hands behind my head.

"You said you owe me. Don't worry, babe. When we're done here, I'll be the one owing you." The sound of his voice is so smooth and full of confidence. It's sexy as hell and sends a shiver between my thighs.

Fear can cause a body to react in many ways. With me, it gives me a rush of adrenaline and turns me on. Gabriel knows this, and I have no doubt he's using it to his advantage. It's one of the reasons that we have such amazing chemistry. He reads my body like a book and knows exactly what to do to get my blood pumping.

I'm watching him intently as he drops his pants and pulls his shirt over his head. With his back still facing me, I take in the rigid scars on his spine and the gauze bandage on his side that covers a knife wound from a few nights ago. I was so angry at him that night. Gabriel is always so careful, but he let his guard down, and in a moment of weakness, he was stabbed. In the end, he made the kill and justice was served on behalf of our client, but it still shouldn't have happened. Part of me worries that I'm the reason he's been getting more relaxed and isn't as focused. I'm in his head and a constant distraction.

"Close your eyes," Gabriel demands as he turns around. I do as I'm told, sinking farther into the bed. My head rests on a pillow covered with a black satin case. My pulse is already racing in anticipation of what's coming.

I can feel him draw closer—hear the sound of his heady breaths. His fingers run along my jawline and I struggle to keep my eyes shut. I want to see his lust-filled gaze staring back at me. He gently lifts my head and I hold it in place as he wraps a piece of silk fabric around my head, covering my eyes. "Nothing crazy, Gabriel. I mean it."

He doesn't respond. Instead, he climbs on top of me. His legs straddle my waist with his knees pressed against the mattress on either side of me. I reach my hand out, wanting to stroke his cock, but he takes a hold of my wrist and places my hand at my side. I can feel his breaths hit my neck as he leans closer. "Do you trust me?" he says in a raspy whisper.

"Yes." I don't even hesitate with my response. I do trust Gabriel.

"Good. I need you to stay very still. I will move you as I need to. Your body is mine and I'm in control."

I don't like the sound of this. But I don't tell him that. Instead, I lie there as stiff as a board, my body his oyster.

Gabriel unties my robe as he sits with little pressure on top of me. A cool breeze hits my stomach when he pushes the sides of my robe down, exposing me to him. "God, you're so fucking sexy, Iris," he purrs, a smooth sound that's music to my ears. His fingers trail up my side, leaving goosebumps in their wake.

I flinch when something cold hits my breast—something *too* cold. Metal maybe? Steel? "What is that?" I ask him, remaining completely still.

Once again, he doesn't respond. He just moves whatever object he has in his hand slowly down my chest until he reaches my stomach. "Is that a knife?" It has to be. I mean, this is Gabriel we're talking about. Of course it is.

"Gabriel, I swear to—"

He silences me with a kiss. A kiss so hard it's painful, but it is a beautiful pain. I crave more, but out of fear of getting sliced, I don't move. I do as I was told and remain still with my hands pressed firmly at my sides.

He tastes so good—sweet and bitter at the same time, like cinnamon.

When he lifts up, he leaves me breathless and wanting more of him. "Just fuck me, Gabriel."

I want to scream at him when he doesn't say anything or give me what I want. Instead, he pushes the sleeves of my robe down. "Lean forward," he says, elevating my body with his free hand.

I lift up, allowing him to slide the sleeves down my arms until I'm lying on top of the robe. I open my eyes, but all I see is darkness. I can't even make out the outline of Gabriel's body. "Let me touch you," I beg. It's agonizing not being able to. I've never been good at obedience, and the more I lie here being told not to move, the more I want to.

The cold metal meets my side. A shiver runs through me that has me instinctively sucking in my stomach. "Don't. Move," Gabriel urges.

My heart begins pounding in my chest. My thighs

clench as tingles course through my entire body. I'm so demented for being turned on by this.

There's a small prick of pain, but it's not really even painful. It's almost...satisfying. A warm ooze of liquid streams down the side of my ass. *Blood.* I'm not sure if it's the fact that this is bringing Gabriel pleasure that turns me on, or the fact that my fucked-up body is enjoying it.

The slight sting diminishes immediately when Gabriel presses his lips to my bleeding skin. I let out a subtle moan when I feel his mouth leave me. "Does that hurt?" His voice is gruff and sexy, sending a new wave of emotions through me.

"No," I tell him. Oddly enough, it doesn't hurt at all. "I want to see." There's a sick part of me that wants to watch him kiss the cut he carved into me. To see him feast on the blood that he brought out of my body.

Gabriel's body slides up mine. I feel his exhale hit the side of my face. I want to grab him and devour him and beg him to pleasure me—but I don't. I lie here at his mercy as his tongue slides across my bottom lip. A metallic tang seeps into my mouth as I taste the blood on his lips.

"Gabriel," I hum. "Please." My back arches, my insides burning with desire. "Just fuck me."

The tip of the blade trails along my jaw, and I freeze. "Gabriel," I say slowly, holding my breath, fearful of making one wrong move.

"Trust me?" he asks again, still moving the point of the knife until it finds my neck, pressed firmly against my jugular.

"I don't... I..." I hesitate with a stutter to my words. "Yes, I trust you."

He won't hurt me. He's careful and in complete control. I do trust him.

"Did you know I got my first pocketknife when I was nine years old?" Gabriel talks as he continues moving the blade down my body, taking care not to pierce my skin. My breath becomes shallow when he lifts up and slides it down my left breast. "It was like fucking Christmas. I spent an entire year learning how to switch, flip, and slice with that thing. Sharpened it every night. Slept with it. I'm the master of my own art. Knives are my weapon of choice, and I have more knowledge than swordsmen." Gabriel leans close, his mouth ghosting my ear. "You're smart to trust me, Iris. I'd never hurt you."

"I know you wouldn't." My voice cracks and vibrates in my throat. "I believe you."

Gabriel kisses me, hard. I can't help myself; my arms lift and wrap around him. My nails dig so deep into his shoulder blades that I know I pierced his skin. I still can't see, but I don't need to. All I need is to feel him. Our tongues tangle in a mess of passion and my clit throbs in agony, wanting more. *Needing* more. "Now?" I ask through breaths of kisses.

Gabriel shakes his head and retreats. His fingers pinch at my sides as he flips me over onto my stomach. "Get on your knees," he demands. I love this side of him. The one that takes control and doesn't give in to me, no matter how much I beg.

I'm on all fours, my forehead resting against the pillow when Gabriel brings the knife back out. I know, because I can feel it trail down my spine, scratching my skin and leaving behind a dull burning feeling. It's not cutting me, just grazing the surface. My back arches again, my ass on full display as he kneels behind me. Shivers waterfall down my spine as he carves out something with the blade on the surface of my skin.

With his free hand, Gabriel slides a finger inside of me from behind. Moving it in and out as he continues to use the knife like it's his own personal paintbrush—my body his canvas.

He adds another finger and digs deep inside of me, twisting and turning. Poking and prodding as if he's searching for that spot that makes my body twitch. When he finds it, I gasp. Afraid to move, but not sure I'll be able to stay still if he keeps pumping his fingers like that. "Gabriel," I cry out, "I can't stay still. Move the knife."

He doesn't stop. He just keeps driving his fingers inside of me like he's injecting me with his own personal poison. Tears stream down my cheeks as I fight the urge to come around his fingers, trying to stay as still as I possibly can with a knife pressed to my back.

"Trust me, baby," he says—and I want to, I do, but I'm scared. I'm so fucking turned on and so damn terrified.

His fingers slide out and I breathe a sigh of relief, but I want them back inside of me at the same time.

I gasp when his dick lines up with my entrance, his head presses in while his piercing teases my sensitive skin. "You're killing me here, Gabriel. One or the other. Fuck me or put the knife down."

Is that what I want? I don't think so. I'm so aroused by the innate object that could potentially end me.

The blade lifts, but only for a second as he slams his cock inside of me. He lets out an airy groan, and I use this moment to rock into him, until the blade is right back on me. He pushes harder and faster, not letting up as the blade trails my lower back. One wrong move and it will slice me.

He feels so good inside me. I'm almost positive that his cock was molded just for my pussy. If any other woman dares to try and touch it, I'll be the one doing the cutting. Gabriel is mine. This dick is mine.

I feel the blade leave me and a loud thud on the floor leads me to believe he's tossed it aside. That assumption is confirmed when both of his hands palm my waist and he thrusts at lightning speed. "Oh, fuck," I whimper. My fingers curl around the satin case on the pillow, squeezing tightly as my blood begins pumping faster. Heat radiates through me, my walls clench, squeezing him tightly. Proof of my orgasm pools around his cock, but he's not finished yet.

Gabriel moves one hand and brings it to my face, loosening the blindfold. I think he's going to untie it, but instead, he pushes it down around my throat and gets a firm grip, causing my head to jerk back. "Did you miss me last night?" he grumbles in a low rasp.

"Yes," I say as the blindfold tightens around my neck, leaving just enough room that I can still breathe.

"I missed you, too, baby."

Gabriel picks up his pace, and I can feel his head swell inside of me. "I'm gonna come inside of you, Iris."

I don't say anything to stop him. I'm on the pill, and it won't be the first or last time, though we try to stay cautious.

"Fuck. I'm coming," he tells me as he thrusts a couple more times before relaxing.

The blindfold hangs freely around my neck as I drop down onto my stomach, Gabriel cloaking my body with his. "That was fucking intense. We should do it more often."

I let out an airy chuckle. "No. No, we should not."

"Oh, come on. You liked it a little bit."

I lift my body to roll over, and Gabriel does the same,

allowing me to move beneath him. Once I'm on my back and he's lying on top of me, I kiss his lips. "Maybe a little. I am curious to see what you drew on my back."

"You've been branded, baby. You're mine forever." He winks, and the look alone sends another wave of shivers through me. A thousand years could pass and I would still get these intense feelings that Gabriel gives me. "Let's get some ice on your back."

He goes to push himself up, but I stop him by throwing my arms around him. "Wait. What is it? The branding?"

"Same as mine." He points to the small heart under his left eye. "We match. Yours will fade, but I'll always know it's there." He leans down for one more kiss before hopping off the bed to go get me some ice while I clean myself up.

Three

ris

Baron and Gabriel are sitting in silence at the dining room table when I come down for dinner. They're both staring at their phones, and I pause in the doorway, where neither of them can see me. For a moment, I just admire them. Gabriel is laughing at a video and Baron is scowling at whatever he's reading.

Just before I walk into the room, I notice Baron glance up at his brother. It's just a split-second movement, but I catch the way he looks at him. There's something contemplative about it, as if he wanted to say something to Gabriel but decided not to. One second later, his attention is back on his phone, and the moment is gone.

Baron and Gabriel don't really talk much. When I first came to this house, there was so much silence between these walls—except, of course, for the guy Gabriel was torturing in the kitchen. As for conversations between these brothers and their dad, nothing.

I like to think I brought life into this house, but just once I wish I could see them being brothers...without me around. I can't possibly be the glue holding it all together. Can I?

"Where's your dad?" I ask, walking into the room. They both look up from their phones, and I stay on the opposite side of the table to keep things neutral.

"His office, I think," Baron answers, glancing toward the closed door. I hate when Silas tries to work through dinner, the only part of the day where I get to have all three of them together. It's those moments where I feel less like a girl living with her three assassin boyfriends and more like we're a family. I mean, I'm not looking for *The Brady Bunch* here, but I never really had a family. It was just me and my dad—and my bodyguards. We spent holidays in Bali and the Riviera, as if that made up for the fact that we were never that family around the Christmas tree with Hallmark moments at Thanksgiving.

Now I have a real family, three people who would literally do anything for me, and as unconventional as we are, it's what I've always wanted.

So, Silas isn't getting out of this.

Marching over to his office door, I don't even bother knocking. Walking right in, I stride up to his desk and place my palms against the old wood surface. He's staring at his computer, looking so puzzled he's going to create a permanent crease in his forehead. Not that Silas doesn't wear his age well. In his late forties, my man has aged like a fine wine. I never thought I'd be into older guys, but that streak of white in his hair does things to me.

"Take a break and come eat dinner with us," I say, as if I have any power over this man. Well, I do have power over him, but it involves the space between my legs, and I'm too hungry for actual food to whip out that weapon right now.

He glances away from the screen but doesn't relax his expression, which means something is actually wrong. Internal alarms go off in my head, and I stand upright. "Silas, what is it?"

"It's nothing." He fakes a calm expression and reaches for me. "Go eat, Iris. I'll be there in a moment."

"No. I can tell when something is up, so tell me."

Silas takes his job as the patriarch of our family very seriously. He takes all the worry, all the responsibility, all the liability on himself, and he carries these burdens alone. It's what I love about him while also being the one thing that drives me crazy. Silas sees me as his girlfriend, yes, but he treats me like one of his kids, constantly shielding me from the darker side of our business. I can help him make deals with new clients and murder in cold blood, in the field, but when it comes to the real things we have to be concerned about, he keeps me in the dark.

"Baby, it's nothing." He stands from his chair and rounds his desk, taking me by the hand, and pulls my body flush against his. With an authoritative touch at my chin, he tilts my face up until I'm staring at him. Then he closes the distance, kissing me gently. He's being tender, not something Silas does often, and I know he's doing it to distract me from whatever I was just nagging him about—and it's working.

"You seem tense," I say, resting my face against his chest. There is nothing quite like the safety I feel pressed against him. As he engulfs me in his strong arms, I know there's not a thing that could harm me here. "I could help you with it. Whatever it is."

"I told you, it's nothing."

I lean back and look up at him. "We're supposed to be a team. Let me help. I hate seeing you so stressed."

"I'm always going to be stressed, Iris. It's part of the job. Keeping you and the boys safe will always be my first priority, but you know..." He nips at my neck and nibbles my ear. "You could always help by relieving some of my stress later on."

A surge of anger courses through me, and I shove him away. He doesn't even have the good sense to look shocked. Instead, he glares at me as if I'm the one who fucked up.

"I'm not your stress-relief whore."

When I try to pull away, he snatches me by the arm and drags me closer. "I thought you liked being my whore." His voice is deep and cold, and it sends chills straight to my treacherous pussy, which lights up like a damn Christmas tree at the sound of his harsh commands.

"I do," I bark back. "But I'm not talking about sex, Silas. I'm talking about being your—"

"My what?" With both hands gripping my arms, he has me right where he wants me, at his mercy. Clenching my jaw, I challenge his ruthless gaze with one of my own. "My girlfriend? My wife?"

My eyes roll instantly at his accusation. I'm not some basic bitch who's going to get caught up on the whole idea of marriage. Yes, I took their last name, but that wasn't about marriage. It was about family. I'm a Black by virtue, and I don't need a fucking white dress and certificate to make it official.

No, I'm not his wife. I'm way fucking more than that—to all of them.

He's taunting me on purpose. Teasing me to make me angry, so I'll act out, and he can punish me. It's so fucking obvious, but Silas Black isn't as sneaky as he thinks. Because

I know him so well, I also know this is his way of deflecting. He's trying to rev me up, so he doesn't have to answer the question I posed first.

What is he not telling me?

Why won't he let me in?

"Your partner, Silas. I'm not talking as your girlfriend, or your little girl, or your *wife.*" I put a little more dramatic emphasis on the last one to remind him how unimportant that is to me. "But I do love you. And that counts for something." I reach up and brush my fingers through his hair.

Suddenly, he softens. He can't argue with that. I'm sending him all the signs that I don't want to be tossed over his knee tonight—although that is fun. What I want right now is a promise that he won't keep secrets from me to protect me, and that's far more important.

Letting out a hefty sigh, he leans back and rests his ass against his desk, running his hold on my arms down to my fingers. Holding them firmly in his hand, he looks at me with the same expression of worry he wore when I walked in. Then, he finally speaks.

"When I said it was nothing, I meant it. I just picked up a new job, and everything about it checks out. There's not a red flag to be found in the case."

"So, what's the problem?"

"I don't know. Something about it just feels wrong."

"It feels wrong? Why?"

He shrugs. "That's ridiculous, right? I've combed over every detail. The client checks out. The money transferred without a problem. His intel is solid, and for all intents and purposes, the mark should be easy money."

"But something doesn't feel right."

His gaze drifts upward, locking onto mine, and we connect in this moment because I understand what he is saying. He's worried without reason, something a parent does. Something I can't help with at all. Which is why he spared telling me. And the helplessness I feel is annoying, so maybe I would be better as a stress-relief whore at the moment, since there's not a thing I could do or tell Silas to make this worry go away.

"So, decline the job. Go with your gut."

He shakes his head. "Gabriel already knows about it."

I let out my own heavy sigh at this news. Gabriel doesn't like the word *no* very much, and once he knows about a job, he doesn't hand over control easily. If he's already on it, then there really is no going back.

"Why don't you go with him?" I ask.

He levels a glare at me that I translate immediately into *yeah right.* These two men were cut from the same cloth... or stone, really. They're both stubborn, strong-willed, and arrogant as fuck. They can share a woman just fine, but a job? Recipe for disaster.

"Want me to go—"

"No," he snaps, cutting me off. "I'll send Baron with him. He has better instincts."

"Good plan. See? Everything is fine. You're overworked and overthinking." I wrap my arms around him and nuzzle close to him, taking another hit of that Silas comfort I love so much. "I know exactly what would make you feel better."

He arches an eyebrow at me, and I can't help but laugh. I swear all these guys think about is sex.

The cool Northern California breeze feels great as we fly down the long country road with the windows down.

Never mind the fact that it's like sixty degrees outside. The crispness of it is invigorating.

Silas is behind the wheel because he's the one with tension to cut, and I swear this car does what a sixty-minute massage and a handful of Xanax can do in half the time. Pressing the pedal down and going nearly a hundred and ten miles per hour down the desolate road is good for the soul.

And he clearly has a lot of tension tonight because we've been out for over an hour and he's not letting up. I love the hilly parts of the road that make my heart drop down to my belly. It's one hell of a turn-on, or maybe that's the vibration from the motor. Either way, I'm in heaven.

I have no clue where we are when he pulls off the main road and takes a turn that dips onto a gravel one. For the record, this is *hardly* the kind of car you take on a gravel road, so I tense immediately.

"What the hell are you doing?" I shriek.

"Relax. I want to show you something."

What on earth could he want to show me all the way out here? We are in the middle of nowhere. The road snakes its way through some trees, and if I was with anyone other than Silas, I would be sure my end was near and I was about to be murdered, hacked into pieces and thrown off a cliff. But after a moment, the trees part and give way to an open expanse of dark black sky splattered with bright stars.

I gasp as the car rolls to a stop. Silas cuts the engine and the dashboard lights go black, making the night sky even more clear. There's not an ounce of light pollution around us, and I don't think I've seen the stars look so bright.

"I used to bring the boys out here when they were little." He puts the car into park and relaxes against the seat as I stare wide-eyed out the window.

"Oh my God, Silas. This is beautiful."

"I almost forgot about this spot. It's perfect on a clear night."

"I bet Gabriel loved it, and Baron complained the whole time," I say, turning toward him. He cracks a rare Silas grin, and stares straight ahead, focusing on nothing. He's clearly caught up in a memory.

"Exactly how it happened. Gabriel would sprawl out on the roof of the car, pretending he was in a spaceship or something. Baron looked bored the entire time. Wouldn't even look at the stars, like giving me the satisfaction would literally kill him. I swear that kid came out of the womb hating me."

"He doesn't hate you," I say, touching his arm. "He's just too much like you to see past his own bullshit."

He's silent for a moment as he stares out the window some more. "That and he still blames me for what happened to his brother and his mother. Even if he says he doesn't, I think he still does." His face doesn't crack or show an ounce of emotion, which I know means he's holding it all inside.

"Silas." I don't know what else to say. The story about Silas's first wife and dead son still unnerves me so much. How can I comment on that part of their lives when I have absolutely nothing I can say to make it better? And how can I possibly comment when the fact is that my being here would never have happened if they were still alive? It weighs too heavily between us, but I have to keep Silas talking. He does it so rarely. "Baron does *not* blame you for that. If he did, would he really still be in this business? Or in this family? Especially with me."

"Yeah, I guess so. I wish Gabriel hated me too."

"Why would you say that?" I gasp.

"Because then at least they'd have something in common."

It's almost funny, and I almost laugh, but I can't because he's right. Gabriel was adopted after Baron's brother died. Baron saw him as a replacement, and Gabriel's constant admiration of their father drove Baron insane. The animosity between them is too ingrained at this point, but I refuse to believe my family could be that easily splintered.

"Hey," I say, climbing onto my knees and drawing Silas's face to mine, "stop it. Your boys love you and so do I. You think it doesn't matter if they like you as long as you keep them safe, but it does matter. They wouldn't be here working alongside you if they didn't love you. You're a good father, so stop this. Baron will come around. I promise."

In the darkness, I can barely make out his face, but I can see his silhouette. I stroke his cheek, pulling him in for a kiss. He spends another moment being tender before I sense the rough side start to take over.

"Thank you for bringing me here," I whisper against his lips.

"You wanna thank me?" he replies in a husky tone while unbuttoning his pants. "Get over here."

Reaching down, I feel for his cock in the darkness. When my hand finds his warm length, I grasp on with a tight grip and give him a long, languid stroke. He lets out a hiss when I do it again. Dropping my mouth to his lap, I take him between my lips with eagerness. God, I love pleasuring him, hearing the sounds he makes and feeling the power in my grasp. I can bring this king to his knees with just my mouth, and *that shit* turns me on.

"Fuck, Iris," he groans when I take him so far down my mouth he reaches the back of my throat, cutting off my air supply. I hold him there until my gag reflex kicks in and I back off, coating his cock with my saliva.

His hand reaches for the hem of my dress, tugging it up until my ass is exposed and sticking straight up. He pulls my lace thong to the side and runs his fingers through the pooling moisture of my pussy. I let out a moan as I go deep again, letting his cock choke me because I know how much he loves it. While I'm gagging myself, he runs his touch over my sex and then circles a wet finger over my tight hole.

I shiver in anticipation.

He slips his finger past the tight ring of muscle, and I cry out, my cries muffled with my lips around him.

"Ride my dick, Iris. Now."

A flurry of heat overwhelms me as I scurry over the console to climb onto his lap. Straddling him in his seat, I lower myself over his cock, and he slides in easily. We moan in unison as he sheaths himself inside me as deep as he can go.

I move hastily, bouncing on top of him and chasing this feeling of pure bliss. Now with his face right in front of me, I kiss him hungrily, tasting his mouth, his neck, his earlobe. I want to absorb him and make him a part of me forever.

Just when I think it can't get any better, his hand finds my back entrance, sliding his finger in again just to drive me crazy. He pulses along with my movements, until I'm slamming my body against his so fast, I nearly die of exhaustion.

With his other hand, he grabs the back of my neck and takes over, sending his hips upward in complete ownership of my body. I am nothing but defenseless prey in his hands.

Our grunts and the slamming of our bodies are filthy sounding, and I manage to hold on long enough to feel him swell and tense inside me, so we can both come together.

It's like perfect harmony, and my hips shudder and shake in his lap while I hold on to my orgasm for as long as I can.

Collapsing my weight into his arms, I let him hold me while I catch my breath. His heart pounds against mine in the now silent, sex-scented car. And with my head against his chest, I soak up this feeling of comfort and safety once more. Nothing could possibly go wrong, I tell myself. Silas's bad feelings about the job are nothing, and everything will be just fine.

It has to be because I don't know how I'd survive if it wasn't.

Four

Iris

Rolling out of Silas's bed, I grab my robe off the floor and wrap it around my naked body. Silas is always up at least two hours before everyone in this house. Sometimes I wish he'd take a break and just enjoy the simplicity of life.

My thighs feel bruised and battered from the pounding between them last night, so my steps are slow. Not that I'm complaining.

I open the bedroom door and step out into the hallway to go downstairs for breakfast. As the smell of bacon fills my senses, my stomach growls. I guess that's what I get for sleeping in so late this morning.

I'm immediately caught off guard by the arguing coming from Silas's office.

For a moment, I assume he's on a call. That is, until I hear Gabriel shouting some nonsense about a job in Mexico.

I walk closer, eavesdropping on the conversation, so

that when it is brought to my attention, I'm not caught off guard. There are times these guys keep me out of the loop. They say it's for my own good, but I wish they'd allow me the chance to choose what is good for me and what's not.

I guess I can't be angry at them for that. They love me and just want to keep me safe. Just as I want the same for them.

Silas holds this tranquility to his tone that I'm all too familiar with. It's intimidating, yet gruff and sexy. "Something doesn't add up and I'm not willing to take any chances. If this client has any connections to Basileus, it's not worth the risk."

Then there's Gabriel who doesn't take no for an answer. He goes from calm to enraged in two seconds flat. "In case you've forgotten, I'm an adult and fully capable of making my own choices.

"So what if the guy runs a cartel? We're not exactly mediocre assassins."

"You're not thinking with a clear head, son. El Basileus has hundreds of men who do exactly what we do at his fingertips. Why us? Why now? Those are the questions you need to ask yourself."

"Because we're fucking badasses. That's why."

"Badasses are not what we are. We are businessmen. We brief every case with detail. We know our clients. We gain knowledge of the hit." A loud thud on the desk takes me by surprise. Silas raises his voice to a near shout. "What we do *not* do is risk our lives to make a few bucks."

"This isn't about the money!" Gabriel yells. "It's about you always being in control, and Baron and I being your little puppets. We're not kids anymore. If we get a job and we want it, we take it and that's what I'm doing."

The door to Silas's office swings open and Gabriel

comes out in a spitting rage. "Babe, what's wrong?" I brush my hand over his shoulder, but he storms off in a huff.

I poke my head in the room and see Silas sitting behind his desk with a cigar pinched between his fingers. He looks up and his eyes catch mine. "How much did you hear?"

I shrug a shoulder. "Enough."

He waves me in, still holding on to his cigar. Bypassing the chair facing him in front of the desk, I go straight for his lap. Sliding his chair back, he makes room for me and places a hand on the small of my back. "You two shouldn't be fighting like that. You're family."

"He's a hothead and if he doesn't get over it soon, he'll end up dead."

I curl my legs up onto his lap and rest my head on his shoulder. "What's the issue with the job?"

"Everything," he spits out, dropping the cigar onto his desk. His body tenses up, so I run my fingers through his hair, hoping to calm him down a bit. "Remember I told you I had a bad feeling about this?"

I nod in response.

"I did some digging and found out the guy who offered us the job has a connection to one of the biggest drug lords in Mexico—El Basileus. He's ruthless, but even more so, he's extremely wealthy and powerful. It could be nothing, but my gut tells me we're stepping into a warzone if we take this job."

I hate getting caught in the middle of this, but I can see both sides. Gabriel is ready for independence in the business, while Silas just wants to keep us all safe. "Maybe you could go with him."

"That won't work. The client wants him there the day after tomorrow. I've got two assignments already lined up.

Before I found this connection, I planned to send both of the boys."

"What is the connection? Like you said, it could be nothing."

"A few years back, El Basileus's men took out the leader of an organized crime syndicate in Russia. The man who put the bullet between his eyes was the brother of Sante Grim—the guy who called and offered us the job."

Biting the corner of my lip, I nod. "Yeah. That does seem odd. Why not just hire his own brother? Unless, maybe they're rivals and don't play nice together."

Silas shuffles around some papers on the table and pulls one out, laying it on top of a Manila folder. "This was five days ago. Those are the Grim brothers. Sure as hell don't look like rivals to me."

I'm looking down at a picture of two guys, who look happy to see each other, outside a cafe. The date stamp is five days ago, as Silas said. The location written on the paper is El Paso.

"Let me go," I blurt out. "I've come a long way and being a woman, I can easily persuade these men."

"No," Silas snaps, "I won't put you in danger because Gabriel wants to prove himself."

"I think Gabriel's more than proved himself. Don't you?"

"He has. But that doesn't erase the fact that he's impulsive, just like his brother." Silas draws back to look at my face, his eyes soften, and he relaxes a bit. "They're quick to react, whereas you're like me. We think things through."

I smile at the compliment. At least, that's what I take it for. "I've learned from the best." I press my lips to his and his hold on me tightens.

Silas breathes into my mouth. "Would you talk to him? He listens to you."

I nod. "I'll do my best, but we both know how much Gabriel hates being told what to do."

Strong hands grip my ass beneath my robe as we fall back into the kiss. Lifting one leg over and dropping it on the side of the chair, I straddle his lap. "Mmm," he hums, "you're making it really hard for me to get any work done."

"It's Sunday. You shouldn't be working." My hand snakes between us and I grab him by the dick, rubbing him through the fabric of his pants.

Silas parts the opening of my robe, exposing my breasts to him. He bites the corner of his lip and lets out an airy breath. "Fuck, Iris. Do you have any idea what you do to me?"

My head drops back when Silas arches my back and takes the bud of my nipple in his mouth. His teeth graze the sensitive skin and my thighs quiver with need.

The door flies open, averting my attention. I sigh and look over my shoulder, finding Gabriel standing there.

"Iris, I need to talk to you," he says point-blankly.

Damn. I look back at Silas with a pout. "Finish later?"

He smacks a hand to my ass and sneers. "Do what you have to do."

My lips press to his before I climb off him and readjust my robe.

Gabriel stands at the door with his hand pressed to it, holding it open while staring down at the ground. He's still coming to terms with the fact that I'm in a relationship with more than just him. It's gotten better, but he's still got a long way to go, considering I plan to be with these guys forever. All three of them.

As I walk out the door, I take Gabriel by the hand and

lead him into the sitting room. He doesn't speak as we walk, and I don't even have to ask to know what's wrong. First the fight with his dad, and now walking in on us. I'm mentally preparing myself for his sour mood because it's apparent he's in one.

Gabriel drops down on the couch, legs parted and a scowl on his face. "I missed you," I tell him straight away, giving him the reassurance he needs.

"Missed you, too, baby." He surprises me and grabs me by the arm, then pulls me down on top of him. "You gonna show me what Silas was looking at, or do I have to take this off myself?" He tugs at the corner of my robe.

"You can look at my body anytime you want." I press my lips to his, anticipating a soft peck, but he fists my hair and forces me into a deep and passionate kiss.

My heart rate excels and the need to finish what Silas and I started is strong. Way too strong. It's not right, though. Not here. Not now. "Hey," I pull back, "why is this job so important to you?"

Gabriel blows out air and looks to the side. "He fucking talked to you about it, didn't he?"

"Not exactly. I heard your conversation when I came down. I asked him about it, but he didn't go into detail."

Running his hands over his face, he shakes his head. "He's too damn controlling. For once, I just want to make a choice for myself."

I grab his hands, pulling them away from his face, so I can see him. "There will be plenty of opportunities for that. Silas has a point. It sounds dangerous."

"It's a simple hit on some member of the cartel who's been leaking information on drops. A knife in the throat and I'm out." Gabriel draws back and looks me in the eye. "Why are you taking his side on this?"

My arms go up in surrender. "I'm not taking anyone's side. I'm just saying what I feel and after talking with Silas, it does sound like a risk. Besides, you're smart enough to know it's never as easy as 'in and out.'"

The cocky smirk on his face is proof that he's not backing down. "It is for me."

He's stubborn as hell, so there is no getting through to him. "If you do this, you'll need backup."

"If you're insinuating that I bring you with me—"

"No. Not me. Silas has already made it clear that's not an option. I'm still learning, so I won't argue about it. If you go, take Baron. That was the original plan, after all."

"He'll side with you and Silas. Probably back out like a little pussy." Gabriel laughs in a mocking tone. "I'd rather bring Punk, the stray cat running around on the property, for backup."

I bite back a smile. "You named that stray?"

"She needed a name."

"You're so fucking cute." I kiss him again, savoring every moment of his touch—his taste. Because there's no stopping him. Gabriel is going to take this job no matter what anyone says. I pull back, taking a serious tone. "Please, just talk to Baron. He's your brother. He'll have your back."

There's a brief moment of silence before he exhales a pent-up breath. "Fine."

"Really?" I beam, wearing my surprise on my face.

"If it'll make you happy, then I'll do it."

This was easier than I thought. I guess Silas was right; Gabriel does listen to me. Now I just need to see if he'll agree to changing the name of that cat. Who names a female cat Punk?

Five

Baron

"What do you want?" I ask between shots fired into the target across the range.

"Wow, thanks, bro."

This is the one place I can come to be alone in a very full house. So, it's either in the armory or out here on the shooting range where I come to let off a little steam. Gabriel rarely ever bugs me, hence why I'm immediately irritated at his sudden presence.

Clearing the chamber, I drop the pistol on the table and turn toward my brother. "Sorry, what's up?"

He shuffles his feet, digging his hands into his pocket. My eyes squint as I wait for whatever he has to say because, judging by his mannerisms, something is bothering him, and I hope to God it's not about Iris again. Gabriel's little tantrums about sharing her are getting old. If I can deal with her fucking my dad, so can he.

"Silas wants to cancel the Tijuana job."

"Okay," I reply, loading the next round.

"And I think it's bullshit!"

I can't help the chuckle that slips through my lips.

"Is something fucking funny?" he snaps.

Oh, my little brother. So damn angsty all the time.

"You sound like me," I reply. "You don't like Silas telling you what to do? Treating you like a child instead of a partner? Thinking about telling him to fuck off because you know better?" I level him a glare. "Get in line, Gabriel."

"Fuck, why do we put up with it? He acts like we don't know what we're doing. Like we can't handle a simple fucking job. We're not his goddamn employees!"

"Well, what do you want me to say, Gabe? I get it. Two years ago, I had one foot out the door. I was ready to work for someone who knew my worth and treated me like a real professional."

"Why didn't you?" he asks, and a hint of a smile creeps across my face.

"Why do you think?" Taking aim, I let another round fly into the target.

He lets out a heavy exhale when I'm done. "Iris."

"Yep."

Honestly, there's more to it than that. I stayed for Iris, but it wasn't just about her. It was what this house turned into after she decided to stick around. It was about having someone in the family who made me want to stay. And Silas started giving me more responsibility, more jobs, more attention. That urge I once felt to get out from under his thumb is gone.

"So what?" Gabriel asks. "I'm just supposed to let him get what he wants...again?"

I finally drop the gun on the table and wipe off my

hands with the cleaning cloth. When I really look at Gabriel, something about his behavior seems off to me, like he's not just throwing another fit, but he's genuinely mad.

And for him to be so mad at my dad, *our dad*, it must be serious.

"You're really pissed, aren't you? What is it about this job that has you so upset?"

He takes in a deep breath and looks off into the distance. "He thinks this guy has some connection to the Mandola Cartel."

"And?"

A little more fidgeting before he finally looks at me. "My...uh, real parents were junkies, and I fucking hate dealers. They're the reason people get addicted, and I'm a firm believer they should all rot in hell."

I can practically see the wheels turning in his head, and I know he's not comfortable talking about this stuff, definitely not with me. He can go to Iris with this shit, but he's talking to me for a reason. I just wish I knew what it was.

"Listen, I get it. You want to go pop some asshole to prove that you're tougher than the fucking cartel, but I gotta side with Dad on this one. Those are crazy fuckers, and we may deal with different types of mafia members all the time, but that Mandola family is a distinct breed."

My brother shoots me a pissed-off glare, his eyebrows pinched together and his mouth set in a thin line. "Thanks, Baron," he spits out, "I knew you'd take his side."

As he stomps off, I hold up my hands. What the fuck did I do? Being treated like the enemy has me feeling really fucking irritable.

"You know what, Gabriel. You think you're so fucking smart, go on the job by yourself then!" I shout after him.

He doesn't even turn around, just holds up his middle finger as he stalks toward the house.

~

Standing by the door, I lean against the frame and watch Iris helping a customer in her boutique. No one would know by the sweet smile and gentle disposition that this woman can kill a man in cold blood, and has. Many times.

After sending the woman on her way out the door, her eyes catch mine, and she lights up.

"What are you doing here?"

"I needed to get out of the house," I reply. She wraps her arms around me, hugging me across my middle as I swallow her up in my arms. With a gentle tug on her hair, I guide her face upward, so I can plant my lips on hers.

When I feel her tongue glide softly against mine, I feel a shit ton better.

"Everything okay?" she asks.

"Yeah," I say with a sigh.

"That doesn't sound convincing."

"Gabriel was being a pain in the ass today. That's all."

Her eyebrows crease in concern as she chews on her bottom lip. "He got in a fight with Silas this morning too. About the Tijuana trip."

"He's pissed it's getting canceled," I say. "But he'll get over it."

A customer walks through the door, and Iris pulls away, so they don't have to watch us making out by the front of the store. Not that I care, but this is her business, so I get it.

"The place looks good," I say, glancing around at the

way she has everything laid out. It's not too expensive-looking, but has the right appeal for this area.

After the blow-up with Maretti, we had the motel that once stood here bulldozed for Iris. I still remember the day I barged into that motel room to find her almost dead at the hands of that piece of shit, Donny Wright.

When we handed her the deed for the lot, it didn't take her long to decide what to do with it. She put together her business plan, had a new clothing store built with a company mission to provide jobs and training to women who needed it. Ex-prostitutes, drug addicts, and homeless women.

It fucking amazes me what this girl can accomplish and how much guts she has. We helped her where we could, but really, she did this all on her own.

"It'll blow over," she says, while adjusting clothes on the rack. "He'll throw his little fit and then he'll give up. You know how he is."

"I don't understand why he has to act like such a little dickhead all the time."

Iris's eyes widen at me as she gestures toward the woman browsing the items against the wall.

"Sorry," I mouth.

"Look at it from his perspective, Baron. He's the youngest. He still feels like an outsider, and he doesn't like to share. He's never really had anything that was just his. And how often does your dad ever really tell him no?"

"I just wish he'd grow up. I keep thinking that when he stops acting like such a kid, I'll be able to relate to him more...but it never ends."

She comes closer, running her hands up my arms. "I'll talk to him tonight, but I have to admit, I'm glad he came to you."

"Even if I didn't tell him what he wanted to hear?"

"Yep."

The sound of a small bell pulls our attention away from each other, and we both turn to see the customer standing at the counter, waiting to pay for her items.

"Sorry," Iris says with a sweet customer-service voice. "Did you find everything okay?"

"Yes, I did."

Iris rings her up and takes her credit card, and just as she's bagging up her purchases, the woman adds, "I have two kids myself, and they're a handful, but you both sound like good parents."

Iris freezes before glancing at me, and I mirror her wide-eyed expression.

"Thank you very much," she says before handing the bag to the woman. Once she passes by and exits the store, giving me a warm smile as she leaves, Iris and I break out in a fit of laughter.

Six

Iris

I end up working longer at the store than I mean to. There were new shipments to inventory and marketing to approve. I hate leaving my to-do list for the next day. Plus, I know Silas is out on a job, Baron said he was going to stop on his way home to recon a few upcoming jobs, so the only one waiting for me is a pent-up and feisty Gabriel.

And as much as I love my angsty boyfriend, I know that sex isn't going to solve this problem. He's going to have to open up and talk to me, and I'm not going to lie—I'm not exactly sure how that will go.

Just after seven, I call the driver to come pick me up, leaving one of the girls here to close. On the way back to the house, I text him.

I'm on my way home. I'm in the mood for something fried. Want me to grab a burger and fries for you?

.   .   .

That's sort of our thing. It doesn't matter that we have a private chef to cook all of our meals. Sometimes you just need the level of saturated fat a home-cooked meal can't provide. So Gabriel and I bond over onion rings and greasy burgers.

But he doesn't text me back, which is strange for him. He must really be upset.

When we pull into the giant underground garage, I jump out and hurry toward the stairs. I need to see him. A wave of guilt for staying late at the store washes over me as I rush toward the main floor, but it's dark and empty.

The TV isn't on. There is no loud music coming from his room.

"Gabriel!" I shout for him, but the only response I get is the echo of my own voice against the empty walls.

Running up to his room, I find it lifeless and cold. I flip on the light, hoping he's at least sleeping in his bed, but it's empty and still unmade from this morning.

The armory is empty too.

On instinct, I open up a text to Silas.

Do you know where Gabriel is?

He replies immediately: *He's not home?*

No.

. . .

I'll check his location, he types back.

Okay.

Leaning over the marble countertop, I can't shake the uneasy feeling in my gut. This just isn't like him. Gabriel doesn't venture out alone. His childhood was sheltered, and he's always felt most comfortable here at home. We don't even go out much as a couple. So, if he's running away as some sort of childish act of rebellion, I'm going to kick his ass when he gets back.

I finally get a text from Silas, but it does nothing to settle my worry.

I'm on my way home.

What's that supposed to mean? If he looked up his location, he should have answers and not this vague reply. Next, I text Baron.

Gabriel is missing.

. . .

Just texting those words has my stomach in knots. Am I overreacting? He could be at a movie theater or off for a walk. It could be nothing. But my gut is telling me otherwise.

My phone chimes and I look down at the one-word response from Baron.

Fuck.

My sentiments exactly.

Fifteen minutes later, I get a notification that both of the guys are home, and I wait eagerly in the kitchen for them. When they walk up from the garage, they're already arguing.

"I'm telling you to relax. I used to do shit like this all the time," Baron snaps at his father.

"I'm aware, which is why I'm pissed at you too," Silas replies.

"Of course, this is *my* fault."

"I really don't need your attitude right now, Baron."

"What is going on?" I ask, yelling over both of them.

Baron doesn't stop as he walks straight to the freezer, pulling out a bottle of vodka and placing it on the counter before retrieving a glass from the cabinet.

Neither of them answers me, and I feel like a nuclear bomb about to explode. "Both of you, stop!" I shout. "Tell me what the fuck is going on *now!*"

Baron shoots back a glass of clear liquor, setting it down

without even flinching. "What do you think, Iris? Gabriel wanted to take that job in TJ, so he went."

My eyes widen, and my head snaps in Silas's direction, seeking confirmation of this. "Wait. Are you serious?" I shriek.

"His last location was listed as San Diego before his phone shut off."

I feel like I'm going to be sick. Gabriel is in Mexico, dealing with the cartel, with his phone shut off, and we have no way of knowing if he's okay or hurt or worse.

"Breathe, Iris. He'll be okay," Baron says, as Silas's warm hand against my back tries to unsuccessfully calm me.

Why didn't I come home from work earlier? Why didn't I talk to him more this morning? Why didn't I give him his night the other day?

"What are we going to do? We have to go after him," I say through gasping breaths.

"You need to sit down. You're going to pass out." Silas leads me to the couch and makes me sit, pushing my head down between my knees.

When my breathing has slowed, he replies, "We can't go after him. It could only make things worse. He'll be home tomorrow. Let's not panic tonight."

"But it's the cartel, Silas. What if…"

A firm grasp around my chin lifts my face until I'm looking at him. "Don't think like that. Gabriel is smart and well-trained. He's out there to prove himself, so he will get the job done."

"He'll be home tomorrow," I reply, trying to siphon Silas's confidence right out of him.

He nods in response. "He'll be home tomorrow."

"And I'm going to kill him," I say. Silas cracks a smile

before pulling me into his lap. He strokes my back again until, this time, I actually calm down. I hear Baron's door slam in the distance, and I try to lift my head to look for him, but Silas only pulls me closer.

"He's fine. Don't worry about him."

But I can't help it. How could I *not* worry about them? I worry about them getting along, staying alive, and still wanting me. I worry *all the time*. I've already lost one family; I can't lose another one.

I knew in the back of my mind the whole time that something bad was bound to happen eventually, but I'm not ready, so Gabriel better hurry his ass home tomorrow.

Seven

GABRIEL

"Stop here," I mutter to the taxi driver. He parks the car on the corner and I scan the street to look for anything out of the ordinary before I get out. This will be an easy job. The target works at the cleaners. Every afternoon at one, he closes up the shop and goes out back to smoke and eat his lunch. The alley behind the store is isolated and out of view of the main street foot traffic.

This shit couldn't be easier. Apparently, he never settled a debt with some guy, and because the guy who hired us used to work with the cartel, my dad had to shit his pants over the whole job. Fucking stupid.

Arrogant old man. He's so fucking caught up in his own ways, and he refuses to see shit any other way than his.

I'll be honest, though. There's a small part of me that hopes this job isn't as easy as it's set up to be. I'm tired of being their little bitch at home. They want me to do the easy shit like getting information out of assholes who don't want to give it up or taking on the easy jobs close to home. I get what they're doing. They want to keep me chained to the house. Because if they really let me flex, they'd be scared as shit that I would take over the family business.

I'm fucking good at what I do. I'm not scared of shit, and I get the job done.

Fuck Baron and his sharpshooting abilities. What a cowardly way to kill someone. How often does he really get to look a man in the eye before he takes his life?

I'll prove to Silas and Baron that I'm not the fucking baby of the family anymore. They treat me like a kid no matter what I do. They take my time away with her, and I see it. But it's only a matter of time before she realizes I'm the only one for her and she dumps those fuckers.

I should have brought her. I wish I could have, but I know she would have talked me out of it. Silas was already in her head. And I know she's going to have my ass for doing this, but it's going to make the next time I fuck her that much better. I can't wait to feel the sting of her slap against my face or the scratch of her claws in my back. My girl is fucking crazy, which is why she and I are perfect for each other.

Right on time, the clock strikes one, and the cleaner flips the open sign to closed.

"Gracias," I finally say to the driver when I think it's a good time to get out. I hand him fifty pesos before slowly climbing out of the car. I do my best to appear casual, looking down at my phone as I walk with the traffic.

There's an apartment building next to the cleaners, and according to our research, we only have to go through the lobby and exit through the staff door to get to the alleyway behind it.

I don't make eye contact with anyone as I slide effortlessly through the lobby of the old apartment building and slip out the back entrance.

The alley is empty. There's an overflowing dumpster to my right and a chair next to the cleaner's door. Ducking behind the dumpster, I keep my presence unknown as I wait for the old man to take his seat in the chair. While I wait, I look around for cameras or open windows, but as promised, it's clean.

Fuck, nothing could go wrong with this job. It's too fucking easy.

But then ten minutes go by and I start to get annoyed. This is Silas's fault. We got bad intel. This is what he gets for not double-checking this shit.

It brings me back to my first job with Silas. I was only fifteen, and we were out at a location like this, leaning up against a wall together while Baron scouted the job.

"This is why we can't do this job alone, Gabriel," he had said to me. "When we're too confident or we aren't careful, we get ourselves cornered in bad situations. Remember, when your brother doesn't have your back, *nobody* has your back."

I nodded back with a stern look on my face. I wanted to prove myself to him so badly. He needed to know that I was meant to be in this family. I was born tough, and I would always be tough. I will never be grateful my parents were killed, but I was forever fucking grateful I ended up in a family where I could be myself and not in some shit-hole foster family that hated me and saw me as nothing but trouble. With Silas, I could live up to my real potential.

And this is my chance to prove myself, once and for all.

Suddenly, the door to the cleaners opens, but instead of an old man walking out, it's a young guy. He's dressed in all black, looking mean as fuck. There's a notch in his brow, bald head, and tattoos crawling all the way up his skull.

I duck behind the dumpster with a very bad feeling. Even though I know he can't see me, he's still looking in my direction.

Desperate to get the fuck out of here, I start walking toward the end of the alleyway, trying to look casual, but before I get there, a large black SUV pulls up and blocks the way.

Fuck, fuck, fuck.

Spinning around, I glance back at the man in black. He's standing with his arms crossed just staring at me.

Fuck this. I reach for my gun, pulling it out faster than I ever have before and aim right at his face. He matches my movement, doing the same thing to me. Behind me, I hear click, click, click. By the sound of it, there are three more guys at my back doing the same exact thing.

My heart beats rapidly in my chest, so fast it feels like it could pound its way right out.

"Put the gun down, Gabriel," the man says. He's so fucking calm, it turns my blood to ice. Fuck this guy and fuck this. If I go down, it's going to be in a blaze of fucking glory.

"Nice try, fucker. You have better chances of growing tits than getting me to put this fucking gun down."

He laughs, and then he does the last thing I expect him to. He lowers his gun and slides it back into the back of his pants.

My blood is still pounding in my ears. "Why don't you tell your boys behind me to do the same?"

When he raises his palms up, I hear the distinct sound of three guns hitting the concrete.

"You want to tell me who the fuck you are?"

"Your turn now," he replies.

"Not a chance."

"Then go ahead and shoot me. But you'll have those three behind you to deal with if you do, and the thirteen inside the cleaners as well as the two dozen guys circling the block."

"Who the fuck are you?" I yell, shaking the gun in my hand to get my message across.

He laughs again, and it makes me want to pull the trigger even more. "What? You don't recognize me?"

Recognize him? What the fuck is he talking about? I looked through the files. I saw the hit and I saw the guy who hired the hit. I never saw this fucker's face anywhere in those photos.

"I've changed a lot since you last saw me," he says with a lopsided smile that still looks mean as fuck.

"Start talking, asshole, or I go nuts on you and all the other fuckers."

"Relax, nephew."

"Don't call me that," I grit through clenched teeth.

"Why not? That's exactly who you are."

No, fuck this guy. Fuck him trying to be clever and catch me off guard. He wants to try and surprise me, so I can't defend myself. I'm all about the mind games, it's a skill I've mastered myself, so I am not falling for this shit.

"Fuck this," I mutter, before pulling the trigger.

The man in black falls to the ground before something crashes against my skull and everything goes black.

Eight

Iris

Watching the sunset from the back patio of the house, I feel like I could literally crawl out of my skin. Silas said Gabriel would be home yesterday, and if everything had gone smoothly, he would have. He could still walk through that door right now, but there's a part of me that knows that's not going to happen.

He's not coming home.

Not today at least. Maybe not ever.

But I can't go down that path again or I'll start crying, and once I start, I'm afraid I won't stop.

I can't speak to Silas or Baron either. The former has been in his office with the door closed all day. And the latter has cleaned every gun in the armory twice. We're staying apart to save arguments. If I look at them, I'll lose it. And if they speak to each other, it will turn nuclear. So we've kept our distance.

Gabriel's phone hasn't turned up on the tracker. There is no car to trace or credit card to follow. He's just...disappeared.

If he's not dead, then I'm going to kill him.

I slept in his bed for the past two nights. After Silas was able to calm me down, I excused myself and crawled between his cool, dark sheets, remembering the first time I was in his bed, when he held a knife to my throat and threatened to kill me. When I was convinced he was truly the biggest psychopath I'd ever met.

I sobbed into his pillows all night, smelling him on the fabric, fearing it would be the last thing I'd have of him.

But the sadness has turned into impatience, anger, and now rage. And I've had it. I'm done waiting and crying and wishing. I'm either going to storm out that door and drive myself to Mexico, or I'm going to burn this house to the ground.

Once the last sliver of sun has disappeared behind the horizon, I storm inside. I don't stop until I reach Silas's office doors, and I swing them open without warning. Silas doesn't even flinch. He's not on his computer, like he normally is. Instead, he's just staring straight ahead with a lost, drunk gaze in his eyes. Fuck, did he even sleep last night? By the look of it, that's a no.

"We have to do something," I announce, standing in the doorway.

"Come here, Iris," he says without looking at me. Goosebumps erupt across my skin as I walk slowly toward him. The cool resignation in his voice sends chills down my spine. He sounds like he's grieving already, but that's ridiculous.

When I reach him in his chair, he takes my hands in his,

and I can smell the whiskey on his breath from here. Instead of pulling me into his lap, like he normally does, he strokes my fingers.

"What?" I say with bitterness.

"It was the Mandola Cartel, Iris. I knew there was a connection, and if he hasn't come back yet, then..." His voice trails, and I snatch my hand away. Using all of the built-up rage coursing through my veins, I rear back my hand and slap him hard against his face. He snaps out of it, but only long enough to glare up at me with anger.

He stands up in a quick movement, grabbing my arms tightly in his hands. I fight against him while he holds my body against his. "Stop talking like that!" I scream at him. "He's your son! And he's missing. We have to go look for him. And if they hurt him, we have to make them pay!"

My screams turn into sobs as I thrash in Silas's arms. "Iris, listen to me. I knew someday this would happen and so did you. You knew the risks when you decided to stay. When you chose to love us all, you knew what could happen." His dark voice is against my ear, and I lose the strength to fight anymore, letting him squeeze my body so hard it hurts.

"You're a coward!" I yell, my voice breaking on the high pitch between the tears and the exhaustion. "I hate you. I hate you. I hate you."

He doesn't let me go, but only holds me tighter while my mind fights against everything I know he wants me to accept. But the rational part of my brain is not working with my heart. Because my heart *knows* Gabriel is alive. My heart *knows* he needs us.

But my mind knows what Silas is telling me.

He never should have gone on that job. It was dangerous. If any one of us follows him, we will be dead too.

And Silas doesn't think with his heart. There is only his rational brain, and that's why he's stayed alive as long as he has. He doesn't make impulsive, life-threatening, *stupid fucking* decisions like Gabriel did. Like Baron used to.

And as I clutch desperately to him, sobbing tears into his shirt, I realize this is probably the only man I'll have left. And I love him, more than anything I love him, but I can't live without Gabriel and Baron. I can't.

So I refuse to accept the truth until I see it with my own eyes. I am not entirely like Silas, and I'm not entirely like the boys. I am a mix of them all.

When Silas sits back down on his giant chair, he takes me with him, curling me onto his lap like a child. He brushes my sweat-soaked hair out of my face and kisses my temple.

"If I send Baron after him, I risk losing both of my sons. If I go, I risk leaving you unprotected. Tell me what you would do, Iris."

I lean back and stare up into his bloodshot eyes. It takes me back to the time two years ago when we thought we had lost Baron or when Maretti's men took me. I never saw this fear in his eyes then, but I know it was there. Because he's right. In our line of business, we both knew something like this would happen eventually. You can only be so careful.

But to know that Silas saves his grief and fear for the privacy of his office breaks my heart. He never lets this show, and now he's letting me in.

"We go together," I whisper, brushing his unkempt hair back. "We go after him as a family."

"And what if it's too late?" he asks.

"Then we burn the whole place to the fucking ground."

His lips crash against mine, hard and unforgiving. I

taste the whiskey on his lips, but I don't let him go. Wrapping my arms around his neck, I clutch onto him like he's the only thing holding me together, which at the moment, he is.

Nine

Iris

Somewhere in the middle of the night, I wake up to the sound of yelling. Rolling over in bed, I see the clock says four in the morning. Silas took me to bed with him last night, but I'm still in my clothes from yesterday when I crawl out of the blankets. I catch a glimpse of myself in the mirror, and I'm a wreck. My two-day-old makeup is streaked across my face, and my unbrushed hair looks more like a nest.

"You're going to put her in danger for him?!" Baron yells from downstairs. I tiptoe down the hall and quietly listen in on their conversation. They're in the living room, just out of my sight.

"You think I would let her get hurt?" Silas replies in a deep, clipped tone.

"It's not worth the risk, and you know it."

My eyes shut tightly as I fight back the tears that burn

behind my retinas. I should have known Baron would hate this idea.

"You're not going alone," Silas snaps back at him, and my eyes fly open. Going alone?

"This is exactly why he left when he did," Baron yells. "You train us for this job and then you try to control everything we do. It's fucking ridiculous."

"It's my fault he left, so I'm going," Silas replies. "Just don't wake her up, please."

My feet carry me so fast down the stairs, I nearly trip over the bottom two and almost face-plant into the marble floor. Their heads both snap up toward me, and I'm sure I look more like a wild animal than the woman they love.

"What are you doing?" I ask through clenched teeth.

"Iris," Silas says carefully, reaching for me, "go back to bed."

"You were trying to go without me, weren't you?" I ask, my voice high-pitched and angry.

"No, I was," Baron interjects, and my head snaps in his direction. Fury burns in my eyes as I glare at him. After all we've been through. After everything with Maretti and my father, he's going to stand there and admit to leaving me here. I don't even need to say what I'm thinking. I'm too fueled with rage.

I want to scream at them both, but there's nothing I could possibly say to them to convey how much this hurts. I know once I start yelling, I'll start crying, and I won't let them see me cry.

"Fuck you both," I snap, pointing a finger at them as I storm away.

"Iris," Silas barks, and I probably would have stopped before, but not now. He doesn't get to control me.

"No," I say, spinning toward him. "We were supposed

to be a partnership, but Baron is right. You are too controlling, and we're not children."

"Where are you going?" he asks as I storm off.

"Back to my room," I snap, waving them both off. When I get upstairs, I head straight for the bathroom. I don't even care that it's not even light out, I need a shower —badly. But instead of switching on the water in the full-size shower, I decide on the large soaker tub instead. Turning it to the hottest temperature, I start to strip off my clothes.

Once I'm down to nothing and about to step into the water, I see the door open behind me. Clenching my jaw, I avoid even looking at Baron as he stalks in. He looks almost apologetic, and it grates on my nerves.

"Get out," I mutter at him as I step into the water.

Without answering, he just starts pulling his clothes off too.

"What are you doing?"

"You're done being mad at me now," he says, as if he can control my emotions, like he gets a say in how I feel or how long I can stay mad.

"No, I'm not, Baron." I settle myself in the tub and avoid looking at him as he strips out of his boxers, all tan skin and lean muscles. I know that once I let my sight drink him in, I'll be done for. And contrary to what he believes, I'm not done being mad at him.

"You're not getting in here," I yell as he starts to step in, but of course, he doesn't listen. And even when I try to fight him off, he only climbs in behind me and wraps his arms and legs around me, clenching my limbs so tightly that I can't move an inch.

I should headbutt him, but then his nose would start bleeding and it would make a mess in my bath. Thinking about that only reminds me of the time I made Gabriel's nose bleed while he was teaching me self-defense, and the memory stings. Anger, sadness, fear, and hope mingle together in my mind, making me want to scream and break something. Instead, I give up the fight against Baron, and I let the tears fall.

"I'm not going to apologize," Baron says, cruelly against my ear. "I wanted to go after him alone because I couldn't risk putting you in danger. So, I couldn't tell you."

"Don't I deserve a say? You're just like your father, trying to control everything. It's exactly why Gabe left in the first place. This is why he's gone." I cry in earnest this time, letting my head fall back against his chest, my tears falling into the hot water filling the tub.

"It's my fault he's gone, Iris. So it's my job to go get him."

"It's not your fault," I reply, feeling terrible that I just implied that. His arms relax their hold on my body, letting his hands slide across my belly and down my legs. I feel myself melt into his arms. "Everything's going to be all right," I say, turning my head to press my lips against his jaw. "But no more secrets. No more lies. We go together or we don't go at all."

"Deal," he whispers. His hands slide up my thighs, and I let out a sigh as he trails them across my sex, playing with me as if I'm a toy. I let out a soft hum, kissing him again. This time, he turns his face and presses his lips to mine. As his fingers find their way to my clit, I'm engulfed in guilt instead of pleasure.

"I can't," I whisper against his mouth. His hand freezes as he looks me in the eye.

"Let me make you feel good." His touch is gentle, and I hate myself for how much I crave it, how much I soften into the pleasure. With one arm across my chest, he holds me upright against his body as the other hand takes me to the brink of pleasure, and just as I feel the climax cresting in my body, he plunges a finger inside me. My back arches, and I cry out, letting myself go.

But my distraction only lasts as long as the orgasm because, once I come down, I'm hit with a wave of remorse. How could I do this with Baron when Gabriel is missing or possibly dead? How can I remain a part of this family without him? It hits me with the strength of a tsunami, and I don't stop the tears as they fall.

Baron clutches me even tighter. Instead of holding this grief against me, he holds me through it, kissing my face and stroking my hair. Pressing his lips against my temple, he whispers, "I've got you, baby. I'm not leaving," and it's exactly what I need to hear.

Ten

GABRIEL

In my dream, I have Iris in my arms; I can feel her long
brown hair against my chest as we sleep, curled up in the
darkness of my bedroom, and it's fucking beautiful.

Which makes it suck even more when I open my eyes
with a splitting headache and my hands cuffed behind my
back. My shoulders ache from sleeping like this, and I let
out a groan as I attempt to roll, but everything hurts. Lying
on my side, I take stock of my surroundings.

I'm in a dark room, and I'm on a bed. There's a ceiling
fan whirling above my head, but that's the only sound in
the room.

What the fuck happened?

It was a trap—that's what fucking happened. Those
assholes ambushed me in the alleyway. I shot one of them,
though, I remember that.

I feel like the guy said something else that was important, but I can't remember what it was, and the more I try

to pull the shit out of my memory, the more my head pounds. Assholes did a number on my skull. I'd feel for blood if I could fucking move.

I struggle to reach the knife in my pocket, but it's gone. The 45 under my shirt is gone too. Can't say I'm surprised they disarmed me. Judging by that show in the alley, this is not a small, rookie operation. If Silas was right, I'm in the hands of the Mandola Cartel, which means I'm as good as fucked. The only question is, why are they keeping me alive and what do they want?

If I had to guess...a way back to Silas Black. They'll use me to get to my father, torture the fuck out of me probably, so they can kill my whole family, Baron and Iris too. Too fucking bad they're not getting a word out of me. Which means I have a lot of goddamn pain to look forward to. Awesome.

Silas was right. El Basileus was setting us up. They took down the syndicate in Russia, and now they want the infamous Black family. Why the fuck didn't I just let him have his way? I could be home with Iris right now, balls deep in the most beautiful, badass girl in the world. Now, I'm probably going to get my eyeballs plucked out of my head and my fingers snapped off before I die a slow, painful death. Why? Because I'm a stubborn fucking idiot.

The door to the room opens, and I stiffen, quickly closing my eyes so whoever it is thinks I'm asleep.

"I was watching you on the cameras. I know you're awake." It's the voice of someone younger than the man I saw today, sounding closer to my age if I had to guess. He doesn't sound half as nasty as that other guy either. There's something strangely familiar about his voice, but I can't put my finger on it.

"Sit up, Gabriel," he says as he opens the curtains, letting the room flood with light.

I peel my eyes open and watch him cross the room to the other window. A man with a complexion a few shades darker than mine stares down at me, and I'm shocked by his appearance, and not because he's terrifying. The opposite, actually. He's tall with cropped black hair, glasses, and a white polo shirt over black pants. He looks like someone I'd run into on the campus of a university, not in the hands of the most dangerous cartel in Mexico.

What sort of mind-game fuckery is this?

"Who are you?" I ask.

"Aw, that hurts my feelings," he replies, crossing his arms.

My brow furrows as I glare up at him. It doesn't help that I'm stuck on my side, having to stare up at him sideways, but if he wants me to remember him from somewhere, he's fucking high. My head still hurts, and I'm, nonetheless, grumpy about the whole going-to-get-tortured-and-die shit, so I just roll my eyes at him and lie my head back down.

"Let's just get this shit over with," I groan.

He laughs. "What shit?"

"Oh, you know, asshole. The part where you demand to know where my father is and rip off my fingernails or something. I'm not a fucking idiot, but I'm telling you now, I'm not talking."

His expression twists in disgust. "That sounds disgusting and not really my scene. We have people to do that for us, but if you'd like me to send them in, I can."

"Fuck off," I mutter.

"Besides, I don't need to torture you to know where Silas Black is. Or Baron or that cute little brunette, Iris. But explain something to me...is she your sister or your girl-friend, because from what I've seen...there seems to be some boundary issues going on in your house. You are aware she's fucking the other two, right?"

I struggle in earnest against the cuffs as I try to kick the fucker standing just a foot too far from me. "You mother-fucker, you even think about laying a hand on her, I swear to God, I'll cut your dick off and shove it down your throat."

He laughs again. "So, I'm guessing she's *not* your sister."

"Who the fuck are you and what do you want?" I spit at him.

"So you all just share—? You know what, never mind. It's not important." He walks away and pulls a phone out of his back pocket, typing something without answering my question. He's not going to. I know how this game works. I don't get answers, no matter how much I want them. The real question is...if they don't want information on Silas and Baron, then what do they want?

"All right, I let him know you're awake and he's on his way down," he says to me. My heart starts to race at the prospect of meeting someone new, someone probably meaner and more dangerous. Then Glasses comes back and sits in the chair by the window, staring at me.

"He's pissed, you know. For the whole shooting him thing. You're lucky he had his vest on or you'd be fucked. I was the one who told him to wear it. I told him you'd be a loose cannon. You always were impulsive as fuck, but he thought he could handle you. I guess he owes me a thank-you, huh? Not gonna hold my breath for that, though."

While he rattles on like we're old friends, I just keep staring at his face, and the more I look at him, the more I see a hint of resemblance, something strangely familiar in his features. Like I've seen him before or knew him from a long time ago.

"Holy motherfucking shit…" I mumble as realization dawns.

His eyes light up and he leans forward. "Finally!" he says, throwing his arms up. "You remember me?"

Rolling onto my back, I shut my eyes and try to calm my brain that's going a million miles a minute. I knew him when I was a kid, not just knew him, but he was…my family? I can see his face in my memory, a big kid, a few years older than me. I can see him in the same memory I see my family.

My mother with her bright yellow hair and crystal blue eyes is sitting at a table with my dad, a tall, broad-shouldered man with a thick beard and chocolate-brown eyes. Another man is at the table with them, and they're laughing. There's a kid there with me…

He's older than me, so I have to look up to see his face, but he's kind, and when his dad barks at him to take me somewhere else to play, he places a gentle hand on my back and ushers me out of the living room. We play on the floor of my room with some action figures he brought with him.

When I open my eyes, I feel like I'm in a different fucking universe.

"We've met before, haven't we?" I ask. I have no clue what his name is or how our families knew each other, but I have a feeling he's going to fill me in soon.

"Uh, yeah, dipshit. We fucking grew up together. You really forgot everything when that asshole took you, didn't you?"

"He didn't take me. He rescued me."

"Yeah, after murdering your family. I know." He rolls

his eyes and I struggle against my cuffs again. This is bull-shit. I'm not going to sit here and argue about my child-hood or Silas with this asshole who doesn't want to give me information.

"Finally," he mutters, staring at the floor, when I hear the *click-click* of shoes against the marble floor echoing through the room.

"He's awake?" he asks. It's the same voice as the man I saw in the alleyway, the same one I thought I put a bullet in.

"Yeah, he's awake," the guy with glasses replies, and I study his behavior. He won't look the other guy in the eye but keeps his gaze unfocused. If I had to guess, these two don't get along too well.

"Hello, Gabriel," the man says, kneeling down to look me in the eye.

"Well, you look more alive than I expected you to," I groan.

"Yeah, thanks to Quentin here for convincing me to wear that vest. He seems to remember you were a little crazy. I'm glad I took his advice."

Quentin. It sparks a deep memory as I stare at the guy in the chair again.

The older man stands and leans against the wall beside the other. "You don't remember us, do you, Gabriel?"

"Enlighten me," I reply, without giving anything away.

He seems to consider this for a moment. Then he lets out an exhale as he says, "Your father, Isaac, was my brother. Quentin is my son, your cousin," he says, placing a hand on his shoulder.

I don't know why this information doesn't surprise me. My jaw clenches as I glare at them. "You don't look happy to see us," the man says with a cold bite in his tone.

"You couldn't send a fucking letter? Pick up the phone? You separated me from my dad and brother just to get me alone, knock me out and put me in cuffs, so we could have this little family reunion?" I yell, spit flying out of my mouth as I ramble on in rage.

"That man is *not* your father," the guy says with an evil sneer on his face.

"Yeah, well he had a choice. Kill me like he killed my parents—like someone *hired him to*, or leave me there with their bodies for CPS or some shit to find me. Where the fuck were you then, huh?"

"I found your parents that night," he booms, smacking his chest. "You should have come with me, Gabriel."

"Well, it didn't work out that way, asshole, and if you expect me to give a shit about you because we share a little blood, you're fucking crazy."

I see the kid's eyes go wide as I rant, and I know I'm probably about to get socked in the face by the old man for this shit, but I don't care.

And just as I expected, the big guy mumbles something in Spanish before grabbing me by my collar and dragging me to my feet.

"Ungrateful little shit," he mutters as he drags me out of the room. I hear Glasses trail behind us. We don't stop as he hauls me into the main living room and then out to the balcony. We're on the second or third floor, overlooking a huge yard with people moving from one side to the other. There are buildings on either side and an infinity pool with beautiful ladies in string bikinis lounging in the sun.

"See this, Gabriel? This is what your parents died for, *mijo*. This is the empire we have built in their honor. They died for *this*."

"My parents died because they owed some dealer

money. They were stupid crackheads who didn't know better," I say through clenched teeth.

He slaps me hard against my head, and I sneer at him. I have a vision of strangling him with these cuffs, but it'd be my death. There are too many assholes around to stop me.

"Your parents were not crackheads. Your father had the potential to be the next Basileus, and if he hadn't been betrayed, he would have been."

"The next Basileus? What the fuck are you talking about?"

"The Mandola Cartel has been around for centuries, naming their leader, El Basileus. When one dies, another takes his place. Your father had plans to overthrow the former Basileus and take his place, but Basileus put the hit on him before he could. After he died, I fulfilled that dream. I killed the man who put the hit on your parents, and I became the leader."

"Wait...you..." My body tenses with his hand still hard against the back of my neck.

"You understand now?"

"You're the new Basileus."

"*Si, mijo.*"

"Motherfucker..." I stammer, looking around.

Well, this shit just got a lot more interesting.

Eleven

Silas

Sitting at a greasy diner in a seat by the window, I take slow, deliberate sips of my coffee and pretend I'm reading something on my phone as I wait for the target to emerge from his beat-up Honda and go back into his house. He left for the store to pick up cigarettes exactly ten minutes ago, and I know he will be gone between twelve and eighteen minutes.

Right on schedule, the white SUV nearly crashes into the parking spot outside his building, and he carries his ugly, fat frame across the sidewalk to the first-floor apartment.

I give him a moment, finishing my coffee and paying my tab. Then I walk across the street to his complex and busy myself with tying my shoelaces while a couple passes by me. Once I'm alone on the lawn in front of his door, I walk straight inside, drawing my gun before he can even flinch.

I already know he doesn't lock his door, probably a habit from always having security to watch over him before, but it seems like a stupid, reckless choice to me. Or maybe he's just resigned to dying at this point after living over sixty years and somehow escaping death in a profession where few ever do.

"What the fuck!" he shouts, reaching for the pistol at his back, but stops when he sees the one currently aimed at the spot between his eyes.

"I wouldn't reach for that if I were you," I mumble darkly, the words stumbling through my lips like steel. I wish I could kill this guy right now. I wish I could watch his dead body fall to the floor along with every other piece of shit involved with the Mandola Cartel, and until I get my son back that is exactly what I plan to do.

And if I don't get my son back…

It's a thought I won't let penetrate my mind. I've already gone down that path, and Iris was there to bring me back. But I can't depend on her to always pull me back to the surface every time I want to drink myself into oblivion. Instead, I've erected a wall between my consciousness and the possibility that Gabriel is dead.

"Sit the fuck down," I bark, nodding my head toward his couch.

He fumbles slowly toward it, dropping into the seat with his eyes trained on me.

"Do you know who I am?" I ask. He should. He hired me fourteen years ago, and although that deal wasn't made in person, I know he would at least recognize my face.

"Silas Black," he says slowly, as if he's expecting his life to end before he gets the last syllable out.

"Very good," I reply. "And do you know why I'm here?"

There's hesitation on his face before he slowly shakes his head. "You hired me to take out the Morales family because they were stealing from your boss."

His brow furrows immediately.

"Why do you look so confused, Mr. Bulson?"

"I didn't..."

My eyes roll as I step closer. I don't have the patience right now to deal with his memory loss. "Three days ago, my son went missing, and your boss is involved. Tell me everything you know about Basileus's operation and I might let you see tomorrow."

"My boss is dead," he mutters, finally relaxing into his sofa. "You don't understand how the title of El Basileus works. Shortly after that family was killed, they came for us. I barely managed to make it out alive, but my boss, El Basileus, was killed."

My patience has run out, and in its place, a surge of rage courses through my veins. I holster my pistol and grab this asshole by the collar, tossing him hard against the wall. He puts up a little fight, so I slam my fist into his protruding gut and he spits onto the floor. Pulling him upright, I give him an uppercut to the jaw. His head jars to the side and comes back, chin to his chest, while blood drips from his mouth.

"Listen to me, motherfucker. You're lying," I bark. "And I don't have time for this shit. He's still running the entire syndicate in Tijuana. You think I'm fucking stupid?"

"It's not the same guy. Basileus is a title," he blubbers. "The man in charge of the cartel now is Baxter Morales. That man you killed...it was his brother, and I didn't put that hit on him. We didn't even know he was stealing from us, and we certainly didn't know he was going to try and kill us. Stabbed us right in the back."

"Make this very fucking clear to me right now. If you didn't hire me, then someone did so with your name. Who the fuck was it?"

"The man who hired the hit on that couple was his own brother—the new El Basileus—Baxter Morales."

Twelve

Iris

"You're going to Mexico?" Camilla asks, following me around the store, helping me unload the new inventory.

"Just for a few days. Silas wants to take us on a little vacation." It's hard to keep the shake out of my voice. I had to come into work today, even though getting out of bed was hard enough. Putting on makeup and doing my hair actually made me feel a little better, but I still feel like a fraud.

When I turn around and look at Camilla, my heart shatters. She has a look of concern on her face, and I basically just told her my rich boyfriend is taking me to Mexico for a few days, which means she can tell something is up.

Camilla is my closest friend, and really, the only best friend I've ever had. After the boys bulldozed the old motel and I built my shop, I hired the one person I knew would work hard and needed a second chance. I found her at the same gas station I met her at two years ago. She was starving and desperate, and we latched onto each other for dear life.

Since then, I've been able to confide in Camilla about everything—well, almost everything. She knows I live with the boys, who seldom show their faces in my store, and although the front is that I'm *with* Silas, Camilla caught on pretty quick. Especially when she caught me and Gabriel having a quickie in the back room.

She doesn't know what they do for a living, of course. And she doesn't know that my father was in the mafia, but I feel like Camilla and I bonded over the fact that we live in different worlds than most. We abide by different rules. We don't have doting mothers or homemade cookies. No one tucked us in at night and the world did not stop turning when our lives fell apart, so although other best friends probably connect over 'regular' things like brunch and pedicures, Camilla and I can relate on matters of the criminal sort.

I did tell her in great detail how I killed Donny Wright —the man responsible for many of her scars and bruises. We happened to be drinking mimosas at the time, so see... we're not that weird, after all.

"Why do you look so worried?" I ask, hiding my face and forcing my voice to hide the terror I'm feeling. Tears begin to well up in my eyes, but I quickly shake them away. Camilla can't know that Gabriel is in danger or possibly dead, and if I start up, I'll never stop.

"Because I can read you like a book, Iris," she replies, touching a soft hand to my shoulder.

When I look up at her, her expression softens, her shoulders slumping and her mouth turning downward. There are a lot of unspoken words between us as the tears return. I wish so badly I could say everything I'm feeling.

It's unfair that I can't express these things that are so intense inside me, like the fear that my family is broken and will never be whole again. Or the rage coursing through my veins that makes me want to draw blood in a way I've never felt before. The violent anger I felt toward Donny Wright and Vincent Maretti is *nothing* compared to this.

If someone hurt Gabriel...just the thought makes me think that I may lose myself to this fury and never return.

"Just promise me you'll keep everything going here until I get back," I mumble through my impending tears.

"I promise," she answers without hesitation.

"I don't know what I'd do without you."

She lets out a laughing scoff and tilts her head as if to say, *really?*

Out of the corner of my eye, I spot a familiar black car pull up in front of the shop. I don't need to see through the heavily-tinted windows to know that Silas is behind the driver's seat. He won't text or get out of the car because he doesn't have to. He's here for a reason.

"I have to go," I mutter quickly, standing up and running to grab my purse behind the counter.

"Please be safe," Camilla cries, grabbing me for a strong hug before I can escape. I let her hug me for a while, wrapping my arms around her tiny frame and squeezing her so she knows how much I care about her.

We let go at the same time, and I force a tight-lipped smile before I run out the front door and climb into the car next to my man. The first thing I notice is his tense jaw. By the looks of it, he must have his teeth clenched so hard it hurts.

"What is it?" I say in a breathless whisper. I'm terrified it's bad news. It feels like there's never good news in this family.

"We need to leave immediately," he replies. I watch his strong hand grip the steering wheel even tighter.

"What happened? What did you find out?" I stammer, desperate for answers.

"I found out that El Basileus, the biggest drug lord in Mexico, is Gabriel's uncle, the same man who put a hit out on his parents."

"Wait, what? Slow down," I mumble, trying to piece this all together. "I thought his parents were low-life dealers...not connected to the head of the cartel."

"I thought that too."

"So his uncle...killed his father?"

He heaves a deep sigh in return, and I take that as a yes.

"And his uncle is now the new head of the cartel?" My heart is pounding so hard, I can feel it throbbing in my skull. I'm trying my best not to panic, but this just got a whole lot more serious. Gabriel's family is tied to the cartel, and he's now in the hands of a Machiavellian uncle who would probably kill him without hesitation to secure his own title.

"Maybe...maybe he just wants his nephew back. What if he found out Gabriel was still alive and just wants to take him back? Then Gabriel is probably still alive, right?"

"I hope so," he says. Sensing my rising panic, Silas reaches over and places his hand on my thigh. Giving it a gentle squeeze, he tries to calm me, but his face doesn't soften, and I know he's even more tense than me. "The sooner we get down there, the sooner we find out."

I intertwine my fingers with his, and try to trick my brain into believing everything will be all right.

Thirteen

Baron

I'm staring out the small window of the private jet as we make our way down to solid ground. I look over and Iris has her eyes pinched closed with her hands folded in her lap. She's not a fan of take-offs or landings, though she does fine once we're steady in the air.

Reaching over, I lay my hand over her intertwined fingers. "Almost there, babe."

With her head rested back, she smiles without batting an eye. Silas is too busy thumbing away at his phone to even notice that we've arrived at the private airfield in Tijuana.

When the wheels touch down, I give Iris's hands a squeeze and her eyes open. My brows rise. "You did it."

She smiles back but the look immediately fades, leaving nothing but pouty lips and tear-soaked eyes. I know she's a mess over everything that's going on. Gabriel is missing and she likely blames herself. That's how Iris is. Ever since she joined our family, she's always tried so hard to keep us all together and happy. The thing is, this is in no way her fault. It's mine.

Gabriel has a way of testing my patience and in a split-second decision, I yelled at him and told him to go on this job. Never crossed my mind that he'd actually take my advice—for once. Sure as shit, he went. Turns out Silas was right. It was a trap and he took the bait. I don't blame him, though. I blame those dirty sons of bitches that he once called family.

The pilot emerges from the cockpit and announces that we can depart the jet. With slumped shoulders, Iris makes her way off the plane and Silas and I share a silent look as we stalk toward her. She's digging the toe of her shoe into the gravel with her hands stuffed in the front pocket of her hoodie.

It's hot as shit out here and I know she's got to be sweating in that thing. "Come on, baby," Silas says, throwing an arm around her waist and shuffling her toward the sleek black Hummer waiting for us.

Once we're all inside, Silas takes a call while Iris and I listen intently.

"Uh-huh," he says, then looks me in the eye. His jaw skates left and right as he grinds his teeth before he raises his voice. "I don't give a damn about their rules. You get me a fucking address or it's your head up your own ass."

He ends the call with a growl and squeezes his phone tightly in his hand. It's not often that Silas shows his emotion, but Gabriel *is* his son. As much as I tried to fight giving him that title, he loves him the same way he loves me. Blood or not.

"You still don't have an address for this Basileus guy?" Iris asks with a softness in her tone. I can tell she's on the verge of another breakdown and I wish we could just lie to her and tell her we've got it all under control. But the truth is, we don't have a fucking clue what's next and we're playing it by ear, so she'd see right through the bullshit.

"We'll get him back. Don't you worry," Silas says in an attempt to calm her. He stuffs his phone in the breast pocket of his jacket and stares out the window as we ride through the battered part of the city.

It's not my first time here in Tijuana, but I'm not exactly thrilled to be back. Anytime I've ever come, it was for a messy job that required great focus. It's a city full of mobs and cartels on every corner. You stick out like a sore thumb if you're not careful. Which is exactly what we're doing now as we creep through Zona Norte.

Iris must have caught onto my tense disposition because she grabs my hand and squeezes. "We'll find him," she says with a calmness in her voice.

Could this girl be any more perfect? Here she is, trying to comfort me when she's the one that is seconds away from tears. What she doesn't realize is that finding Gabriel isn't what's gnawing at me. I know we'll find him. It's keeping her safe in this fucked-up situation that has me on edge. If I had my way, she'd be home where she's put out of harm's way. Iris is tough as nails, but the men around here would snatch her up and sell her to the highest bidder, without giving it a second thought.

"Yeah," I squeeze her hand back, "we'll find him." I flash her a brief smile before we hit the highway and pick up speed.

I glance down at the map pulled up on my phone and see that we're five minutes away from the hotel. "Did you get an address yet?" I look at Silas, who's deep in thought.

He snaps out of it and glances at his phone. "Nothing."

Minutes later, we're pulling up to the hotel. It's the

same one I stayed in the last time I came to Tijuana with Silas. I was only thirteen years old then. My mom and David had died two months prior and Silas was hell-bent on settling the score with the rest of the Rossi family. We took care of the brothers who killed my own brother, but their father was still alive and well. Until that day. It wasn't a job, it was personal. There were howls and bloodshed and images in my head that I won't soon forget.

The driver opens the door and I slide out, then offer Iris my hand and help her to her feet. "Wow. This is beautiful," she says, peering up at the twelve-story hotel that hides the setting sun.

Silas takes her hand while the driver sets our bags on a luggage cart the bellhop brought out. "Don't get too comfortable. We're getting Gabriel and getting the hell out of here."

Let's hope it's that easy. El Basileus is powerful and corrupt, which means there's no doubt he's expecting us.

What appears easy never is. Not in our line of business.

Silas opted for his own room while Iris will be staying with me—at least for tonight. Tomorrow, she'll likely stay with him, which I've learned to deal with. What we're doing works, and as long as she's happy, we're all happy. Just being with her is enough for me. Her love for me doesn't diminish just because she loves them, too.

"Are you almost done in there?" Iris asks behind the closed bathroom door.

I rub the towel across the mirror, wiping the fog away, then drop it to the floor. "Come on in."

The door opens and there she is. A goddess in the

highest form, wearing nothing but a black T-shirt—I think it's mine, though it could be Gabriel's. Regardless, she's stunning in it. Her hair is let down and her tired eyes only add to her natural beauty.

Her eyebrows dance across her forehead as she gapes at me. I back up, pressing my palms to the sink vanity behind me and bite my lower lip, wearing absolutely nothing but a grin on my face.

"I could have waited," she says, looking me up and down, mostly down.

"Maybe I didn't want you to." I point and bend my finger, calling her over.

Slow steps raise a smile on her face and I'd do damn near anything to keep it there. She stops a foot away and the pleased look instantly fades as her lips press together. "He's still missing, Baron. I don't think—"

"Shh." I grab her by the waist and pull her close. "Don't think." My arms wrap around her waist, hands gliding under her shirt, feeling the heat of her skin.

Her eyes close and her head drops back as I suck on the thin skin of her neck, planting kisses down her collarbone. Balling the ends of her shirt in my hands, I lift up and remove it, then drop it on top of the towel on the floor. Her perky breasts greet me and my cock aches to be inside of her.

The worry in her eyes mimics mine. We're both lost. In this situation, in this moment. Nothing is known. The future of our family is bleak. All I know is that I won't lose her. Not now. Not ever.

"Baron," she grumbles as I cup her breasts and press my mouth to hers. "I need you," she says between breaths and kisses.

Everything intensifies. Our emotions get the best of us

as we beg our minds to stop going to that dark place where Gabriel isn't okay. Where he's never found—or doesn't want to be found.

We tear into each other. Kiss for kiss. Bite for bite. Our teeth clank together in this raw, real moment. Iris's nails claw their way down my back until she's holding my cock in her hand. My hips sway to her movements momentarily as she gives me a few pumps, but I stop her, not ready for this to end. I know if she keeps going, I won't last long.

Pulling back, I drop to my knees. She questions me with her eyes, while I stare into them as I pull her black, silk panties down her legs. She steps out of them one foot at a time while weaving her fingers through my hair. Before I can even spread her legs, she's slamming my face into her pussy.

With two fingers, I part her lips and flatten my tongue, licking the length of her slit. My free hand slaps her ass and then I squeeze, filling the gaps of my fingers with her flesh. "Leg up," I tell her as I drop my hand to the crease behind her knee. She raises her leg and sets her foot on the toilet to the side of us, spreading her thighs far and wide. Arousal drips from her pussy, and I sweep it up with the tip of my tongue then lick my lips. "Mmm. You taste so good, baby."

Iris groans, rolling her hips and moving my head with her motions as I suck her clit between my teeth. My cock twitches in agony at the beautiful sounds she makes. The need to be inside her is torturous, but her pleasure is a necessity.

I slide a finger inside her heat, then another, filling her up. I dig deep, massaging her on the inside. My tongue swirls around her clit. Lips parting, then closing as I suck the delicate skin.

"Oh God, Baron," she whimpers, dropping her head

back and grinding against my face. I go faster, agonizing over the pleasure I'm bringing her. It's as if my life mission is to please this woman. Make her happy, make her feel good. More so than Gabriel and Silas can. It's not a competition, it's about pride. Knowing I can give my girl something more than they can or do.

"That's right. Come for me, baby." My tongue returns to its rightful place and I lick in long strides, relishing in her taste. My fingers don't stop moving as she clenches her walls and cries out in euphoria. I growl a husky sound as she reaches the height of her orgasm.

Before she comes down, I get up and grab her waist, flipping her over the vanity onto her stomach. I ram my dick inside of her and she whimpers in delight.

Iris braces herself with two palms pressed to the vanity. Grabbing a fist full of her chestnut locks, I tug her head back until she's looking at me in the mirror. Her mouth falls open as I penetrate her pussy at rapid speed. Her tits bounce, and I reach under her, pinching the bud of her nipple. She shrills at the pain, but I know my girl likes it rough.

"You like that, baby?" I groan through a cracked voice. She nods in response while I hold her head upright.

Pressure builds inside of me. I thrust once, twice, three times before I fill her to the brim. "Fuck, Iris." I growl as I slow my movements, until I'm motionless inside of her. My cock pulsates as I come down.

Leaning over her back, I cup her chin and tilt her head, pressing a chaste kiss to her forehead. "I love you," I tell her.

She blinks a few times, then smiles. "I love you, too."

Fourteen

Iris

I'm walking down the hall of the hotel in sweatpants and a sweatshirt with a pair of house slippers to go and check on Silas. I know he's just as much of a mess over everything as I am. Gabriel is his son. It doesn't matter that Silas has a hard exterior; he's soft when it comes to matters of his family—even if I'm the only one who sees that side of him, which is also a rarity.

Warmth radiates through me at the thought of these three men of mine. I've never felt so cherished and protected. Growing up, I was always under a watchful eye, but it was always by men who were paid to keep me safe. Now, it's men who want to keep me safe. The thing is, I want to do the same for them. I know they're grown men, who are trained to take care of themselves, but there isn't a job out there that doesn't have surprises pop up occasionally. Unfortunately, in this line of work, surprises can turn deadly. My chest hurts at the thought of something terrible happening to Gabriel. I don't just love him; I am madly in love with him—just like I am with Silas and Baron.

As I approach Silas's door, I hear shouting coming from his room. At least, I think it's from his room. The closer I get, the more certain I am. It's definitely Silas shouting.

The tone in his voice has my stomach twisting in knots. He's angry, which means he's likely getting bad news. I'm not sure how much more bad news I can take, but regardless, I press my ear to the door. I don't like invading his privacy, but I also don't want him to sugarcoat things and make me feel like everything is fine when it's not.

"It's about fucking time," Silas huffs. "No. I'm going alone. I don't want anyone else put in danger."

He's going alone?

A couple seconds later, the room is silent. He must have ended the call abruptly. I knock my knuckles to the door, and when he doesn't come, I knock louder. "Silas," I say in a whisper-yell.

When the door flies open and startles me, I jump back. "Iris. Is everything okay?" Silas pokes his head out the door and looks left then right.

He's standing in the doorway with a scorned look on his face, wearing nothing but a towel he's gripping around his waist. All his sexiness causes me to lose my train of thought as my eyes give his body a lazy sweep. "Umm, yeah. Everything is fine. Is everything okay with you?"

"Come in," he says, stepping aside with his palm pressed to the open door. Once I'm in, he closes it. "I was just getting ready to jump in the shower. Would you like to join me?"

God, would I ever. But a shower is the furthest thing from my mind, even if he is standing there looking so damn enticing. "Were you on the phone?"

He quirks a brow in all seriousness. "You heard?"

"I heard you talking to someone when I got to the door. What was it about? Did you get an address to where Gabriel might be?"

Silas scratches his neck as if he's thinking of a response when it should be as easy as a yes or no. I look past him and notice a pad of paper lying on the still made bed.

He doesn't want to lie to me, but he also doesn't want to tell me the truth.

"You know," my hand sweeps through the air, "we can talk about this in the morning. Why don't you just go finish your shower and get some rest? It's been a long day."

Silas leans forward and presses a soft kiss to my forehead. "Go back to your room and get some sleep. I'll see you in the morning."

I nod under his touch. He disappears into the bathroom, leaving me here with temptation lying right on his bed. When I hear the shower begin running, I stare at the address scribbled on the paper. He's planning to follow this lead. If my instincts are correct, that's exactly why he wants me to go back to my room and get some sleep. And as much as it pains me to betray the person I trust more than anyone, I can't resist this.

"I'm sorry," I whisper, before tearing the page off the small notepad.

Folding the paper in half, I tuck it in my bra and grab his pistol from the holster on his nightstand and tuck it in the other cup. It's a good thing I went with an oversized sweatshirt tonight. Wasting no time, I leave the room and hurry down the hall to my and Baron's room. With a swipe of the room key, I'm in. "Hey," I say to Baron, who's lying in the bed, wearing nothing but a pair of gray joggers, ankles crossed and hands folded behind his head. "Anything good on?" I ask him jokingly.

"As a matter of fact, yes." He reaches out and grabs me by the waist, pulling me down on the bed with him. "You see, there's this image in my head of you bent over that bathroom sink and it's been my favorite show of the day. In fact," he kisses my neck, nuzzling his face in the crease, "I think I should watch it again."

Ugh. So much temptation tonight and I'd love nothing more than to eat it all up, but I can't. "Actually, I told Silas I'd go for a walk outside with him. I think he needs some fresh air. I just came in for my shoes."

Baron sulks, dropping back on the bed.

"I'm sorry, baby." I lean forward and kiss his perfectly parted lips. "I promise I'll make it up to you."

"Don't be sorry. As much as I'd love to have you all to myself, I can't be selfish."

I draw back with a crooked grin. "Who are you and what have you done with my boyfriend?"

Baron laughs. "I guess I'm just...accepting everything."

I kiss him again through our smiles. "And it makes me love you even more." Getting to my feet, I squeeze his hand on the bed. There's an unsettling feeling pooling in my stomach that feels like this is goodbye. "I won't be long. And Baron, I do love you."

"Love you, too, baby."

I walk away with a guilty conscience, an address, and a gun stuffed in my bra.

I've been gripping the paper so tightly, the moisture from my hands has seeped through, dampening it. I'm a ball of nerves as the Uber driver coasts down the suburban road. There are houses lined in rows and I find it odd that anyone would hold someone prisoner in such a nice, quaint area.

"How much longer?" I ask, leaning forward to get a look at the GPS on the gentleman's dash.

"*Cinco minutos, muchacha*," he responds. I don't know Spanish well, but I do know numbers. Five minutes until I could possibly see where Gabriel is being held.

I'm terrified of what I might find. He could be hurt, dead, or perfectly fine, not wanting to be found—which scares me just as much. Silas said that this big cartel leader is Gabriel's uncle. He could be happy to have this reunion with his blood family. But where would that leave us? Me?

I can't go there. As long as he's safe, that's all that matters. Patting my bra, I make sure the gun is safely secured. The last thing I need is for it to fall out. If I'd had a minute to prepare, I would have grabbed my holster, but there was no time for that.

Minutes later, the car comes to a rolling stop. It's completely dark outside and hard to see where we're at, but we're definitely not on a street with compacted houses. The surrounding area looks desolate—both empty and slightly terrifying.

"*Buenas nochas*," he says from the front seat.

We've arrived.

I've paid through the app.

There is no reason for me to still be sitting here, but something doesn't let me get out.

"Thank you very much." I grab the door's slippery handle, take a deep breath, and push it open.

My feet hit solid ground and I swear I can feel the vibration shimmy through my entire body. Chills skate up my spine in the seventy-five-degree air.

I look out and notice a gate, then look up and see a row of cameras peeking down on me. Well, it looks like my presence will be known.

"One hour," I remind the driver as I poke my head in the door. The arrangement was a ride here and a ride back, hopefully taking Gabriel with me. Am I naive to think that's even a possibility? It sure as hell feels like it, but I'm not giving up hope. I can't.

The driver nods and I finally close the door behind me. Before I can even blink, he's driving off. I watch, internally begging for him to come back because I'm so fucking stupid for even coming here. But it's too late. His taillights become just a speck in the night.

I fidget nervously with my hands as I stare ahead at the tall wrought-iron gate, wishing I had come up with some sort of a plan before reacting. I'm just going to press the buzzer and request entry. I'm a measly tourist who took a walk and got lost. Once I'm in, I'll see what I'm up against.

My knees wobble, hands trembling as I reach out and press the buzzer. I look up, left, and right, knowing damn well that I'm under a watchful eye.

A minute passes and there's still no response, so I press it again. The buzz echoes through my ears and I almost jump out of my shoes at the sound before I realize it's not the buzzer, it's the gate opening. I take a step back, feeling a mixture of lightheadedness and eagerness to get this over with.

Once the gates are completely open, I take a few steps forward until I'm hovering between being inside the gate and outside of it. I'm thankful for the lights that line the driveway; otherwise, I wouldn't see a thing. Not that it matters. All that's in front of me is an endless paved driveway.

The slamming of a car door has my heart jumping into my throat. I take another step, hoping to see where it came from, but there are no headlights in sight.

Then I see him. A tall, dark shadow of a man coming toward me. It's hard to make him out, but he has a slender build and there's a glimmer of a reflection from his glasses. The closer he gets, the more I realize he can't be much older than I am, which settles my nerves slightly.

"Hello," I call out, trying to get his attention, although he's still at least ten yards away. He doesn't respond, just keeps walking toward me at a leisurely pace. "I seem to have taken a wrong turn and I was wondering if I could use your phone."

Still nothing.

He comes closer, the scorned look on his face obvious. He's wearing a pair of black dress pants, shiny black shoes, and a white button-up shirt with the sleeves rolled and the top three buttons undone. There's no way he's a day over twenty-five, and that's pushing it.

Once we're only a foot away from each other, his expression changes from angry to surprised, but I'm too distracted by the brightness of his copper eyes and the black-and-white tattoos snaking out of his sleeves. He's gorgeous in a way that's almost...familiar.

I shake myself out of my daze and finally speak.

"Hi. I'm sorry to intrude, but I..."

"Iris?" he mutters, cutting off my words. My mouth hangs open and my mind moves a mile a minute.

"How do you know my..." *Gabriel*, my mind registers. Gabriel must be here. He must have told this man about me, shown him my picture. Panic and hope mingle in my gut as I stare up at the mansion before me. If he's in there, then I need to go in there to find him.

"I know why you're here," he mumbles with a wicked expression in his eye that makes my blood run cold.

"Where is he?" I ask, changing my tune from innocent tourist to pissed-off girlfriend real fast.

"Right this way," he replies, guiding me toward the large, ornately decorated home.

I hesitate. "Why should I trust you?"

The man responds with a warm smile that's convincingly innocent, which actually unsettles me more than anything. I was ready for a fight, not a warm welcome. "I don't see a whole lot of options for you right now," he says with his subtle Spanish accent and soft tone, giving me hope that this guy isn't a total psychopath.

Relenting, I take a step with him. He hovers a hand at the small of my back and I want to rip it off, but I'm too afraid the wrong move could ruin everything and end up with me dead and no closer to my boyfriend.

Then, the man mumbles darkly, "I sure hit the jackpot with you."

Fifteen

GABRIEL

"Get me the fuck out of here," I scream, my words bouncing off the four walls surrounding me. I got a little handsy, so good ole Uncle Bax decided it was best if I was locked up for the time being. Apparently I needed to cool down or some shit. Not that I have. Not that I ever will in this fucking place.

I push myself off the cot and walk over to the door, feeling defeated but far from giving up. There's a square, plexiglass window on the door, but the dirty film on it makes it impossible to see out.

"Do you hear me?" I shout even louder, "let me out, you dumb fucks."

They're dead. Every last one of them. I don't even care that they're family. I vaguely remember my uncle as it is, so teetering on the idea of strangling him to death fills me with zero empathy.

I knew I had family out there somewhere. They didn't

all die the day I lost my parents. Sure, I had a last name, could have searched and probably would have found them with the connections I made as part of the Black family, but I never cared to. Silas is my father. Baron is my brother. I have no aunts, uncles, or cousins, and I don't need them. Especially not that geeky-looking boy, Quentin.

"Fuck," I bellow, gripping the sides of my head and tugging. Should've just listened to Silas. He was right, as always. I should be home right now with Iris, curled up in bed and arguing over that stray cat's name—although, she's Punk, and she isn't changing my mind. Unless, of course, she gets on her knees and begs around my cock. Who am I kidding? I'm weak when it comes to Iris. I'd give that girl anything she wanted.

Just the thought of her makes me smile, but it diminishes as fast as it came when I hear the clicking of the lock on the outside of the door.

It comes open, and I expel all the air from my lungs in one breathy huff. "You again?" I shake my head, turning away from my uncle and walking back over to the cot, or should I say, Basileus, the almighty leader of the underground drug world.

"Yes, it's me. It will always be me. Would you like to know why?"

I drop down on the cot and glower at him as he stands in the doorway. There's an army of men behind him, so attempting to fight my way out is senseless.

When I don't respond, he keeps going. "I will not give up on you, Gabriel. You are blood, *mijo*. My blood. I fight for my family, and I will fight for you."

What is this asshole going on about? "Family isn't about blood, it's about loyalty. I've got that. So, if you don't mind," I stand up and eat the space between us, "I'll see myself out."

Glaring, I walk around him, and I'm pretty surprised when he lets me. I'm surrounded by brick walls, and it looks like some sort of catacombs.

"You can leave the room, but you're not leaving the property. I've got men surrounding this place who are under strict orders to keep you here."

"Fuck off," I grumble as I make my way through the maze. I follow the lights on the wall until I come to an open door. Unsure what's behind it, I open it up and make my way up the staircase.

"I knew you'd be angry, Gabriel. Knew you wouldn't just agree to stay, but you've also not heard my offer."

"You're still here?" I huff, making my way up the enclosed staircase. I reach another door and don't even hesitate to open it. Stepping out, it's like I've walked into an entirely different world from the one I've been stowed away in for the past twenty-four hours. The basement was dark, damp, and cold. Everything in this kitchen is shiny, clean, and white. I walk around the counter to the sliding glass door.

"You can go out, but you won't go far."

I growl back at him as I slide the door open. *We'll just see about that.*

There are three ladies in skimpy bathing suits basking in the sun on the deck. A large underground swimming pool and a bar with a bartender behind it. They know how to live here, I'll give them that.

It's not the girls that catch my eye first, though. It's the gate surrounding the area. Behind it, another gate. At least ten feet tall, wrought iron with daggers on the tops of each post. Cameras are everywhere. On the gates, the bar, the house. If I had to guess, there isn't an inch of this property that's not under twenty-four-hour surveillance.

"Mojito?" Uncle Baxter says, handing me a drink.

I look at him, snarl and turn away to observe my surroundings. "What the fuck do you want from me?"

"Gabriel," he chuckles, "we're family. You, me, Quentin. You've got cousins. A great-aunt who'd be very excited to see you. She's a firecracker, Aunt Lucille. Wouldn't hesitate to smack you over the head for disregarding your *familia*. She makes the best damn tamales in Mexico, though, so we let her insolence slide."

Swinging around, I slap the drink out of his hand. The glass crashes to the cement patio, shattering into shards, and the girls in the pool yelp in surprise. "Are you really talking about fucking tamales right now? Are you delusional? I'm not staying here. I've got a girl. I've got a family. Not to mention, a job. Now point me to the damn exit and forget you ever found me."

Uncle Baxter snaps his fingers at a guy walking by and points to the broken glass shattered all around us. The guy nods and scurries away before Uncle Baxter redirects his attention to me. "How's it feel to be employed by someone who doesn't know your worth?" His expression is calloused, but there's also a glint of sympathy. Sympathy I don't want, or need.

"What the hell are you talking about?"

"Silas Black. From what I hear, he keeps you boys on a tight leash. Chooses your jobs, turns down the ones he doesn't think you can..." he air quotes, "handle."

"Fuck off." My hand sweeps the air and I turn to face the pool. A tall, thin blonde winks at me before diving in and making a splash.

"You're in the same spot in that business you were in

when he took you in as a child. Where's the growth?" He rubs his thumb and forefinger together. "Where's the *exhilaration*?"

"You've got no idea what you're talking about. Our business is just fine."

"Yeah," he blows an airy chuckle, "for him."

It's no lie that Silas is vigilant with the jobs we get. Any father would be when it comes to the safety of his children. Hell, if I ever had kids, I'd probably be the same way. Not that I want any. I get where he's coming from. He lost a son once, and doesn't want to lose another. We came close two years ago with Baron when he was shot by Maretti's goons. Sure, he's been extra cautious, and many times it comes down to us making the decisions for ourselves. Much like this time. Baron wouldn't come, so I made the choice to leave and take the job on my own. Granted, it was a trap, but if I didn't take this job, it would have been another. Uncle Baxter claims he's the kingpin of the Mandola Cartel —Basileus—so he wouldn't have stopped until he had me in this exact spot.

I'm staring into the clear water when the blonde emerges. Her eyes set on me as she rests her arms on the edge of the pool. "Looking pretty hot up there. Care to go for a swim?"

Hell no, I don't wanna go for a swim, especially with her, or any chick that isn't Iris. I shake my head and turn back to Uncle Baxter.

"You'd live like a king here, *mijo*. All your dreams are within reach. The only rules you follow are your own."

My curiosity is piqued. "So, what do you want me to do for your *business*?"

"You'd sit beside my son and I on the throne, of course. A lord of the business. A leader. We're family, after all."

I ask the question burning in my stomach. Because forever is off the table. "How long?"

He shrugs his shoulders, grumbles a bit, then finally says, "As long as you'd like to stay. Let's start small. A few days? What do you say? Just enough time to catch up with your *familia*?"

I can tell that he doesn't use the word *family* lightly. It's apparent he'd die for those who carry his blood. He avenged my parents' death by fulfilling my dad's dreams of being the next Basileus. Assuming he wasn't jerking my balls and just telling me some bullshit story. Something tells me he wasn't. I think he really just wants me to work for him—to be part of this family. But I can't shake the feeling he wants more than that, a price I'm not willing to pay.

"What's the catch?" I ask.

"No catch, Gabriel. Just your loyalty to your family, your *real* family."

What about the one I've already got? If he's asking me to choose my birth family over the Black family, he's fucking crazy. Silas may piss me off, but I can't turn my back on the man who raised me.

And what about Iris? Without her, I am nothing.

Sixteen

Iris

My eyes flutter open and I smack my dry lips together. Disoriented, I scan the room and try to remember how the fuck I ended up on someone's bed, knocked out cold. Then I see him, the dark-haired guy with glasses and warm copper eyes, standing over me with a glass of ice water that looks more like liquid gold right about now. Shoving away the fear that wants to bubble to the top, I scooch myself into a sitting position and mumble vulgarities as I grab the glass from his hand. It could be poison, but I don't even care at this point. I'm so thirsty that I'll gladly drink to my death just to satisfy my thirst.

Once I've taken down half of the contents while he lingers over me, just watching and waiting for me to say something, I clench the glass with both hands. "Where the fuck am I?" I finally say.

It's not a dudgeon or some rundown shack, like the places I've been held prisoner in the past. No. This room is nice, with dark gray painted walls and a large bay window covered in heavy drapes. I notice some personal items on a large desk across the room and expensive-looking clothes hanging in the open closet. The bed I'm in is really damn comfortable with silk sheets and heavenly soft pillows.

The last thing I remember is walking through the gate with the same guy who is peering over me like I'm some sort of prized possession in threat of getting taken from him.

"My bedroom."

I set the glass down on a nightstand beside the bed, making a mental note that I could easily break that glass and stab him in the eye in two seconds flat if he tries to pull anything.

"Obviously. And why am I in your bedroom, asshole?"

He rounds the bed, running his index finger over the black, silk fabric of the comforter. "My name is Quentin, but asshole works, too. You're a feisty little thing, I'll give you that. We hadn't even made it down the hall and you were pulling a gun on me. Lucky for me, I think fast. Unlucky for you, I had to knock you out."

He's right. It's all coming back to me now. I realized my mistake in trusting him when I noticed he had me cornered in the hall. When I tried to escape, he grabbed a hold of me. I kneed him in the balls and pulled out my gun, and that's the last thing I remember.

"You son of a bitch. You chloroformed me!"

"Yeah, sorry about that."

"What the fuck? You just keep chloroform on you when bringing girls into your home?"

He laughs, and I can't help but notice the deep dimples chiseled in his cheeks when he smiles. Gabriel has those same dimples. "No, but when I saw you on the cameras, I came prepared."

I tuck my knees to my chest and nonchalantly pat my ankle for my gun, even though I know damn well it's gone.

"Looking for this, Green Eyes?" He reaches into his pocket and pulls my gun out, dangling it around his finger like a yo-yo string.

"Where is he?" I grit through my teeth. I don't say the name because he knows exactly who I'm talking about.

His eyebrows hit his forehead as he plays stupid. "Who? Your driver? Slapped him a few Benjamins and sent him on his way when he returned."

I throw my feet over the bed and stand up, my hand lingering over the glass. "Not my fucking driver. Where is Gabriel?" His response is an egotistical smirk as he pushes his glasses up on his nose, so I shout louder, "Where the fuck is he?"

"Exactly where he belongs. With his family," Quentin says as he pulls back the heavy curtain over the window. "And right now, it looks like he's having himself a drink."

"What the hell are you talking about?" I scoff, hurrying over to where Quentin stands in front of the window. I suspect he's trying to rile me up, but when I look out the tempered-glass window, I'm proven wrong. Ignoring the fact that an ocean view on the street I got out when I arrived was actually nowhere near the ocean, I only focus on him.

It's far away, toward the main house, but I can easily spot Gabriel's familiar frame.

Banging my fist against the window, I scream his name.

Behind me, the dark-haired boy laughs. "Don't bother. It's soundproof. Besides, they wouldn't hear you from all the way over here anyway."

I lower my hands in defeat.

Gabriel's there. Standing next to an older guy by a pool full of girls with a drink in his hand. A small sound escapes my lips at the sight of him, relieved to see him alive, but so confused to see him talking to the man in front of him and not rushing back home to me.

Smacking my hands against the window, I scream, "Gabriel!" My hands don't stop until I realize it's no use. He can't hear me.

Bile rises up my throat, but I swallow it back down. "You've brainwashed him, haven't you?"

"Iris," he says my name like we're old friends. "Gabriel was reunited with his family—his *real* family. Did you expect him to be shackled to a chair? We don't want to hurt him."

Something isn't right. Gabriel should be fighting his way back to me. He should be fighting for the family he's had since he was a child. The ones who took him in when he had nowhere to go. I turn away from the window and cross my arms over my chest. "I want to see him," I demand, keeping my voice steady and hiding the emotion. The desire to run into Gabriel's arms and feel his touch on my skin is torture, but I have to keep my cool.

Quentin shakes his head. "No can do, *señorita*. Gabriel hasn't earned the right to guests just yet. You see, we need to know we can trust him and, right now, you're getting in the way of that. You'll run down there and destroy all the progress we've made. So right now, you need to stay far away from him."

"Progress?" I laugh. "Do you think you're dealing with a couple of average civilians here? Gabriel is a trained profession-al." I raise my voice. "*I* am a trained professional." I don't elaborate what I'm insinuating, which is that Gabriel is using a little reverse psychology, it's what he does best. He's biding his time and earning *their t*rust while they think they are earning his.

He's okay, though, and that's all that matters right now.

"I know exactly who I'm dealing with. A quad of mediocre assassins," he tilts his head back and forth and clicks his tongue on the roof of his mouth, "a girl who talks too much. Oh, and my cousin—who I've known half my life. So yeah, *Iris*," he enunciates my name and it makes my blood boil, "I know everything about you, your father, and your boyfriends."

Refusing to let him get to me, I just do what Gabriel is doing and bide my time. My hands plant to my hips and I smirk back at him. "I see you've done your research. You should also know that I start my mornings with coffee—two sugars—so unless you want to hear me talk too much while shoving your balls up your ass at the same time, you should probably go fetch that for me."

Quentin drops his head back laughing then snaps a finger at me. "Talks too much and makes jokes." His humorous expression drops immediately. "Get your own damn coffee. I'm not a servant."

With that, he crosses the room and walks out the door, leaving it wide open. Does this mean I have free rein of the house? They're putting way too much faith in me because I could easily walk out that door and leave. Or maybe I'm putting too much faith in them. There is no way they'd allow that to happen. Something tells me they have me right where they want me.

I shoot back over to the window to get another look at Gabriel, but he's gone.

"Where are you and what the hell are you up to?" I mutter under my breath.

I'm gnawing on my thumbnail to the point that I'm at the skin while I walk down the hallway. This place isn't that big. I'm guessing a two-story, three-bedroom condo. I've got no idea why this Quentin guy thought it was a good idea to put me in his room, unless the others are occupied. It's possible he doesn't live here alone. A lot of these cartels keep all their men on the same property, so they are readily available. The house behind where Gabriel stood is most definitely not a condo. It's a mansion three times the size of the one the guys and I live in. There's no doubt the leader lives there—their king—their *Basileus*.

I go down the white, plank wood staircase and trail my fingers along the stainless-steel banister. The scent of bacon floods my senses and when I reach the bottom, I see an older lady in an apron standing over a stove. "Good morning," I say, in a whisper hush, "is...is Quentin down here?"

"Back patio," she says point-blankly, pointing her spatula at a pair of open French doors.

There's a nice breeze coming in, and I draw in a deep breath of the fresh air, hoping to rid my lungs of whatever that asshole used to knock me out last night. Chloroform wouldn't have kept me out all night. I look at my arms to see if he could have injected me with something, but don't see any signs of a needle puncture. Whatever it was, it worked.

I should have known he would move me to a different location. If he hadn't, then Silas and Baron would have easily found me based on the address Silas procured last night, and seeing as how there isn't a bloody shoot-out and dead bodies scattered around the property, they must not know where I am—yet.

I pass by the lady and head straight out the open doors. Quentin side-eyes me, mumbling something into the phone, then ends the call.

He smirks as he tucks his phone into the pocket of his pants. "Well, aren't you just a sight for sore eyes, wearing the devil's grin and my T-shirt."

Looking down, I gasp when I realize that I am, in fact, wearing his T-shirt. How did I not notice? I guess I'm so used to wearing the guys' shirts to bed that it didn't even faze me. I cross my legs and tug the black cotton shirt down, at the risk of exposing myself.

"Where the hell are my clothes?" I shout. "And who the fuck took them off me?"

Quentin raises a brow and that smug look returns. "Me, of course."

"You son of a bitch." I raise my hand to slap him, but he grabs me by the wrist.

"More like son of a whore. Nothing like waking up to your parents bringing home every Tom, Dick, Harry, and Jane every night."

I snarl in disgust while attempting to free my arm. "Let me go."

Quentin glowers as his grip strengthens. "But you know all about that, don't you? After all, you're fucking a trio of men."

My stomach twists in knots, and I swear to God, as soon as he lets me go, I'm knocking his ass out.

I jerk away again, and this time, he releases my arm, but the egotistical look on his face never fades. Even as I cock my fist back and release it on his left cheek.

Quentin rubs his hand over the imprint of my knuckles and laughs, but I waste no time, running like hell off the patio and straight to the back of the landscaped property.

It's like déjà vu, as memories hit me like a tidal wave. I was running through the woods at one of Maretti's houses. Lost for hours, I ended up walking in a circle and ended up right where I started. It was only minutes later that I found out Baron had been shot. At that moment, it felt like a small part of me died until I heard that he was going to be okay.

I keep running until I'm hidden amongst rows of trees. I glance over my shoulder, expecting him to be there, but he's not. Stepping around a tree, I look out, and Quentin is taking casual steps off the deck with his eyes on me. I snap my back to the tree and steady my breaths before I take off running again.

"Come on, Iris. You're not going anywhere. Save your energy," Quentin hollers in the distance.

Like hell I'm—

I scream as my body flies backward and my back slams into the hard ground. Shoots of electricity run through me, and it takes a second before the burning sensation subsides, and even then, it's still there.

"What the fuck?" I screech, pulling the stick from under my ass. Quentin makes it to me, peering over me as I lie on the ground. "You look pleased with yourself," I grumble through heavy breaths.

He smirks, hands pressed to his knees as he bends over. "I always wanted to watch that happen." With the stick still in my hand, I swing it up and attempt to hit him in the face, but he grabs it. "And you call yourself a trained assassin." He blows out a laugh.

"Fuck you!"

His hand reaches under my armpit, and he pulls me up. "You sure? I think you've got enough guys doing that already."

"I wasn't insinuating that I wanted you to. Ever," I snarl in disgust, as I jerk my arm away. "Don't touch me."

"You sure?" His brows rise. "You just got hit with fourteen thousand volts of electricity. Might wanna eat your pride and accept the help."

Walking with a limp from having a three-foot stick rammed into my ass cheek, I growl with each step back to the house while I wear my pride proudly. I don't need his damn help. "Why the hell do you need an invisible fence like that anyway?"

Quentin walks in step with me, ignoring the buzzing of his phone in his pocket. "Did it stop you from leaving?"

"I could have run through it. All it did was piss me off and make me want to leave even more."

"Beyond that is another, and another, until you come to a visible fence that you would only want your enemies to try and climb, because chances are, they'll die trying."

"You all are fucking sick."

Quentin shrugs his shoulders nonchalantly. "We keep people in, and we keep people out."

I'm well aware of the lengths people go to so they can protect themselves and their families. I grew up a caged animal. Never free to roam, always had eyes on me and a bodyguard at my side. I know the importance of privacy, but it doesn't mean I like it. Being told what to do pisses me off. Being held against my will enrages me.

We get back in the house and the pain in my ass is getting worse. Not Quentin—though he is a pain in my ass —the jab from the stick is what hurts. I reach back and touch the puncture, expecting it to be a small surface wound, but gasp when I look at my hand and see that it's painted in blood.

Quentin looks from my eyes to my hand, then back up. "Damn, girl. What did you do?"

"You did this," I shout, rubbing my bloody hand up and down his crisp white shirt. "Your stupid fence knocked me on my ass and I fell on a stick."

"All right, calm down." He looks around my body to get a look at my ass. "It's not that bad. We've got a doctor that can look at it."

"No! I don't want a damn doctor. I want to see Gabriel."

Quentin shakes his head, pushing his glasses up. "I can't allow that, but I can promise you that if you don't get that looked at, it could get infected and you could very well lose half of your ass." The grin on his face leads me to believe this is funny to him.

As I walk away, I huff and puff, mocking him under my breath, "You could very well lose half of your ass. I'll shove something up your ass, asshole."

"What's that?" Quentin says, hot on my trail.

I sigh and walk up the stairs, clenching my cheeks and hoping like hell I don't need stitches.

Seventeen

Silas

"It's been fourteen goddamn hours," I growl at Baron, clenching the glass of bourbon in my hand. My frustration is not with him, though. It's with her. "Why the hell is that girl so damn stubborn?" As soon as I know she's safe, I have every intention of laying her over my knee before fucking her so hard she never pulls a stunt like this again.

"Iris is tough, and so is Gabriel. They'll be fine. We have to do this right. If we go in too early then we risk all our lives."

I take down the rest of my drink and slam the glass to the mini bar in my room. "She took my fucking gun. Stole the address and ran off to play hero."

Dammit, Iris. You and my boy better not get yourselves killed or I'm not sure if I'll have the strength to keep going.

"Where the hell are they?" I glance at my watch. "It's been forty-five minutes."

"It's been ten. They'll be here."

We've got six men on their way here to go over a plan. Originally, I was going to go alone and make a deal with Basileus—an agreement to overlook a shipment that he's got coming in worth billions. It's the biggest deal the Mandola Cartel has had in fifteen years. If he didn't oblige, then I planned to put the deal at risk. All that went to shit.

"They're here," Baron says. He peers up from his phone, gripping it tightly in his hand. "Let's do this."

I snatch my jacket off the bed, grab my Glock off the nightstand and put it in the holster around my waist. "About fucking time."

As we walk down the hall of the hotel, I put my jacket on and button it in place. "Remember, we're in control, not them. They work for us."

Baron nods in agreement as he adjusts his own gun.

My nerves rarely get the best of me, but this feels too similar to the time that Iris was taken and Baron was shot. We finally put that mess behind us and we're at a good point in our lives. Business is booming, everyone is safe and happy, and I found love after thinking it wasn't possible for me. It might be unconventional, but I don't focus on their relationships with Iris—I focus on mine.

Three minutes later, we're walking out the back door of the elevator where two black SUVs are bumper to bumper. The driver's window of the front vehicle rolls down halfway.

"Mr. Black?" the man says in question behind black shades in the dark of the night.

"Rico?"

He continues rolling the window down, resting his arm on the frame. His tongue clicks on the roof of his mouth. "I hear you need some assistance."

"I need men who aren't afraid to get their hands dirty. I certainly don't need assistance."

Rico pokes his head out the window and looks at the vehicle behind him. "You're in luck, 'cause we're your men."

The thing about not forming relationships is that when you need a hand, you don't call friends, because you don't have any. You have allies who work for money. I have connections, but I pay for them. Some cost more than others, and when it comes to going up against the leader of the Mandola Cartel, you pay a pretty penny.

"We'll see about that," I scoff. "We need to get into El Basileus's lair. Every inch of his property needs to be searched, and we don't leave without *my* son and my girlfriend.

Rico drops back in his seat and takes in a deep breath. "Which property?"

"Cabo Street." Like many other leaders, Basileus has homes positioned all over the world, but this is the street address that my PI confirmed Gabriel was taken to.

"I see," he nods again, as if he's contemplating his sanity for considering this offer, "it won't be easy. They've got top-notch security and we're putting our lives at risk. Might cost you extra."

Baron steps up to my side. "Money's no object. Do we have a deal?"

Rico thinks for a moment, surveys the car behind him again, then holds up a finger. "*Uno momento.*" Then he rolls his window back up.

Baron nudges my shoulder then backsteps. "You think they can handle it?"

Biting the inside of my mouth, I look at Rico's tinted window and nod. "They'll get us in. That's all we need."

Seconds later, the window rolls back down, and Rico says, "Six a.m. tomorrow morning, we meet on the corner of Sanchez and Cabo. There's a little convenience store there. My boss says that Mr. Morales has a meeting at the docks and he's bringing primo men. That will be our best time to gain entrance."

A low grumble climbs up my throat. "Tomorrow?" I snap. "I want this shit done tonight."

Rico shrugs a shoulder and tsks, like he's the one in charge. "Sorry, sir. All the money in the world ain't worth that risk."

Baron grabs my arm, but I jerk away in a heated fury. "Fuck what your boss says. Right now, you're working for me, and I'm telling you to get us in there *tonight*!"

Rico holds up his finger again and proceeds to roll the window back up. My patience is running thin with this man.

"Dad," Baron spits, "the guy's got a point. We need to wait until the time is right. I want them back, too, but we need to be safe about this or we can get them killed, and ourselves."

"Dammit." I take a few steps away to collect my thoughts, running my fingers along my jawline. I know he's right. I'm just really fucking worried about what could happen between now and morning.

The sound of the window coming back down has me back at the vehicle door. "Forget it," I tell him, "meet us in the morning and don't you dare be a second late or you won't even have to worry about Mr. Morales."

With that, I walk away while Baron follows. It's only ten hours. They'll be fine until then.

They better be.

Eighteen

Iris

It's just my luck that I end up with six stitches on my ass cheek. I'm currently resting on an ice pack in Quentin's bed because Doc's orders were to stay put, so I don't split it back open. Apparently it's right above my gluteus medius, which is the muscle used when walking. I've screamed a few times at the world for hating me so much, then I calmed down and decided to use this time wisely and think of a plan to get me and Gabriel out of here.

Gabriel is here somewhere and he's safe. Somehow, I need to make him aware that I'm here, too. Once he knows, he'll get us out of this mess. I've learned a few things during my short stay: these condos are closed off from the main house and employees of Basileus live in them—apparently there are dozens—Quentin is Basileus's son, and there's roughly two hundred surveillanced acres.

My chances of doing anything and not being seen are slim to none.

Therefore, I can't leave this area and go to the main house to find Gabriel.

"Fuck!" I shout, throwing my hands up and feeling defeated once again. I'm back at square one, but I refuse to give up.

Throwing open the door, Quentin comes bursting in. "What are you screaming about?"

I give him a side-eye snarl then roll my eyes to the window. "Just let me out of here!"

When I hear his footsteps come closer, I slowly turn my head to look at him. He goes to sit on the edge of the bed, but I stop him by throwing a hand out. "Whoa, what are you doing?"

His hands press to his knees as he inches his ass closer to the mattress. "Umm, sitting."

"No, you're not! You said I had to stay in this bed, therefore, you can sit somewhere else. If you think for a second you're going to worm your way into my pants then—"

A burst of laughter cuts me off. "Worm my way into *your* pants? That's hysterical, Iris."

My arms cross over my chest tightly and I feel slightly offended. "Why is that so funny?"

Against my demand, Quentin sits down anyway. I scooch over until I'm at the very end of the opposite side of the mattress. "Ahh," I shriek as pain shoots from my ass down to my thigh.

"Easy, girl. Remember what Doc said, you don't wanna spread that ass hole back open."

With knitted eyebrows, I sneer, "Don't you worry about me or my ass hole."

"Fine with me. I think all this talk about your ass is

giving you a complex. Now you think I actually have an interest in getting in your pants."

Sliding up until my back rests against the headboard, I get myself comfortable again. "I know men like you. You kidnap girls, beat them down, then rape them." I should know, it's happened to me. Only difference is, I wasn't in a king-size bed with room service. I was in a cellar and the man was bearded, burly, and reeked of body odor. Quentin, on the other hand, is actually easy on the eyes. He'd probably be sexy in a smart, nerdy type of way, if it weren't for the fact that he's the enemy.

"Men like me?" He laughs again. "You don't know me at all, Green Eyes."

"Would you quit calling me that?"

"Why? You don't like it, Green Eyes?"

"No," I breathe out forcefully, "I hate it. My dad used to call me Green Eyes." I don't know why I just said that. I wish I could take it back and swallow the words.

Quentin tucks his leg as he turns his body toward me. "You wanna talk about it?"

I shake my head in slow movements as I speak, "You're not doing this. This reverse psychology bullshit, where you try to earn my trust. You beat me down and then the next thing I know I'm telling you my life story. Not happening."

"You're the one who raised the subject."

He's got a point. Why did I bring it up? It's been so long since I lost my dad that sometimes I feel like I'm losing the memories, too. Something about being here just has me missing him so much more. Maybe it's because Quentin reminds me of one of the guards I used to fool around with. Same slender build, same messy, coal-black hair, black-framed glasses, and a sharp jawline. That guard had a big cock, though, and Quentin leads me to believe he uses big words to make up for his small package.

"What time is it?" I ask, changing the subject. I haven't eaten all day. The pain medicine I've been taking has me feeling groggy and nauseous and the thought of food makes me feel like I'm going to vomit. But, I know I need to eat. I need my strength if I'm going to fight off this jackass.

"Nine o'clock."

My eyebrows shoot to my forehead. "At night?"

"Yeah," he laughs, "you've slept most of the day away."

Ripping the blanket off me, I fling my legs over the bed, ignoring the pain. "I have to see Gabriel."

Quentin rushes over to my side, grabbing me by the waist as I steady my feet. "No. You need to lie down and rest."

"No!" I shout, "You don't understand. I have to see him. You can't keep us here. Please, Quentin." This guy might be a hardass and he might've captured me, but I can see emotion behind his eyes. He's not completely desensitized, like a lot of the men in this profession are. "Please," I say again, tears pricking the corners of my eyes.

His expression goes blank while his head tilts slightly to the side as he stares into my eyes. Just when I think I've persuaded him, the corner of his lips tugs up. "Sorry, Green Eyes. I can't let you leave. It's too much of a risk."

My shoulders drop in defeat as tears fall carelessly down my cheeks. "What risk? What do you all want with him?"

Standing there poised with power, he bites his bottom lip, likely contemplating his response. The long pause leads me to believe I shouldn't trust whatever he's about to say.

"We've missed him. I grew up with Gabe until Silas Black killed his parents and took him away from us."

"Why now? It's been over a decade since his parents' death. Why wait until he's built a life with a new family?"

Quentin drops back down on the bed, his hands folded under his head as he stares at the ceiling. The muscles in his bicep flex underneath the black ink that runs down his arm. "After my aunt and uncle were killed and Gabriel went missing, we'd assumed he died. My dad tried to find him that first year or so, but there was no trail. Last year, an acquaintance of my dad's reached out, seeking revenge for the murder of his own parents. It was at that meeting that my dad realized it was your little group that took them out. My old man killed the guy on the spot. He saved your asses. You should actually—"

"Wait a damn minute. Who was the acquaintance?"

"Niles Barton."

I drop my head back in a sigh. Mickey Barton's son. His wife was my first interrogation. I got the intel I needed so that Baron could track down Mickey and take him out. I was pretty damn proud of myself that day.

There's still so much that doesn't make sense, though. "Why would your dad wait an entire year after he'd found him?"

Quentin stretches his arm back and grabs a pillow—the pillow I've been using—and tucks it under his head so that his eyes are level with mine. "Watching. Waiting. Come on, you know that impulsiveness is reckless."

I do know that. Not quite as well as Silas does, but I'm learning his worry all this time was for good reason. Gabriel, though, he's smart, but he's the most impulsive person I've ever met. "But no one wants to hurt him? You all just want him back in your lives—in your family?"

"Pretty much." Quentin's gaze shifts back to the ceiling. "At least, the old man does. Gabriel was always the golden child. My dad's his godfather. Would've given that kid the moon if he could've. Even at a young age, I was an outcast—the book nerd, the computer whiz. I preferred solitude, whereas Gabriel stood out in a crowd."

I'm definitely getting a sense of envy on Quentin's part. This is useful information that I can work with. "Do *you* want him here?"

His shoulders waggle against the silk comforter he's lying on. "Of course I do. He's blood."

He's lying.

"Even if it means him stepping back in as the golden child?"

Quentin's eyes shoot to mine, wide and observant. Suddenly he's sitting up and agitated. "I think this therapy session is over. There's food in the kitchen if you're hungry." He gets up and starts heading for the door, but I need him to stay. I need to somehow convince him that he doesn't want Gabriel here.

"Wait," I spit out, eating the three feet of space between us, "what if he doesn't want to stay?"

Quentin turns back around and rolls down the sleeves of his shirt, one at a time. "Iris," he grins, "he'd be a fool not to. The business he's in with the Black family is anthills compared to the mountain he's been placed on. And he didn't even have to climb it. He made it by simply being born into the right family. *His* family. He's not going anywhere. Even if he doesn't realize it yet."

I swallow hard as Quentin leaves, closing the door behind him. Dropping back, I fall onto the bed. My arms sprawled out at my sides.

Don't give in to them, Gabriel. Fight for the family who has loved you all these years.

Fight for us.

Baron

With any hired job, we are able to shut off all emotion and get the job done. Hell, up until two years ago, I didn't even know I had sentiment to offer. Today, this isn't about work. We weren't hired. There's no mastermind behind the plan. The enemies are ours, not someone else's.

They took my brother, took my girl, and the heaviness in my chest is attributed to the fact that it's all my fault. I pushed Gabriel away. Told him to take the job alone because his stubborn ass wasn't taking no for an answer. If I'd just sucked up my pride, I could have prevented this. If we lose them, their blood is on my hands.

Suiting up this morning feels all too familiar. The last time I was prepping to ambush a home, it was Iris's house. Hired by Maretti, while trying to earn my stripes, so I could join his side and finally have the freedom of choice. I took part in the demise of her family. Never gave it a second thought as her world was crumbling down one gunshot at a time.

The tapping of knuckles on my hotel door sends my heart into my throat. *It's time.*

I pull the door open, knowing full well there's a good chance I won't be coming back to this room if things go south. I refuse to let my mind go there. We're bringing them back here and then taking them home.

"Let's go," Dad says as soon as I open the door. He wastes no time as he starts down the hall ahead of me.

The plan is to meet these goons, who are supposed to help us gain access to the Morales estate. Once we're in, we take out anyone in our path to the son, then we take him hostage to get what we want, which is Gabriel and Iris. It's not solid, but with the little time we've had to prepare, we have no choice but to see it through.

Our driver is waiting for us at the entrance loop in front of the hotel. He stands tall with his hands folded in front of him. "Good morning, Mr. Black," he says to Silas before tipping his head to me, "and Mr. Black."

"Good morning, Carlisle," I say, before undoing the bottom button of my jacket and sliding in the open door. Once Silas is in, the door closes and we take the ride in complete silence, both of us caught up in our own thoughts.

I've replayed all the ways this can go wrong, but no matter how much I dwell on the what-ifs, nothing can prepare us for what is really waiting on the Morales property. Truth is, we have no fucking clue. No time to do our research, map out the property, or run background checks on his employees—we're at the mercy of luck today.

We drive up to the rundown convenience store where we planned to meet. Cracked concrete makes up the parking lot. There's a couple girls smoking cigarettes in skimpy dresses and heels, standing under the tall sign that reads *Jack's Quick Stop*. Another sign flashes from the broken window of the store that says 'closed' with the 's' light burnt out.

It's five minutes before six a.m., so we're early, but so are the men who are meeting us. The same two black vehicles from last night are parked in front of the building. Carlisle pulls up beside the front car and Silas rolls down his window as the driver does the same.

Marco stares straight ahead as he speaks, "Follow us to the right edge of the property. It's a gated community, all occupied by Basileus and his men. Lenny here is working on hacking into their security system." A guy from the passenger seat raises a hand then resumes tapping away at the computer in his lap.

"You've double-checked the timestamp on his meeting, I presume?" Silas asks while checking his wristwatch for the time.

"Three cars left the property approximately twenty minutes ago. We've got a good couple hours, but let's hope we don't need it. We get in, and we get out."

Normally Silas would be the one resisting. He's never this impulsive and his calmness about this entire thing really has me questioning what we're getting ourselves into. "All right. Let's do this." I drop back into my seat, rubbing my hands up and down my legs. My nerves rarely get the best of me, but something feels off. Hesitation gnaws at my stomach, but I ignore it because we have no choice here but to try.

Marco rolls his window up and Silas does the same. "Follow them," he orders Carlisle before looking at me. "We're bringing them home." He reeks of an arrogant confidence that is not my father at all. His words do nothing to soothe me because I can see right through them. He wants to believe this, so much so that I can tell he's never wanted anything more.

Tapping my fingers to my leg, I take in our surroundings. I was taught to always be aware of what's around you. You never know when you might need the information that seems useless at the moment. If we have to take off on foot, we need to know where to go, where we can hide, who we can use to our advantage. That's never happened, though. We don't run; we fight back.

The car comes to a stop behind the other two vehicles. Marco steps out, leaving his door open and holds up a finger halting us. A minute later, he's waving us out. Eight men come out of the two vehicles, armed and ready, in all black with face coverings. All aside from Marco, and Lenny, who is still holding his small computer in the palm of his hand and tapping away at it. He looks at Marco and gives him a nod of approval.

One of the men hands me and Silas each a walkie-talkie. "Test it," he orders, and I don't like the way these guys act like they're running the show.

"The place is disarmed. Use these to communicate," Marco says. "There's a back entrance about three yards down the property line."

His men begin walking away toward the back end of the property, but Marco and Lenny stay put. "Aren't you coming?" I ask him, confused as to why he's still standing there.

"I don't do the dirty work. We'll be out here keeping watch and making sure the system stays disarmed. We'll keep in touch, if we need to abort the mission."

"Pussy," I mumble under my breath.

"Baron," Silas snaps, nudging me along. "We've got no time to waste."

He's right, we don't. Even seconds of wasted time could be a matter of life and death.

The guys in front of us crouch down like soldiers as they walk with their rifles tucked under their arms. Silas and I stroll casually behind them in our ironclad suits with our weapons tucked away until they're needed.

The sun is beginning to rise beyond the clouds, giving us more light than when we'd arrived. Outside of the estate, the property is unkept with overgrown weeds and cobbled soil. You'd never guess that beyond the brick wall fence is a kingdom run by a self-made billionaire, who runs the biggest cartel in the three nations.

A big guy leading us looks left then right, before using a pick gun to crack the lock on the gate. He looks behind him, nods, then pushes it open and shuffles inside.

Not making a sound, we make our way through the property. It feels like we've walked a mile before we finally see the house in the distance. A white concrete structure that's at least twelve-thousand square foot. We walk onto the manicured landscaping and slow our steps. Now's the time to be extra cautious. I glance behind me, to my left, to my right, back in front. Repeating the process with each step.

"We're in. Is the system still down?" the guy in the front asks, his voice coming through all the walkie-talkies.

"The system is down, including the invisible fencing. All clear out here." Marco's voice comes through. "We just received confirmation that Mr. Morales has arrived at the docks with his top three guys. Proceed."

Silas and I share a silent glance as we continue to make

our way up to the house. This is our mission and we're in control.

"Spread out," Silas orders. A few men go left while the others go right. Silas and I walk the middle, until we're on a ground patio beside a pool.

The guy leading us presses his back to the house beside the door and reaches out to open it. He gives it a push then points his gun as he looks in. "Clear," he says in a hushed tone.

Once the guy is inside, Silas and I follow. My hand hovers where my holster sits beneath my jacket. Prepared and ready.

We come face to face with a guy who's holding a bag of chips in the large kitchen. "What the—" he begins, before Silas draws his gun and puts a bullet between his eyes. There's no sound, thanks to the silencer. His body drops to the ground and we walk around him.

It'd be nice if we had a map to this place, but I know criminals, and if they're keeping prisoners, they'd likely be on the lowest level of the house.

Cautiously, I open a door off to the side of the kitchen and gesture toward the staircase. Silas nods and I walk down as he follows behind.

A motion light comes on as we walk down, but it doesn't stop us. There's a large open room with a couple doors, so I pick one and give it a try. Just as I turn the handle and push it open, gunshots ring from upstairs. Someone comes down the staircase, one of the men that came with us. With my hand still on the handle, I look at the guy as he comes toward us.

"Place is empty aside from a couple freeloading guards, who stuck around to watch the place. What's in there?" He tips his head toward the door I just opened.

"Hopefully what we came here for." The house being empty isn't necessarily a bad thing. It makes our job a bit easier, as long as Iris and Gabriel were left behind.

I step into the dark room and gasp when I see the backside of a girl bound to a chair with her head dropped to her shoulder. "Iris?" I say, stepping closely. My voice startles her and her head shoots up, and she begins squirming and making sounds through the gag in her mouth.

"Baron. Get your ass in here." Silas hollers from another room, but I ignore him. Placing a trembling hand on the girl's shoulder, I hope like hell it's Iris, but when I round the chair, my heart drops when I see that it's not her.

"Stay put," I say, immediately regretting my choice of words. She obviously isn't going anywhere. "We'll get you outta here. Just give me a minute."

"What is it?" I ask Silas as I enter the room that he's in. There are more girls—bound and gagged in chairs. "What the hell kind of business is this man running?"

I pull the gag out of one of the girl's mouths, and she immediately screams. "Hush," I snap, but she doesn't listen. I raise my voice. "I said shut the fuck up if you want to get out of here." She immediately stops, breathing heavily as her chest rises and falls. "Why are you here?"

"*Ellas me llevaron a mi y a mi amiga.*"

I look at Silas and the other guy who came down. "I've got no idea what she's saying."

"They took her and her friend," the new guy translates.

"*Por favor ayuda. Ellos nos venderán.*"

"Please help. They will sell us."

"Son of a bitch," I spit. "Motherfucker is running his own sex trafficking ring. I should've known a dirty bastard like that wasn't just selling drugs." My heart begins pounding in my chest. "What if—"

Silas shakes his head, stopping me from even saying the words I'm thinking. "Don't go there."

If he did something to Iris, so help me, I will walk to the ends of the earth to find him and kill him.

"We need to get these girls free and keep searching," I tell Silas and his man. They have to be here somewhere.

"This is not our business," Silas says. "We didn't come here to play their hero and we don't interfere with another man's work."

It's totally like him to say something like that. Regardless, there is no way in hell I'm leaving these girls. They could be someone's Iris. I start untying them one by one, leaving them to escape on their own. They're free now, and that's something I won't have on my conscience for the rest of my life.

Silas finally huffs and puffs and gives a helping hand. I go into the other room where one single girl sits alone. Something stops me from leaving her. "Why are you alone?" I ask her. She's young, probably seventeen or eighteen years old.

"I don't know," she cries. "I was with my mother and they...they killed her and took me. I think they want my dad. He worked for the man in charge."

I'm glad she speaks English. It makes this a little easier. This isn't a case of trafficking. She's here for the same reason we brought in Barton's wife last year. They need her for information. Letting her go would go against everything I've been taught. She's so young, though. So much life ahead of her.

I glance over my shoulder when I hear the shuffle of feet draw near. Silas is standing in the doorway with a stern look on his face. He shakes his head, telling me no.

Can I really just leave this poor girl here? Fuck. When

did I start letting my emotions get the best of me? It's Iris. Her sweet voice is in my head, telling me to let her go. Her passion in life is empowering women.

Besides, it was Silas who took Gabriel all those years ago.

Screw it. I pull out my knife and flip it open then slice through the rope before leaving the room.

"What else did you find?" I ask Silas and the guy whose name I still don't know.

Silas waves an arm toward the staircase, where some of the girls are still hurrying up. "Not a damn thing. They're not here."

"No. They have to be."

"We've been duped, son. They were here at one time, but they've been moved." Silas holds up a hair scrunchie. The same hair scrunchie Iris was wearing the last time I saw her.

"Dammit," I shout, stomping across the kitchen floor to exit the way I came in, "we're back at square one."

Iris

It's been six days since I made the stupid decision to try and rescue Gabriel on my own. Six days that I've been holed up in this condo with this Bill Gates wannabe. Upon my search of the condo for anything that could help me, I came across a room that Quentin has set up with a half dozen computer screens and an array of technical garbage that I know nothing about. Apparently, he's really good with computers, like really good. I got a little snoopy and tried to hack into footage of the main house, just so I could see what Gabriel's been up to, but I was caught by another camera zoomed in directly on me.

"What exactly is it that you do?" I ask Quentin as I walk through the computer room, looking at all the screens.

He spins around in his swivel chair, elbows pressed to the arms as he drums his fingers. "Watch people, find people."

"For the family business?"

"For the family and for the business. I'm the one who tracked down Gabriel and got all the info needed on the Black family—and you." He winks, sending a breeze of chills down my spine.

Aside from the fact that he won't let me leave, Quentin really isn't that bad. He's surprisingly normal. When he caught me in here, he didn't yell or drag me back to his room I'm staying in. Instead, he sat down, pulled up a screen at the main house and zoomed in on Gabriel pacing a study while deep in thought.

They're getting to him. I could see it in his eyes.

I'm caught off guard by a screen that shows a car coming through a gate, but it's not the same gate I walked through when I arrived. "Where is this?"

Quentin slides his chair over to my side, bumping me in the leg. "Front entrance. Why?"

My eyebrows pull together as I glance from him to the screen. "Are there multiple entrances? That's not the gate I came through." It's a big property, so it would make sense. Then again, when I saw Gabriel from the bedroom window my first day here, I saw the ocean. I didn't think much of it then, but now it has me wondering if I'm even at the same house. Quentin doesn't say anything, just swivels back and forth in his chair, wearing a shit-eating grin. "Quentin," I emphasize his name, "where the hell am I?"

"An undisclosed address in a private community owned by my family."

"You asshole," I punch his shoulder, softer than what I should have, "you knocked me out and took me somewhere else that night, didn't you?"

Quentin grumbles and rubs his arm like I actually hurt him. "You would have been found there. We had no choice."

Pressing my hands to the arms of his chair, I stop him from moving. "You moved Gabriel, too, didn't you?"

"Well," he drawls, "not me personally, but he was escorted off that property and brought here shortly before we arrived."

All this time I was focusing on the fact that Silas had access to the address and they'd come for us. Now, I'm not even sure if he knows where to look.

I swallow hard, Quentin focused on the bob in my throat. His eyes skate up to mine as a tear falls down my cheek. "They're not coming for us." Pushing myself off the chair, I straighten my back and brush my fingers against my cheek, anger rippling through me as I scream, "How long do you plan on keeping us here?"

"I told—"

"Yes, I know," I spit rage-infused sarcasm, "as long as it takes for Gabriel to decide to stay. Then what? Huh? What do you plan to do with me?"

"I guess that'll be up to him. My guess is, he'll want you to stay."

"Stay?" I laugh, as if it's an option. Staying means never seeing Silas and Baron again. Staying means waging a war that they will never stop fighting. Two divided families with Gabriel in the middle of them. His future will be doomed —mine, empty without all three of them.

"It's not so bad here. Gabriel will work and you could... take up a hobby or something."

"Gabriel will never agree to this. Never!" I shout. "Your dad is the reason his parents are dead. You're all fools to think he could forgive him for that."

Quentin scratches his head and gives me a side-eyed glance. "What the hell are you talking about?"

"Don't act like you don't know." I stomp across the

room, ignoring the pain shooting through my lower half.

"Wait," Quentin hollers as I pull open the door and leave the computer room.

I won't wait. I don't even slow down as I walk briskly through the hallway to the room I'm staying in. Once I'm there, I slam the door shut and lock it.

He must think I'm some sort of an idiot. I know that his dad is the one who put the hit on Gabriel's biological parents, Silas told me so. There is no way in hell that Quentin doesn't know that.

Or is there?

He was just a child himself. I'm sure he wasn't invested in the family business when he was only eight years old. I suppose it's possible he doesn't know, but he works so closely with his dad, it would be far-fetched to think he doesn't.

Although, if it's true, and he has no idea, this could also work to my advantage. Maybe once Quentin and Gabriel both know the truth, they'll turn against this Basileus guy.

"Unlock the door, Iris." Quentin knocks his knuckles repeatedly on the door. "Tell me what you were talking about."

His voice is strained. He sounds serious. I'm not sure that I can trust Quentin—in fact, I know I can't—but I have nothing to lose aside from him telling Gabriel. That could actually be a good thing.

I click the lock, not bothering to turn the handle, then backstep until I'm sitting on the bed.

The door flies open, and Quentin stands there, catching his breath like a fifty-year-old smoker who just ran a mile. "My dad didn't put a hit on my aunt and uncle. So what's this nonsense you're spewing?"

Grimacing, I cross my legs and fold my hands in my lap,

trying to take the upper hand. I observe the chipped polish on my nails then look at Quentin. "Believe what you want."

Small, cautious steps bring him closer to the bed. "Why'd you lie?"

"Did I, though?"

His expression goes bleak before his mouth twists into a snarl. His steps heavy against the hardwood floor as he closes the space between us. Two hands press to the mattress on either side of me. Warm breath hits my cheek and the scent of his mint gum fills my senses. "What game are you playing, Iris?"

It's clear now that he did not know. This is good. This is very good.

"Were you close with your aunt and uncle?" I ask, swallowing the air he breathes into the thin space between us.

"Very," he deadpans.

"Wow. That's really a shame." Sarcasm drips from my words as I work him up to a boiling point. "You were probably pretty pissed at Silas for killing them, huh?"

His jaw ticks furiously, molars grinding, as he seethes, "I hated the man who *did* put the hit on them. But my dad killed that man and took his place."

"Ahh." I nod. "The former Basileus, I presume?"

"Yes," he grumbles. "Now get to the point. Why the hell did you say my dad had them killed? Who fed you that bullshit lie?"

My response is nothing but a smirk.

"Dammit, Iris. Tell me why?" He pushes me onto my back. Climbing on all fours, he hovers over me. Warmth pools in my stomach. It's taking everything in me not to buck my hips up. It's been six long days since I've been with one of my guys and God, do I miss them.

What the hell am I thinking?

I push the thoughts away, hating my hormonal body.

"I guess I was wrong."

Quentin bites his bottom lip, continuing to try and read my expression. "You're lying."

Why does he smell so good? My nipples pucker against the fabric of my T-shirt, and I have to get the hell out from underneath him before I torture myself any further. I shouldn't feel this way. Silas and Baron are out there frantically trying to find us. Gabriel is in the process of being brainwashed. And here I am, getting turned on by a twenty-two-year-old stranger, who has me on my back in his bed.

"Get off me," I order, squirming beneath him. Instead of doing what I ask, he takes my hands and pins them over my head.

"Not until you tell me everything you heard."

His pelvis drops down and my chest rises and falls rapidly when I notice that I'm not the only one turned on.

I have to just tell him. If I stay in this position any longer, I'll need three hot showers to fully satisfy myself.

"It's true. Silas took the hit, but it wasn't the former Basileus who hired him to do it. It was your dad. He knew that your uncle was trying to take down Basileus, but he wanted the title for himself. He's the reason they're dead. He killed them, then killed Basileus."

Quentin doesn't say anything as his grip on my wrists slowly loosens. He pulls himself up, practically sitting on my legs but not with his full weight. "Son of a bitch," he finally says as he stares off into space.

I lift my shoulders off the bed and see his cock straining the fabric of his pants. "Can I get up now?"

His eyes shoot to me, alluring and seductive. "You want up? Ask nicely."

Who is this guy and where is the computer nerd I was hanging out with twenty minutes ago?

"How about get the fuck off me or I'll throw you off."

Quentin laughs. "Ya know, I'm pretty pissed off with my father right now. Might not want to piss me off further. I've been known to have mood swings, and I wouldn't wanna do something I might regret."

Against my better judgment, I press, "Oh yeah? Like what?" My pulse quickens as he leans forward, his eyes burning into mine.

"This," he whispers into my ear as he grinds his cock against me. "Or maybe this." His hand slides up my side, working its way beneath my shirt.

"Don't." I gnash my teeth together.

"You're in no position to tell me what to do, Iris."

In a swift motion, I shove him to the side, lift my knee and drive it straight between his legs.

Quentin rolls over, dropping to the bed. "Fuck!" he bellows, "I was just playing around."

"Next time, don't!" I climb off the bed and walk over to the door and pull it open. "Now get the hell out."

Quentin lies there for a moment, likely waiting for his nuts to drop back down. A few seconds later, he gets up and walks slowly to the door while cupping his crotch. His eyes never leaving mine until I slam the door shut behind him.

Once it's closed, I press my back to the door and steady my breaths. That was too close. I can't allow myself to get in that position again. I'd never cheat on the guys—*ever*—but that doesn't mean temptation wasn't knocking. Something about Quentin draws me in and I refuse to believe he's not on my side through all of this.

Now I need a shower—or three.

Twenty-One

Iris

I'm wrapped up in warmth, someone's lips gently kissing my neck and another pair trailing their way up my legs. I'm covered in soft, familiar hands, touching my stomach, breasts, face, and the wet, needy place between my thighs.

"Baron," I moan. I can feel him, but I can't see him. No matter how hard I try to open my eyes, I can't. I just want to gaze into those familiar brown eyes. "Gabriel!" I cry out as he thrusts himself inside me. I know it's him—even without seeing his face, I know it's him by the size and movement of his cock. He's here with me.

Silas is watching us. His heavy gaze is like a warm blanket covering my body. I'm safe. I'm *home*.

"Iris," he bellows angrily, "wake up!"

"No," I cry, my face wet and my words slurred. *Please don't leave me,* I plead in my mind.

"Iris!" he yells again.

The pleasure of their hands and lips fades away. Now

the touch is rough, shaking me, and I cry out again. It's a wordless howl of agony. When my eyes fly open, the moisture pooling between my lashes makes it impossible to see, but I swear it's Gabriel standing over me in the dim bedroom light. The eyes are the same, but this face is longer, the lips fuller, and the familiar heart tattooed under his eyes is gone.

A high-pitched gasp escapes my lips when I realize it's Quentin, not Gabriel. He's not wearing his glasses, and without them, he could almost pass for Gabriel's twin. He's lying next to me, one strong arm on my shoulder and a look of frustration on his face.

I move to fight him off, but I'm too overcome with grief to muster the energy.

"I was with them. I was happy, and you woke me up!" I shriek.

"Well, you were fucking moaning and grinding against me like a cat in heat."

Oh shit. I was?

"No, I wasn't," I reply defensively, turning away.

"Baron," he moans in a high-pitched voice. "Gabriel."

He's teasing me, and it makes my blood boil. Spinning on him, I go to smack him across the face, but he throws his hands up defensively, laughing as I assault him. "You're an asshole!" When I land a knee to his stomach, he loses his patience and grabs my wrists in his hands. In a quick motion, he spins me onto my belly and lays his body over mine, holding his weight on the uninjured side of my ass, instead of the stitched up one.

"You're such a feisty little bitch," he mumbles into my ear. "You know I was just fucking with you, but all you want to do is fight."

"Well, you are holding me here against my will, so

excuse me for not being the little sweet demure girl you think I should be!" I struggle against his hold, but he has me pinned with my face pressed against my pillow and my hair covering my tear-soaked cheek.

Holding my hands in place with one of his, he uses the other to brush my hair out of my eyes. "You realize I'm keeping you safe, right? Do you know what my father would have done with you if he had found you before I did?"

I tense and think for a moment. Before I can answer, he continues, "Think about it, Iris. You're a liability. One look at you, and Gabriel would have bolted. It would have been an easy decision to kill you and let Gabriel think you were never coming for him. Then kill your other two boyfriends when—*or if*—they ever decide to show up. I'm keeping you alive, Iris, because I know it's what Gabriel would want. I'm not a complete fucking monster."

Bile rises in my throat at the thought, but I know he's right. Basileus doesn't act on emotion or empathy; he acts on logic.

"Will you please get off of me?" I ask.

He hesitates, and I feel his eyes on my face for a moment before he rolls away. He's on top of the covers and I'm beneath them, but since I sleep fully clothed in his sweats, because I don't trust him, the covers continuously end up at the foot of the bed each night. Once he rolls away, I sense him reaching for something on the nightstand. A second later, he's handing me a tissue.

I glare at him as I take it, wiping the tears and sweat off my face. My pillow has dark tear stains from crying in my sleep. Even in my dreams, I must have known they weren't really there.

The room is quiet as we lie next to each other, but then

Quentin breaks the silence by asking, "Three boyfriends? Really?"

Unexpectedly, a small laugh slips past my lips. I've been here for almost a week. He admitted on the first day that he knew about my arrangement with the guys, but it took him this long to finally ask. And for some reason, it's funny to me. Like being away from the house and out of the situation for this long has made me realize how it must look to outsiders.

"They don't seem to mind," I reply.

"No one gets jealous?"

He's lying on his back, and I'm curled into a ball on my side facing him. I have to keep reminding myself I'm not here by choice, so why do I feel a sense of guilt for lying in a bed with another man. Even if I'm not doing anything I shouldn't, it feels wrong.

"Gabriel does. Sometimes." I don't know why I just told him that. Something about it feels like ammunition, and maybe I'm just tired or going crazy from being stuck inside this tiny condo for six days. I cannot trust Quentin—that would be reckless, but still...

His head turns in my direction. "But the other two... father and son. Isn't that weird?"

There's a genuine look of curiosity in his eyes, and it's making me want to open up instead of knock him out, like he's actually curious instead of patronizing.

I shrug. "It was a little weird at first, but it just happened. We're a family. I guess it seems strange to others, but it's not strange for us. We already lead unusual lives, so we might as well be an unusual family."

He nods, and I notice the way his eyes trail down my face from my eyes to my lips, and I have to swallow down the tension that's suddenly filling the room. I'd give anything to know what he's thinking.

"It's a pity really," he mumbles quietly.

"What is?"

His warm golden eyes find me again. "It's hard enough for a guy to compete with one boyfriend, but three…"

I watch him as his jaw clenches, and I don't reply. Quentin can't possibly look at me like that, can he? He hates me. He's constantly tormenting me, laughing at me, and treating me like I'm nothing but a pain in his ass. Does he really think he can compete with Gabriel for me?

"No one is competing with them," I reply dryly, trying to shove the topic away. "What about you? Don't you have a hot girlfriend like one of those babes hanging around the pool all the time?"

He scoffs. "Yeah, right. They're here for Basileus. They don't care about his lame, nerdy kid."

I playfully shove his shoulder. "Liar! You're snatching up pussy left and right. Don't be shy!"

He grins, dimples piercing his cheeks as he does, and I swear he's actually blushing. "When I was younger, I did. Fifteen, sixteen years old, when my dad started letting me party with him. He'd throw girls my way like it was a game, and I thought I was hot shit. But those girls were boring. They were good for sex, but they never cared about anything I liked. Then they'd leave. And it's not like I ever get out of this place. I'm not hitting up the local clubs."

He laughs again, this time without the humor, and I do actually start to feel bad for him. In fact, it reminds me so much of Gabriel, my heart actually aches in my chest.

"Want to hear something crazy?" I ask in a whisper.

Shifting one arm over his head, he leans in closer to me

until we're only inches apart. "Of course," he whispers back.

"Gabriel was a virgin when I met him," I say, and although there's a smile stretched across my face, I feel nothing but sadness as I tell him. Not because I'm giving away some big secret Quentin could use against us, but because it dredges up those memories of the first days, when Gabriel and I started out our relationship much like this one. Full of hate for each other, and passion fueled by jealousy.

"Shut the fuck up," he replies, flinching backward as if he really is shocked.

"Yep. Turns out Silas Black was *not* throwing pussies at his kids."

Quentin's laughter fades, and it's almost like I can see his wheels turning. Forcing a fake smile, he turns away. I know what he's thinking. Silas Black actually cares about his sons, more than the business and the fame and the power. He might have gone overboard protecting them and isolating them from the outside world, which led to Gabriel ending up an eighteen-year-old virgin, but at least he cared about his sons.

"Well, now I'm glad Silas Black didn't abduct me all those years ago. I might have ended up a virgin too. Or worse...one of your boyfriends."

This time when I shove him, he flies off the side of the bed, landing with a resounding thud on the floor, and his laugh is real again.

"You can sleep down there then." I toss his pillow onto his head. He doesn't climb back onto the mattress, and the room grows quiet again.

For the first time all week, I'm not on edge. I'm feeling almost confident. I know Quentin is mostly kidding, but I might actually be succeeding at getting him to empathize for my family over his. If I can make him understand that Silas Black isn't the villain and that Basileus is the real enemy, I might actually stand a chance at getting my boyfriend back alive and getting the fuck out of here.

Before drifting off to sleep again, I peek over the edge. He's still on his back, one arm over his head, staring blankly at the ceiling. My eyes catch on the thick muscles of his bicep, and the warm tone of his eyes as he stares back at me.

"Thanks, by the way," I say.

"For what?"

"Not killing me."

We stare at each other for a moment, lost in a loaded gaze. And it makes me think...maybe if things were different. Maybe if I didn't have my guys, I could see myself with someone like him. I like that he makes me laugh, because I can't remember the last time I did.

Then again, maybe I just desperately need to get laid. This lack of sex is going to my head. The sooner we—no, *I* —get Gabriel out of here, the better. Then I'm sure those three are going to fuck my brains out for days to make up for lost time. And after what I pulled, I don't expect them to be nice about it either.

"Anytime," he replies with sarcasm as I roll back onto my pillow.

My body is practically buzzing, and it takes me another hour at least before I finally drift off to sleep.

Twenty—Two

Gabriel

I'm standing in the middle of a dark room in the basement, directly beneath the main living area of the mansion. Standing near the wall with me is my uncle and three of his men. In the center of the room, a man is tied to a chair with a burlap sack over his head.

Two men with their sleeves rolled up are in the process of extracting information from him regarding the whereabouts of three million dollars' worth of missing cocaine.

I know why Baxter brought me down here. His men are doing a piss-poor job, probably on purpose, so he can entice me to do what I do best. He's offering me a position where I can shine, in hopes it'll convince me to stay.

I have no fucking clue how long he's going to keep this thing up, but I'm not going to change my goddamn mind, and I keep reminding him of that.

I don't care if Silas Black is an asshole sometimes.

I don't care if Baron hates me and sees me as competition all the time.

And I don't fucking care that Baxter is my blood. This isn't my fucking family.

He won't let me call, text, email, or even send a fucking smoke signal to let Iris know I'm okay. She must be going out of her damn mind with worry—or at least, I hope she is.

I don't believe for a second that she's just accepted the fact that I'm dead and moved on...with them. Now that she only has two boyfriends instead of three—

No. Fuck that. My brain keeps wandering down this dark, pity party train of thought, and it's pissing me off. My family will come for me—I know it. And I'll just bide my time until they do. I just hope they don't bring her because I know these assholes fight dirty, and I don't know what I'll do if anything happens to her.

The big guy lays another heavy punch in the bagged guy's face, knocking him out, and I don't succeed in stifling my groan of annoyance.

"Not enjoying the show?" Baxter asks.

I roll my eyes and scoff. "So now we have to stand around and wait for the asshole to wake up. Quit fucking around and get the information," I yell at the burly monster of muscle currently glaring at me with hatred. He could charge at me, ready to rip my head off, and I wouldn't give a fuck. I hope he punches my lights out at this point. It'd be better than watching this shitshow of an interrogation.

"Think you can do better?" Baxter asks, getting me exactly where he wants me.

I almost say no, but fuck it. Might as well have some fun while I'm here. I'm dying to hurt something right now anyway. I haven't broken a bone in over a week, and I haven't fucked anyone either, both making me horny as hell —for sex or violence, I'm not quite sure. Maybe a bit of both.

Marching past the giant fucking idiot, I rip my shirt off and toss it at Baxter. Grabbing the back of the chair, I drag it over to the corner where the large basin is, and I drop his chair so it lands with a loud thunk against the edge of the tub. It doesn't wake the man up, so his bloodied face is hanging off the back of the chair.

When I turn the water on it's ice cold, and I quickly fill the bucket and pour it onto his face. He gasps and shakes after a moment, desperate for air, but only getting enough to keep him alive and still make him feel as if he's drowning.

"Good morning, motherfucker," I growl with my face next to his ear. "I need to know who took off with the coke and where they went. Maybe, just maybe, if you fill me in on those little details, I'll let you keep your pathetic fucking life."

He continues gasping and wheezing before muttering a weak, "Fuck you."

Letting out a sigh, I grab the bag over his head and tear it off. The two goons who were torturing him before me hold up their hands giving me a wordless 'What the fuck?' Meanwhile, Uncle Bax just smiles.

Kneeling down in front of the man, I try to remain casual as he stares at the suits behind me with wide eyes. He knows he's fucked now. He's seen their faces, which means he's not walking out of here alive. Unless I give him hope.

"You're fucked now," I say.

"Might as well kill me then," he mumbles, trying to look as tough as he can, but the first two guys have already done a number on him. By the looks of it, his nose is broken, he's missing a couple teeth, has some burn marks on his scalp, and he's short of one eyeball.

Wow, they treated him so nicely, and he still wouldn't talk. Wonder why.

"I'd love to, trust me. I'm in the mood to spill some blood, and I'm sure you want nothing more than a painless, quick death, but I think you and I both know that's not going to happen without those names. So...the choice is yours, *amigo*."

"I'll never talk," he replies, his voice shaking with his violent shudders.

Standing up, I smile down at him. "All right then...let's have some fun."

I look over the tray of tools and see nothing that catches my eye. There's a door off to the right, and if these people are as well-prepared as they pretend to be, then there has to be something more to work with besides fists and scalpels.

The guy groans and tenses as I cross in front of him to go to the door. "Whaa...what are you doing?"

Ignoring him and the questionable stares from the men watching me, I jerk open the door. My fingers run down the wall in search of a light switch.

Bingo.

"Holy fuck," I mutter. This room is like a dream for an unhinged interrogator.

Me. It's a fucking dream for me.

The walls are lined with hooks, holding torture devices I've never seen up close and personal. I know what they are, though. My years spent reading opened my eyes to a whole world of methods. In the far back is an electric chair. Looks like it's a few centuries old, but I bet I could get the thing to do what it's meant to do.

"We ain't got all day," someone hollers from outside the room.

I walk deeper inside, running my fingers over some of the most grueling weapons I've ever laid eyes on. I stop on one in particular. Used during the Middle Ages, mostly on women—until today.

Snatching it off the hook, I turn around without a second thought.

"You've gotta be fucking kidding me?" the tall guy with a lazy eye snaps. "What are you gonna do, cup his dick with that thing?"

Not a bad idea, actually. But I had other plans. It's apparent these men are amateurs. If they'd done a little research, they'd know exactly what I intend to do.

I rejoin the perp, smacking the pear-shaped tool against the palm of my hand.

Crouching down, I level with him. "Who's the thief?" My tone is stoic and all-business. Even if I have no affiliation with this case. When I'm given a job, I get the job done.

"Fuck you," he finally groans out.

I extend my hand, grabbing his limp neck, fingers pinching into the skin of his vertebrae. "Last chance, asshole."

He looks me in the eye, practically begging for mercy. But when he doesn't respond, I shove the pear of anguish right into his mouth, knocking out a few teeth in the process. He gags, chokes, tries to cough around it.

Showing him none of the mercy his eyes were begging for, I click it a few times, spreading his mouth far and wide, so that I can see the back of his throat. His tongue flops around as he squirms, trying to free himself from my clutches.

"Name," I deadpan.

He shakes his head, tears sliding down his cheeks and colliding with the blood rolling out of his mouth.

When his response is nothing but a few whimpers, I click it again, spreading his mouth even wider. The corners of his lips disconnect and the sound of his ripping skin is oddly satisfying.

He tries to cry. Tries to save himself, but it's no use. I click it again, hearing the pop of his jaw.

One of the men behind me begins shuffling his feet, so I turn to look at him. He's white as snow with his hand over his mouth, shocked by my depravity.

"You okay back there?" I ask, returning my attention to the perp.

The other guy laughs. "He's a newb. Can't handle this epic show."

"Last chance before your jaw is completely disconnected. Who the fuck stole the drugs?"

More squirming, gagging, and the next thing I know, the asshole's mouth is filling with vomit. It rolls freely out and onto his lap, and it smells fucking repulsive.

He goes to talk, I know because I can see the muscles in his neck spasm, but the words are muffled. Likely because he's got a fucking iron pear in his mouth. He can talk, though. All I need is one name, and he has the ability to give it to me.

More gurgles, spasms, and vomit.

"Car..." he sputters through the liquid pooling around his tongue.

I tap my ear sarcastically. "Come again. Seems the cat's got your tongue."

"Carlisle," he finally chokes out.

Baxter rushes over to my side. "Did he just say fucking Carlisle? That son of a bitch."

"Know him?"

"Yeah, I know him. He works for me." Baxter runs his fingers through his hair before his glowering eyes look at me. "We're done with him."

With that, I click the lever one more time, splitting his jaw. I pay no attention to the sounds of pure anguish as I release the tool that's still in his mouth and leave the room.

"I'm proud of you, *mijo*," Baxter says, clapping a hand on my shoulder as I wash my hands in the main floor bathroom.

The muscles in my arms ache, but it feels good to be working again. It took some effort, but the guy finally fessed up. It was the delirium that finally set in. Making him so disoriented he didn't know his own name anymore after so much pain.

He spilled the names, dates, locations, everything. Then Bax walked in and slit his throat.

"Thanks," I reply, because I'm too exhausted to even bother being antagonistic at the moment. "It was fun, but I don't work for you. So don't think this is going to be a habit now."

"Why not? You don't like my interrogation room? I can get you a bigger one. More tools, a table, some big contraption for you to torture every piece of shit who steals from me."

"I'm good, thanks." I have a perfectly good workspace at my own place, but I'm not going to open up to him about that.

"What is it that's stopping you from working with me,

Gabriel? Your girlfriend?" He scoffs as if Iris is nothing, just a pair of tits. My blood boils. "We have plenty of women here."

He pauses for a moment, and I watch him, knowing he has more to say. "A man like you shouldn't have to share." There's a hint of mischief in his eyes, and it grates on my nerves.

"She's more than my girlfriend, and it's not just her. I already have a job and a family, and I still don't fucking trust you."

He looks so offended it's comical. Everything is such an act with this guy.

"Fine. You want to know if you can trust me?" He holds out his arms as if he's letting me walk right out the door.

"What?"

"The place is yours. Free rein. Go anywhere you'd like."

"But I can't leave?"

"Not yet. Give me more time, Gabriel. If you look through every room of this compound and you don't find anything interesting, then you can leave."

What is he playing at? What could he possibly have that I would want?

"Fine." I stare out at the front door of his giant house. There are three damn floors in this building, but there are also about a dozen other buildings on this property that I don't have access to.

I think what he's teasing me to see is the scope of his operation. He's basically showing off the size of his balls, trying to prove just how alpha dog he is. I don't give a shit how much drugs or money get filtered through this place. It doesn't impress me.

"I'm too fucking tired," I reply, heading toward my

room instead of the front door. Whatever he's trying to do, I'm not playing along. I'm already kicking myself for doing his interrogation for him for free, since that's obviously what he was baiting me to do. I can't keep giving in to this asshole.

As I reach my room, I drop onto the giant bed and stare up at the ceiling.

Baxter may be my uncle, but he didn't come for me when it counted. He waited over ten years, so he obviously wants something more than just my loyalty. I'm sure he wants nothing more than to dismantle my entire family and everything we've built, but why go through the trouble? What could Silas Black have on Baxter that makes our family so crucial to eliminate?

GABRIEL

It's not even dark out, and I'm lying in my bed in this fucking mansion with more questions than answers and a growing restlessness in my bones.

Something is not right. It's been six days, and I can't tell if Baxter is giving me time or biding his. So what if he has some massive operation here. I don't need that.

But a fancy room to work in and freedom to grow on my own without someone cutting me off all the time? That would be nice.

Fuck, what am I thinking? I don't want to live here. Or be a part of the Mandola Cartel.

I need Iris. At the very least, I need her. And maybe, *just maybe*, if she gave up Silas and Baron to be with me, I could stay here. But she wouldn't. I know she wouldn't.

And Baxter was right about one thing—I shouldn't be expected to share.

I can't sit here and think about this anymore. Instead, I

jump out of my bed and head straight out the door of my room and down the long hallway toward the grand staircase. It's quiet, so there's no one to stop me as I reach the front door.

"Fuck this," I mumble to myself as I pull it open. I'm facing the mountains as soon as I step outside, and somewhere in the distance is a gate I know I won't be able to walk through. He's giving me free rein of the grounds, so that's what I'm going to take.

Heading left, I see a giant building that looks like a warehouse on the far end with two or three smaller buildings sandwiched in between. There are people walking around, but no one seems to pay me any mind. I'm a fucking *Morales*, right? El Basileus is my fucking uncle. I shouldn't be afraid of anyone here, and they can't tell me shit.

The first building appears to be empty. It looks like a meeting space with a small kitchen and some storage. The door is locked, so I peer through the windows.

The second building is another living quarter, but there are people coming and going. I have no reason to go snooping in someone's house, but I would assume by looking at them that they are staff quarters. It's expensive-looking, but the people all keep their faces down, scurrying past me without a word.

The third building is farther away and takes me on a paved pathway that goes downhill and off to the left. There are no people out here, but when I get closer to the building, I hear voices.

It's a woman, and she sounds like she's—

"Stop, stop, stop! That hurts!"

I freeze, waiting in the silence for her to speak again, so I know I'm not fucking crazy and I actually heard the voice I thought I heard. A man's voice replies in a muffled tone, and I can't make out what he's saying.

Then, she laughs. She fucking laughs, and my heart skitters to a halt in my chest.

Iris.

My Iris.

My feet carry me in a sprint toward the front door of this small condo building. It's unlocked, opening with a deafening thud as I barrel through the doorway. In my head is an endless cadence of 'she's here, she's here, she's here.'

There's a scream as I burst into the living room, but the voices seem to be coming from the bedroom off to the side. As I run into the room, I'm staring down the barrel of a gun, but it doesn't stop me.

"Put the gun down!" Iris screams.

"Just calm down, Gabriel," he says in a panic, shoving her behind him.

Quentin is pushing *my Iris* behind him, away from me. I attack him with a roar, grabbing the gun out of his hand and knocking it to the floor. Then, my fist flies, connecting with a harsh impact against his face. The sound of his glasses cracking is all I hear as I lay down another punch.

"Don't hurt him!" Iris screams, and I swear I must have blacked out because nothing is making any sense. She's hanging on my arm as I throw a third punch at my *cousin,* but this time, he blocks it and rams his shoulder into my stomach, driving me against the opposite wall. We slam into a desk, and the chair flies to the floor.

"Both of you, stop it!" she screams. "Someone is going to find us!"

But I'm hyperfocused on killing this fucking traitor, who had the nerve to *hide my fucking woman from me,* then point a gun in my goddamn face. If he touched her, I'll kill him.

No, I'll fillet him. I'll take my time too. Making it the world's longest, most painful death.

"Gabriel!" Soft hands wrap around my bicep, pulling me away from Quentin. My arms are still wrapped around his neck, trying to choke the life out of him, but he's quickly escaping my grasp. When he finally does snake himself out of my arms, I'm flipped onto my back, but before he can climb back on to attack me again, she's there.

Straddling my waist, Iris covers my body with hers. Then she settles her face just inches from mine, holding my jaw in her hands.

"Baby, relax. It's me," she whispers. Then her lips press softly against mine, and I lose all of my fight. My hands slide around her waist and I squeeze her tight. She's so warm and smaller than I remember. My cock doesn't seem to care that I was just intent on murder a moment ago or that Quentin is just a few feet away, because it jolts in my pants from being so near the only place it wants to be, buried deep inside her.

There are so many questions on my mind, but my brain isn't the one in charge anymore. I flip Iris onto her back and grind my hips into her as I own her mouth with mine. Fuck, I've missed her. She moans beneath me, wrapping her legs around me.

I'm going to fuck her right here on the floor. I don't care about anything else at the moment, and Q must have taken a hint because he's not in the room anymore.

Trailing my mouth down to her neck, I use one hand to unfasten my pants. She's in nothing but her underwear and a long T-shirt, so after getting my pants undone, I drag her panties to the side to feel her warm, wet pussy in my hand.

Wait. I freeze and look down at her, my brain finally catching up.

"Where are your clothes?"

"What?" she asks in a breathless pant. Her eyes are dilated and filled with lust as she stares up at me, trying to pull my face back down for a kiss.

"Where the fuck are your clothes, Iris?" I bark, and she flinches.

"Quentin was changing the bandage on my stitches—"

"What stitches?"

"I got six stitches on my ass, trying to escape this place."

"Escape? Wait, Iris, why the fuck are you even here? Did he kidnap you?" I shout in her face.

"He was protecting me," she replies, and I swear to God, I see red. Jumping up from the floor, I march out to the main living area. Iris is hot on my tail. We find Quentin in the kitchen, holding an ice pack against his face, which is already turning blue and swelling.

"I've seen you a dozen fucking times this week," I yell. "You failed to fucking mention that you had my girlfriend hidden away in your fucking condo!"

"Keep your voice down. I'm keeping her safe."

"Safe? Bullshit!"

"What if I had told you she was here? What would you have done, Gabriel? You would have caused a big scene, my dad would have found her and then she'd be dead. Plus," he adds, wiping the blood from his swollen nose, "that was before I knew what I know now."

"And what exactly do you know now?" I say through clenched teeth.

His eyes dance over to Iris, who is standing behind me, and no one talks. I swear I'm going to fucking explode. A minute ago, I thought my girlfriend was safe at home and now I find her here keeping secrets with the asshole who abducted both of us.

Iris passes by me toward Quentin and takes the ice pack from him, inspecting his nose before grabbing another paper towel from the roll and wiping up more blood. "Let's just say Uncle Bax is responsible for more than we thought."

"What does that mean?" I snap.

When she turns toward me, I stare into those familiar green eyes. Why do they feel so unfamiliar now? Has she changed, or have I?

"This has been a lot already, baby. Let's just take this one thing at a time."

I grab her by the waist and haul her against my body. Taking her face in my hands, I search her for any sign that Iris would lie to me or betray me. I swear my mind is playing tricks on me. Why has she been here all this time and not with me? Why has she been here with *him*?

"Listen to me, baby," she whispers. "We have to make a plan, but we have to play it cool. If we blow up and cause a scene, we're dead."

"Princess," I mumble against her mouth, "you're here. Come back to my room with me. Be with me. I'll tell my uncle you came and found me. I'll protect you. If he knows how much I love you, he won't hurt you."

She pulls away. "He'll know I'm taking you home, Gabriel. He won't like that."

"We don't need to go home right away." I lick my way up her neck, savoring the taste of her after eight long days without her, but she pulls away too fast. Staring at me with horror in her eyes, I furrow my brow.

"What do you mean we don't need to go home?"

"Not right away. If we play along, learn what we can, I

think we could actually create an alliance with them. Morales and Black families working together."

She shoves away from me. "You can't be serious. He's brainwashing you," she snaps.

"He is not. Not as much as this nerdy fuck has been brainwashing you!"

"Gabriel, you can't seriously be saying this. Baxter abducted you. And he—"

A beeping noise in the back of the house begins to blare, cutting her off. Quentin rushes to the computers along the back wall of the second bedroom, and I find him in there, scrolling through video footage on about six computer screens.

"He's coming. Iris, you need to hide."

"What?" I stammer.

"Baxter is coming. If he finds your girlfriend here, you're not going to like the outcome."

"You have to go, Gabriel," she says, staring at me with wide eyes.

"I can't leave you here!"

"You have to. Come back tomorrow. I'm fine. Quentin isn't going to hurt me, I promise. Just go and come back when you get a chance."

My feet won't move. I can't believe what she's asking me. I just got her back, and she wants me to leave her again. Leave her with him in her fucking underwear.

"Please," she begs.

Quentin chimes in with his two cents, "He's probably looking for you. He never comes out here."

It feels like minutes crawl by while I stare at her, unable to tear myself away. Finally, she's the one to leave me, running to the bedroom and closing herself in. But just before the door shuts, she whispers toward me, "I love you."

One glance at Quentin with a frantic look on his face, I know that Baxter can't find me here. Not with his son's face looking like ground beef and furniture tipped over from our fight. Giving him one last scowl, I point at him. "Hurt her and I'll fucking maim you."

"Got it," he replies with an eye roll.

Then, as fast as I can, I rush out the front door and down the paved path, meeting Baxter halfway down the drive. It takes everything in me to remain casual.

"There you are," he says when he spots me.

"This place is fucking boring," I mutter with resentment.

"Well, this is just Quentin's place. Let me show you the good stuff."

Then, he leads me down a different paved path toward the bigger warehouse building. He can call it the good stuff all he wants, but the only good stuff I want is back in that condo.

Twenty-Four

Iris

"It's not broken, so stop your whining."

"Your boyfriend knows how to throw a punch," he replies in a nasally wheeze. "He broke my glasses." His voice makes me laugh as I slip a small bandage over the bridge of his nose.

I always loved tending to my guys' wounds. They don't get them often, but on the rare occasion Baron or Gabriel (never Silas) would come home from a job with a little glass embedded in their skin or cuts from a fight, I would sit them down in the bathroom and mend what needed to be mended.

The thought makes me homesick. And homesickness reminds me of what Gabriel said. Did he really mean what he said about staying for a while? Staying for what? Silas will never agree to an alliance, not after this. And what for? We don't need affiliations with the cartel, we never did. That was the whole situation with my father and Maretti.

Gabriel didn't want any part in that because his father raised him to never take sides. Don't get involved. Do the job, collect the payment, and move on.

What am I going to do if Gabriel won't leave? I can't stay here forever. Baron and Silas need me. What if I'm forced to choose?

"I have to tell you something," Quentin says, and my hands stop, waiting to hear what he's about to tell me. I'm not afraid to admit that in the past few days, I've actually grown fond of Quentin, and not in a romantic way. But he's my friend now.

"What is it?"

"I got some security footage the other day, but I never planned to tell you about it. I don't even know why I'm telling you now..."

"What footage?" I say flatly, my blood running cold.

"At the false location...where I found you, there was an ambush."

"What happened? Quentin, *what happened*?" I shriek.

"Your guys are fine. They shot up a few of the guards my dad left there, and they released all the girls he was holding, but your guys seemed to get out alive."

My lungs relax and the air rushes out of me. My shoulders actually ache from holding in that tension. Sitting on the stool across from him, I let this information sink in. Silas and Baron came looking for us, but they'll never find us here. I don't even know where *here* is.

But why would Quentin tell me this?

"I was on board with the whole Gabriel plan from the start. My father wanted his nephew back, and I was sure it was a family vendetta thing, but now..."

"Now what?"

He tosses his towel against the counter. Then he storms

away from me, and I feel as if I'm on the brink of something good. If we can get Quentin on our side, he could easily help us get out of here.

"My father preaches about family and loyalty, but he only cares about you so long as you provide him with something. If you're useless, you're of no value to him."

"So, what does he want with Gabriel?"

"Another member of his team? Someone else to protect him and his legacy." He's heated, throwing his hands up in frustration.

"But you're his son. Aren't you supposed to hold up his legacy?"

"He doesn't care about me! The last three years it's been nothing but Gabriel, Gabriel, Gabriel. As soon as he heard his long-lost nephew wasn't just alive, but a trained assassin, he was obsessed! Like he didn't even have a son at all."

Standing up, I cross the room and put out my hands to try and calm him down. Placing one on his shoulder, he seems to settle.

"Gabriel and Baron have this argument all the time. Gabriel doesn't feel like his father gives him enough attention. And he acts like Baron is the golden child. It's the same old thing over and over. But, Quentin…if you want Gabriel gone, then you know what to do…"

"Help you get him out of here?"

There's a long moment of tension between us as we stare at each other. "I know you can do it easily."

Solemnly, he nods. A pinch of guilt gnaws at my stomach. What will happen to Quentin if he's caught helping us? Will his own father hurt him for it? This is the man who had his own brother killed just to claim a title. I wouldn't put it past him to kill his own son for treachery.

"I don't think your boyfriend even wants to leave at this

point. Wait until Baxter shows him the warehouse operation. This is all part of his master plan, I promise. He is playing mind games with him."

"Well, don't you worry about that. I can play a few mind games of my own."

Twenty-Five

Iris

I'm picking at my breakfast when Gabriel finally comes back. It took him longer than I expected. In fact, I made Quentin sleep on the couch in case Gabe showed up in the middle of the night and found us lying in the same bed together.

Q didn't take that too well. He said I was too vulnerable alone—and all this time I thought he was sleeping next to me to make sure I didn't escape, not protect me.

Gabriel doesn't say a word as he charges through the front door, snatches me up by my waist and hauls me into Quentin's empty bedroom, draped over his shoulder like some war prize. Just before the door slams, I catch sight of Quentin in his computer room, closing his own door without looking at me.

Yeah, he's probably not going to want to hear this.

Gabriel tosses me hard onto the bed. There is something wild in his eyes as he snatches my pants and tries to tear them down. I kick away from him before he can pull them all the way down.

Don't get me wrong. I want—no, I *need*—him, but right now, he owes me an explanation.

"Gabriel, stop!" I yell as he yanks me to the edge of the bed.

"No. You were here this whole time and I didn't know. You're mine now, Iris Black."

His hands fumble again for the waistband of my pants, but I fight him. "Fine. Tell me we can go home. Tell me you didn't mean what you said last night."

There's no response. He simply grabs the hem of my shirt and rips it off with one quick swipe. Then his warm hands are on my breasts and he drapes his body over mine, traveling up my body with harsh kisses, nipping and licking his way to my neck.

My struggle dissipates. Especially when I feel his hard cock against my leg.

God, I've missed him.

But I need him to tell me we can go home. I need to hear him say that he's still mine and not El Basileus's new pet. I need to know we are still us.

Drawing my leg up, I plant my foot on the top of his thigh and shove him hard. Taken by surprise, he flies backward, and I flip onto my stomach in a rush to climb away.

"No! I'm not giving you what you want until you tell me what I want to hear."

His arm hooks around my waist and draws me back, slamming his hips against my ass. "Fine, Princess. Then I'll take it."

Heat floods my body, and I grip the sheets tight in my hands. God, I'm weak.

Because the moment I hear his zipper drop, I'm a goner. I can't even pretend to struggle anymore. When he aligns his cock at my entrance, I feel just how hard he is. And I'm so wet for him already, he slides in easily, thrusting hard and piercing me deep, I let out a cry that shakes the walls.

With the sheets still in my fists, I hold on as he pounds into me relentlessly. His heavy grunts echo in the room mingled with my cries of pleasure. His hands travel up my back, and I feel his thumb work small circles over a familiar spot between my shoulder blades.

"I fucking branded you, remember?" he growls, slowing his thrusts but pounding even harder.

"Yes," I gasp, recalling the heart etched into my skin by his knife only a couple weeks ago. "I'm yours, Gabriel."

His hand snakes its way up to my throat, pulling me upright and pressing his lips to my ear. The other hand finds my clit, working harsh circles and making my body squirm, overcome by the sensation. Keeping up his momentum, my body builds and builds in pleasure, sending me into a mind-blowing orgasm.

"I'm coming!" I scream. Gabriel licks his way up from my shoulder to my mouth and bites my jaw as my body seizes in a climax. A moment later, I feel his cock jolt inside me, and his groans turn breathless.

Once we are both spent, we collapse together on the bed, his cum already leaking out of me and onto Quentin's sheets—which I'm sure he'll be thrilled about.

But I don't care. Right now all I care about is that I have Gabriel with me, my face nuzzled comfortably against his chest and his broad arms around me. Neither of us say a word for a while, and I listen only to the erratic pounding of his heart against my ear.

Gabriel and I are so alike. No, we're more than alike,

we're the same. I love each of my men so differently, but I love Gabriel because our hearts recognize each other's, as if they beat in unison. And I never realized until this moment how wrong it feels to be away from him, how I'm not even myself when he's gone.

Squeezing my arms around his waist, I find his lips and kiss him with every ounce of emotion in my body. Turning onto his side, he wraps me up in his arms, draping his legs over me and covers me like an armor until all I can see, smell, and feel is Gabriel.

Something about this feels dangerous, because I know him all too well. Gabriel wants me to himself—he always has. I mean, he loves his brother and dad, but this situation was always harder for him to accept. There was always a part of him that understood that if he wanted me to be happy, he needed to let me love them as much as I love him. I am incomplete without even one of them.

Instead of easing him into this conversation again, I rip the Band-Aid clean off.

"I want to go home."

He tenses before pulling back and letting out a heavy sigh. "You didn't see what I saw yesterday, Iris. The operation he has here, the size of his empire..."

Jumping out of his arms, I glare down at him. I don't believe what I'm hearing. "I. Don't. Care."

"Well, I do!" he argues. "This isn't like Maretti, Iris. It's not one measly mafia boss to defeat. It's an army. And I have the choice to stay on his good side, take my place by his side where I could literally give you the world—"

"And what about your dad?" I shriek.

"He's dead, Iris," he replies, and my eyes go wide.

"Silas. I'm talking about Silas, your *real* father. And

Baron, your brother." I swear I think I'll be sick. It's like Baron all over again, but at least Baron understood what he was doing. He realized his mistake when he betrayed his family and when he betrayed me, and he almost paid for it with his life. I can't lose Gabriel like that. I just *can't*.

Gabriel bursts out of the bed, grabbing his pants from the floor as he rambles on, sounding insane.

"Silas is content with mediocrity. He never wanted to make our business what it could really be."

I quickly jump up to get in his face. My palms itch with the need to just hit him with the way he's talking right now. If I could just knock some sense into him because, apparently, I can't fuck sense into him.

"What good is this empire when you have to kill your family to get it?"

"What are you talking about?"

Fuck. I can't let that secret about Baxter and Gabriel's parents out yet. If he knows the truth, he'll go on a rampage and get himself killed. So I quickly change the subject.

"You don't think someone could easily take down Baxter and take his place the same way he did the one before? If you stand next to him on that throne, then you'll have a target on your back too, Gabriel. And so will I."

"Have you seen the level of protection they have here? Think about it, Iris. If we go back home, we're passing up the opportunity to be something really great. More than we could ever be with Silas, and you know it. We're too good at what we do. We deserve *more*."

He tries to take my hands, and I quickly snap them away. Tears fill my eyes, and I hate it.

I won't leave without him—I *won't*. But I could never truly give him what he's asking me for. Leave behind two people I love for one? Who could possibly make that choice?

But I'm not the one making this choice, he is. And he's not choosing me.

Twenty-Six

Iris

Quentin is gone when we come out of the bedroom. Not surprisingly. We were not quiet, and that couldn't have been fun to listen to.

Well, we're quiet now. Both of us fuming and exhausted, Gabriel leaves me in the condo after an empty kiss on my forehead and a promise to come back later. It pains me to watch him walk away. Especially knowing that I'm losing him.

Whatever bullshit Baxter has been feeding him has been working. He's gotten into Gabe's head, but I can't really blame him for believing it. This really is his birth family, and I can only imagine how torn Gabriel is feeling right now. His mother and father died for this dream, and now it's within his grasp.

Fuck, am I being too hard on him?

It's a few more hours before Quentin comes back, and

it gives me enough time to wash his bedding and get myself cleaned up. To say it's awkward after he walks through the door would be an understatement.

But it's more than awkward—he almost seems...angry. He slams the cabinet door after grabbing a glass and slamming it down on the counter so hard I'm surprised it doesn't shatter.

I don't ask what his problem is, mostly because I'm too fucking tired of fighting with men today. I'm missing Baron and Silas so much right now, and it has me feeling irritable. I wish I could just send them a message to let them know we're okay, but I know that's a dangerous idea. One little whiff of where we're at and they will bring hellfire upon this place, getting themselves killed in the process. I can't put them at risk like that, so for now, they will just have to worry. And I hate that.

"He's too rough with you," Quentin barks out after throwing back a shot of tequila.

My brow furrows as I glare at him. Is he serious?

"I can handle myself," I argue.

"That's what you're willing to die for? A man who throws you around and yells at you and carves into your back. Yeah, I saw the heart."

I grimace. It's still scabbing over, and it looks pretty gnarly, but nowhere near as bad as the giant gash in my ass cheek.

"Well, you drugged me, electrocuted me, and let me take a stick in the ass. Only two inches over and I really would have been fucked!" I throw my arms up at him. He chose the wrong day to pick a fight with me.

"Yeah, but I'm not your boyfriend," he shouts back.

"Thank God for that!"

So done with this conversation, I turn to head to the

bedroom, so I don't even see him coming as his hand finds its way around my neck and I'm slammed hard against the wall. He covers my body with his own, pressing his face only inches from mine.

"You should watch your mouth, Iris. You're being a little bitch again."

"Get the fuck off me!" I scream, trying to shove him away.

And he's saying Gabriel's too rough? Hypocrite much? Somewhere in the back of my mind, I know that if I really wanted him off of me, I could do it. Gabriel taught me all the moves to evade an attacker, and it would be easy, but I don't. And I don't think he's buying my struggle either.

"You're just jealous!" I snap, choosing words as my weapon, instead of my fists or a knee to the groin. Which, let's be real, words hurt more anyway. "You're jealous that Gabriel gets all the attention from your dad. And you're jealous that I fucked him and not you!"

When his mouth slams against mine, I let out a yelp. And maybe I knew this was coming or I pushed him on purpose because I knew it would lead to this, but I fight him anyway.

Grasping his shirt in my fist, I push him, but he doesn't let up, tugging my bottom lip between his teeth and licking his way into my mouth. He tastes like mint and he smells like him, and I hate myself for even noticing that, let alone *liking* it.

The more I shove him away, clawing and pounding at his chest, the harder he kisses me. I refuse to give up this fight, and when he trails his mouth from mine to my neck, lighting my body up in flames, I panic.

"Quentin, I can't!" I shriek, driving his body away in earnest.

Finally, he lets up, moving away, but not far. There's only a foot of space between us, his hands still against the wall, framing me in. We're both panting and staring at each other, not quite knowing where we go from here.

"You can't? Or you don't want to?"

Fuck. I won't lie to him.

"I...can't," I reply, and I can't believe what I'm even saying. Quentin is hot and funny and I like him—I really, really like him, but I could never, ever do that to my guys. Never.

And I hate myself for even admitting that I might want to.

He leans in again, but instead of kissing me, he presses his hips against my belly, grinding his hard cock against me. I let out a small sound. Not quite a moan, and not quite an argument either.

"You're already fucking three guys. Is this really even cheating if you fuck one more?"

"Yes!" I shout without hesitation. "I'm not just fucking them, Quentin. I'm in a relationship with them."

He grinds his molars, but doesn't pull away. My hands are still on his chest, his shirt still grasped tightly in my fists, so I gently let him go and touch his face. If I was the person I was three years ago, I would have spread my legs for him days ago. It would have been such an easy decision to make. I would have let Quentin fuck me until I forgot my own name.

And what's worse is that I probably would have fallen in love with him. Because Quentin isn't like any other guy I've been with, and I'm finding it easier and easier to be around him, to be *myself* around him.

That's what he wants, isn't it? No more quick fucks

with nameless women. Quentin wants the real thing, and it breaks my heart that I can't give it to him.

"I'm sorry," I whisper, but the indignation on his face doesn't dissolve. Instead, he flares his nostrils and storms away, slamming the door to his office behind him.

Great, now both of them are mad at me.

Gabriel

"We need to talk," I say to Quentin with my elbows pressed to the center island in the kitchen of the main house, a short glass of bourbon staring back at me.

He stops walking, shoulders slouched, with his eyes deadlocked on the white wall in front of him. "So talk."

My fingers pinch the glass, giving the liquid a swirl as ice clanks against the glass. "She's not yours. She will never be yours."

A low grumble climbs up his throat, followed by a mocking laugh. "Oh yeah?" He spins around to face me. "And I assume that's because she's yours—and your brother's, and your adopted father's?"

With the glass still in my hand, I straighten my back and level with him, though he's still ten feet away. Lucky for him, otherwise I might lay him out just for his condescending tone. "That's right. Is that a fucking problem?"

"Well," he drawls, "it wouldn't be a problem if you

knew how to fucking treat your girl. She's practically begging you to leave this place and here you are wanting to keep her here. Trust me, man, I don't wanna see her go, but I also prefer she be happy and not miserable."

Miserable? How could she be miserable if she's here with me? Right now things are intense, but we could build a fucking awesome life here—together.

I take a sip of my drink, licking the excess on my bottom lip. "She'll understand eventually. I'll make her."

"Is that so?" He finally turns to face me, indignation all over his face. "Just like you make her do everything else? With force and disgrace?"

Squeezing the glass harder, anger ripples through me. "What the fuck is that supposed to mean?"

"Hmm. Let's see." Quentin taps his chin with smugness. "You toss her around like she's a damn toy. Fuck her like you own her. Not to mention, you try to dictate her life."

Who the fuck is this guy to try and analyze *my* relationship with Iris?

My teeth grind, jaw popping. "You don't know a damn thing about us so keep your fucking mouth shut when it comes to me and my girl."

"Your girl?" he laughs. "From what I've heard, she's the community fuck."

That does it.

My fingers clench so tightly that they bust right through the glass. Tiny shards digging into the skin of my thumb. I toss it down quickly as glass scatters on the center island. In two second flat, I've got Quentin by the collar of his shirt, his eyes wide, but not as fearful as I'd like them to be.

"What are you gonna do? Kill me?"

"I just might." I tug aggressively, pulling him into my personal space, so he hears me loud and clear. "Mind your own fucking business or it *will* get you killed."

There's a beat of silence that has my heart rate steadying, before Quentin finally says, "You're breaking her heart."

Something odd stirs inside of me. A feeling braided with dread and anguish. "What'd you just say?"

His expression goes solemn as if he truly does care about Iris's feelings. "You heard me. You're breaking her heart by making her choose. It's not fair."

"You don't even know her. Why the hell do you care so much?"

Hanging by my hold, he doesn't even try to fight me off. Just stays put, thinking he can get through to me. He can't. I haven't seen this guy since we were kids. A week and he suddenly acts like he knows the ins and outs of my relationship. Fuck that.

"I do care about her. In case you've forgotten, I'm the only face she's seen in over a week. We've talked—gotten close."

I jerk him forward aggressively, sneering in his face.

"Not like that," he spits out. "She'd never betray you like that. And I can't believe I'm trying to talk you into this, but I'd rather she leave and be happy than stay and be miserable. Even if I had half a shot with her, I'm willing to make that sacrifice for her. Are you? She just wants to go home, Gabriel."

She just wants to go home.

Back to the place where we live in Silas's shadow. There's no freedom there. He's so damn worried about keeping us safe. How can anyone grow to their full potential with so many limits?

But, it is Iris's home—our home. She loves them as much as she loves me. Probably more right now.

Fuck. I'm such a selfish asshole.

Iris is my world, my everything. Here I am trying to pull her away from the life she's built, and for what—money and power?"

I release my grip on Quentin's shirt and let him down, turning away immediately. My fingers rake through my greasy hair as I approach the counter. With my back to him, I lean forward, elbows pressing down, and my head between my hands. "Fuck," I grind out. My head shakes as all the reasons to leave race through my mind, beating all the reasons to stay.

It all comes down to one thing—her happiness.

That's all that matters. I'm nothing without her, so staying while she leaves is impossible.

"You okay, man?" Quentin asks from only three feet behind me.

My body shoots up, back steeled. "Get the fuck out of here," I hiss, hating that he's seeing me like this—questioning my own motives, giving thought to what he said.

It's all because of him. If he'd just left well enough alone and stayed out of my fucking head, he wouldn't have me questioning such a big life choice.

He's right, though. As much as I want to deny it, the fucking nerd is right.

I'd do anything to protect Iris. Anything to keep her happy. She wants to go home to her family—to our family.

Now I just have to be sure I'm ready to leave behind the blood family I just found.

Twenty-Eight

Iris

I'm going stir crazy. Each day goes by the same. Gabriel comes over, Quentin leaves. Gabriel and I fuck, we argue, he leaves.

I'm getting nowhere. The longer Gabriel spends with Baxter, the deeper he seems to sink into this mindfuckery. Something needs to shake him out of it; because even though the sex is great and I use every second of it to try and soak up everything I love about him and revive our connection, I feel him slipping away.

He leaves angry, and Quentin swoops in every day with some way to make me laugh or talk me down from really losing my mind. I've been in this condo for almost two weeks. I haven't spoken to Baron or Silas, and the fact that they haven't found us is a relief, but it's also making me worry. Are they okay? Did they run into Basileus's men and get themselves killed? What if I never see them again?

No. I can't let myself go down that road again. That's all I do. Sit around here and worry.

Quentin will help Gabriel and me escape, but we both know we're running out of time. If we don't make a move soon, Baxter will either find me and kill me or finally have Gabriel hooked and he'll never want to leave.

I'm cornered, and restless, and the fact that the tension between me and Quentin is growing stronger each day isn't making any of this easier. I see the pain in his eyes, and I recognize what it's like to be the child of a powerful person who sees you more like property than kin.

But he is not a member of my family, and I can't think about him right now. I'm under too much pressure as it is to get the rest of them together. He can take care of himself.

"I have good news," Quentin says when he comes back in one afternoon.

"Oh my God, please tell me we're going home," I reply from the living room floor in the middle of a deep stretch with my ass in the air. Not being able to leave the condo has meant little to no exercise. I've had to take up yoga, of all things.

When I sit up, I catch Quentin staring at my ass before turning away. "My dad is going on a business trip for a few days at the end of the week. He wants me to stay here and keep an eye on Gabriel."

I jump up onto my feet, feeling a buzz of excitement race through my veins. "It's our chance. It'll be perfect."

He nods, turning toward the kitchen and busying himself by making a drink. He's not doing a very good job of hiding his disappointment.

"You don't think it's a trap, do you? Like he knows you're going to sneak Gabriel out?"

"No. He goes on these trips all the time, and I genuinely think he wants me to bond with Gabriel more. He's noticed how much he comes out here to see me, so he's taking that as a good sign. Your boyfriend is putting on a good show."

"I don't think it's a show," I mumble quietly, too afraid to say those words out loud because it means I'll accept them as true.

He's keeping his back to me and I can tell there are a lot of things on his mind that he won't voice. I don't know why I even trust Quentin when I have no good reason to. Obviously, things between us have changed since I got here and he clearly has feelings for me that I can't reciprocate, so it's not insane to think he might betray me. If he did something that could get Gabriel killed, he'd have me to himself, not that I would ever let that happen, but he doesn't know that.

And he hasn't really reacted much to the news that his father killed his uncle and aunt. I'm sure he's dealing with a lot over that right now, too.

I need to ensure that he's truly on our side. Settling up next to him at the counter, I look up at him, but he doesn't return my gaze.

"Pour me one?" I ask.

Without a word, he does, and we each take a shot together. I hate tequila, and I grimace and squirm as it goes down while Quentin hardly even reacts.

"I'm going stir crazy in here. What do you say we go for a walk or something? Can't you hijack the cameras long enough to let me get some fresh air?"

His warm, golden eyes find mine, and I resist the urge to melt under that weighted stare. "What if your boyfriend comes back?"

"Then, he can wait for me here. I'm sure he'll be fine."

I watch the rise and fall of his chest, waiting for him to respond. Finally, he nods. "Sure. But we have to wait for it to get dark, okay?"

"Okay," I reply, bouncing up and down on the soles of my feet.

It takes him a few minutes to work on the cameras in his computer room before he walks out just a few minutes past sunset. He hands me one of his sweatshirts, and when he's not looking, I hold it up to my nose, taking a long whiff of his scent infused into the fabric. Seriously, what is it about guys' sweatshirts?

His condo is secluded enough on the property that we rarely ever see people walking by and no one can really see us from here. Once we're clear, we head down toward the tree line, where I was electrocuted two weeks ago.

"Don't worry. I know where the fence line is. I won't let you get shocked again," he says with a trace of humor in his voice.

"I'm sure you'd just love to stitch up my ass again."

"No way. You whine too much when you're in pain."

I scoff, knocking my shoulder against his. "I do not! I'd like to see you take a stick up your ass and not complain about it."

"It wasn't *up your ass*," he replies, mocking my tone with a playful smile stretched across his face. Those dimples are back, and with a smile like that, he's really not playing fair. How could a girl possibly resist those eyes and dimples?

"Well, it was pretty damn close!"

"I don't think you would have complained at all if it was *up your ass*."

I freeze, staring at him with my jaw hanging open. "I can't believe you just said that to me!"

"Oh, come on!" he laughs. "You have three boyfriends. Three dicks...three holes."

"Quentin! That is none of your business!"

"Is that why you stopped at three? No holes left for a fourth?"

"You're dead," I snap as I throw my hands against his chest. He stumbles backward. Instead of fighting back, he takes off in a run, and I sprint after him, both of us laughing as we do.

It feels so good to run and sweat and breathe in the fresh air. And to laugh. I needed this. And yet it feels so wrong. I was kidnapped, and I should be trying to get home, not laughing and smiling with the man who abducted me.

When I finally reach Quentin, I slam into his chest, and we stumble together to the ground. This time, I use the moves Gabriel taught me, so when Quentin tries to get the upper hand and pin me to the ground, I snake my way out of his grasp, hooking my legs around his neck and bringing his arm down in the perfect position to snap it at the elbow.

I won't, of course, but it's enough to make him finally tap out.

By the time I release him, we're panting and laughing and covered in dirt. And even after I relax my grip, his head is still squeezed between my legs, only inches from where it really shouldn't be.

Once he climbs out of my grasp, he doesn't stand up. Instead, he crawls over my body and stares down at me. The playfulness is replaced by tension as I look up at him.

"You're amazing, Iris. I just want you to know that."

My heart practically splinters in two as I gaze into his eyes, wishing things were different. I wish Silas took him that night along with Gabriel. I wish Quentin was there two years ago when I met the others. I wish I didn't have to leave him when I go.

It's so fucking unfair, which is the only reason I don't feel bad for pressing my body up to meet his lips. My mouth meets his for a moment, and I think he's not going to kiss me back, but then he rests his weight on my body and deepens the kiss. His tongue snakes its way into my mouth, and I hum against his lips. The kiss is full of passion and angst, desperate and hungry for everything we both know we can't have.

I tug on his jacket, pulling him closer as he buries a hand in my hair, holding me tighter, and we stay like that, devouring as much of each other as we can in this secret moment before we have to go back to reality and eventually say goodbye. I feel his erection growing against my belly, and I shift my hips, wanting to feel any friction I can, but I stop myself. This is so wrong.

We both pull away from the kiss at the same time, gasping for breath. Resting his forehead against mine, we breathe the same air for a moment before he finally climbs off of me.

The walk back to the house is silent. We're no longer laughing or joking, and something sour begins to form in my gut.

It only gets worse when we arrive back at the condo to find Gabriel sitting outside with a look of pure wrath on his face. Quentin and I are still covered in dirt, my hair is disheveled, and our mouths are still red.

But I don't bother looking ashamed or sorry. He was the one who got us in this mess by leaving us for this job alone. So I march past him and straight into the condo. They both trail behind, and I can tell something is up.

"Iris," Gabriel calls after me in a softer tone than I

expect. I'm too wired, too anxious and angry to respond, so I head straight for the bedroom, but he's quick. Grabbing me by the arm, he jerks me backward, and I stumble.

The next thing I know, Gabriel is shoved hard against the wall with Quentin's forearm holding him there, pressed against his neck and blocking his airway.

"You fucking touch her like that again," Quentin snarls.

"You'll what?" Gabriel replies.

"Both of you, stop it!" I yell. The sight of them fighting like this, hating each other so much has my blood turning cold. I hate it. Their faces are pressed so close together, I can't help but notice just how similar they look. They have the same facial structure, same eyes...and I never quite noticed it before.

"You sure hurt her a lot for a girl you supposedly love so much."

"Because I know she can take it. I know she *likes* it, because I fucking know her. You think you do, but you don't know shit," Gabriel replies through gasps for breath as Quentin shoves him harder against the wall.

"Yeah, well, I know she wants to go home, and I know she thinks you're being a selfish, ignorant asshole!"

"Quentin, you're choking him! Stop it!"

"If Iris was mine, I'd give her anything she wanted, but you're being a fucking idiot instead and choosing this fucking place over her—"

"I'm not," Gabriel manages to hiss while turning blue.

"Quentin, seriously!" I yank hard on his elbow, trying to dislodge his arm from my boyfriend's throat. "Please," I beg.

Finally, he releases him, and Gabriel collapses to the floor, gasping for air like a fish out of water. I kneel next to him, desperate to touch him and bury my face into his neck.

After a few minutes, he can finally breathe regularly, and he looks up at me. "I'm serious, Princess. I'm sorry for being so fucking stupid. I'm ready to go home."

My eyes widen, and I stare at him. "Seriously? What changed your mind?"

His gaze only flicks to Quentin for a moment, but it's enough for me to understand that they must have had a talk today at some point. Whatever they said, it was enough to convince Gabriel that it's time to go.

"When Baxter goes out of town, we'll make our move. Should be easy enough. I just have to loop the surveillance feed to the main security building, cut the power to the invisible fence, and you guys can walk right out."

"Won't Baxter know you helped us?" I ask, staring up at Quentin with a feeling of dread coursing through my veins. I can't stand the thought of worrying about him after we go.

"We can kick his ass and tie him up before we go. Make it look forced," Gabriel replies, his voice still strained from the fight.

Quentin doesn't respond, just holds up a shot of tequila as if he's wishing us well and tips the clear amber liquid back, spilling it down his throat.

My nerves are still shot, the idea of getting drunk sounds so enticing. Standing up, I walk over to where he's pouring another. I don't look him in the eye as I pull a glass down from the cabinet and set it in front of him. "It's cause for celebration, isn't it?"

"Guess so," he replies coldly.

Twenty-Nine

Iris

"I hate tequila," I squeal as my fifth shot burns its way down my throat. Or was it my sixth? The room is fuzzy, and I'm feeling light and happy. Like everything will be okay. Soon, I'll see Silas and Baron, and all will be right again.

"We need some music!" I say, getting up to mess with the security screen on the wall near the door. After tapping a couple buttons, Quentin hooks me by the waist and drags me away.

"Don't touch my computer, Green Eyes."

"Yes, sir," I reply, looking up at him. How is he still sober? He's taken almost twice as many shots as me. Even Gabriel is starting to look tipsy. He's currently melting into the couch, just watching me with a dark expression.

Suddenly, the condo is filled with the sound of music, and I practically shriek in delight. The music is sexy with an upbeat tempo and a sultry beat.

"Dance with me," I say, grabbing Quentin by the hand

and dragging him to the middle of the living room. He shuffles his feet, grimacing as I pull him to where I want him. This is totally the tequila talking because I know what I'm doing is stupid, flirting with another man in front of my boyfriend, but I'm too happy to care.

Gabriel doesn't react when Quentin's hands rest just above my ass. With our bodies pressed together, we grind against each other in the middle of the room, moving with ease to the music blaring through the speakers. Looking up at Quentin, I get lost in his golden-brown eyes.

"Why aren't you drunk yet?" I ask.

"Oh, I am…" he replies. There's darkness in his tone, something unfamiliar about it since the Q I've grown to know these past two weeks has been cocky and playful.

"You don't look drunk." Our faces are dangerously close to each other.

"Because I'm too busy thinking about how I'm going to get you alone."

I swallow, still gazing into his eyes. "We…can't."

"I don't give a fuck anymore, Green Eyes. Don't you want to know what I want to do to you?" His eyes are heavy, and there's not an ounce of playfulness in his tone.

"I think I know exactly—"

"No, you don't."

I glance sideways at Gabriel, who is still watching us, this time with a little more interest than before. "Then, why don't you tell me?" the tequila asks.

Quentin leans his face down closer to me, pressing his lips almost against my ear as he whispers, "I want to take you to my room and watch you strip for me, slowly until you're naked and I can see that perfect little pussy. Then, I want you to lie on the bed and give me a front-row view as you play with your cunt. Fingerfuck yourself until you can't take it anymore. I want to see you pinch that perfect little clit so hard you scream, and I want to watch every second as you come, legs shaking and your cunt leaking for me. You'll scream my name when you do it.

"Then I want to fuck you, Iris. God, I want to fuck you so bad. You'll never want to go back to them. My cock will be all yours, and it'll be the only one you'll ever want. Your pretty little cunt will weep, soaking your panties for me, Iris, because when I fuck you, you'll stop all this talk of leaving."

With a hand on my ass, he grinds himself against me again, and I feel his hard length pressing against my stomach. I gasp. I can hardly breathe as it is, after that little picture he just painted for me, but now that his cock is hard for me, I feel just how impressive it is.

Holy shit.

Quentin kept up this hot-nerd performance so well, but apparently, he has a dark, kinky side, and I'm not going to lie...my panties are already soaked, and the hunger for everything he just described is torture.

"That's enough," Gabriel barks as he wraps his hands around my waist and hauls me away. I'm slammed against his body, and now it's his turn to grind against me to the music, and I don't miss how he's already hard too.

"I see you still don't know how to share."

He's staring down at me with hunger in his eyes.

"I already share you with my brother and my dad...now you want me to share you with my cousin, too?"

I glance at Quentin, but he's back in the kitchen pouring himself another shot. I know I'm playing with fire here, and I can't quite decide if fucking Quentin counts as cheating, if *one* of my boyfriends is here to give his approval. When I look back at Gabriel, it's like he's reading my mind.

"Don't even fucking think about it," he mumbles darkly, squeezing me tighter.

The alcohol running through my bloodstream warms my cheeks as I let a sly smile stretch across my face. "I just wish you understood that even though I love them, it doesn't mean I'm not yours. We don't live normal lives, baby. Sharing me might be good for you..."

"I'm not sharing you tonight," he snaps, kissing my neck so hard, I squeal. It grabs Quentin's attention, and he glances over at us as he throws back another drink.

"Fine," I breathe, "then, show him."

"What did you say?"

My eyes are still locked on Quentin's as I reply, "Let him watch. Show him who I belong to."

I can tell by the heavy rise of Q's chest that he has feelings about this idea—whether they are good or bad ones, I'm not quite sure yet. I'm taking a risk, and I hope it pays off. This is my last night with Quentin, and I want to make it memorable.

"What do you think about that, cous? You want to watch me rip this dirty little girl in two?"

Quentin's eyes are hooded as he watches us. With his gaze on me, he slips out his tongue and runs it across his lower lip.

"I don't know...she's looking at me like she wants my cock right now."

Heat blazes down my spine. He can read me like a book.

Gabriel grabs me by the hair and spins me around, so I'm facing Quentin, his hard shaft digging into my lower back. "I don't know if Dad or Baron would like that very much," he whispers.

Slowly, Quentin walks over, closing the distance

between us, and I swear each step steals the breath from my lungs. Once he's only a foot away from me, he takes my chin in his hands. "I'd love to see these perfect lips wrapped around my cock."

Gabriel kisses my neck, his teeth biting harshly on my sensitive skin, as his fingers dig into my hips as he grinds into me again. This possessiveness fuels his lust—I know it does. I wish he could see how good this could be.

"She's very good with her mouth," he says with his lips against my jaw.

"What do you say then? Lend me your girl for one blow job?"

Gabriel reacts by bruising my hip, his other hand clutching hard onto my right tit, and I squeak out a cry, but it's a good pain. He's showing me who I belong to, and I answer by rubbing my ass against his cock. He knows I'm his.

I keep waiting for him to say no, to throw me over his shoulder, to take me to the bedroom and stop everything before it goes too far. What I don't expect is his hand finding its way back to my hair as he puts his lips next to my ear and mutters, "Fine. Get on your knees and show him how good *my* girl is."

The air leaves my chest and my heart flutters so fast, I think I might pass out. With a harsh tug of his fist, I'm forced to kneel between them. Gazing up at Quentin, I wait for his next move. There's a new light in his eyes and a wicked smile forming on his face.

He leans down, stroking my chin. "Show me how good you are, Iris. Show me how much you love cock."

It's Gabriel's hand still holding my hair in his fist as my face is shoved toward Quentin's crotch. I'm so fucking aroused, I can't think straight, so Quentin begins unbuttoning his pants before I have the chance to.

Suddenly his hard cock springs free of his boxers, and my eyes feast on the sight of him. I can't keep my hands away now, grasping him tightly around the base and marveling at how perfect his cock is—thick, long, and the flawless shade of tan and pink. There's a little moisture leaking from the tip as I stroke him, and my tongue goes out on instinct, quickly lapping up the precum.

He groans when I do, and Gabriel's fist tightens against my scalp. I welcome the pain. If Gabriel wants to pull me away from this cock now, he's going to have a fight on his hands.

After dragging my tongue along the underside of Quentin's shaft, I finally open my lips and welcome him inside, feeling the head hit the back of my throat before my lips even reach halfway down his length. My sex pulses with need when he responds with a long, satisfied groan. "Fuck yes, Iris. Take it."

Covering his cock with saliva, I work my mouth over him, deeper and deeper each time. Gabriel's hand never leaves my hair, and it's like he's guiding me, moving me like a puppet as I suck Quentin's dick.

"Hurry up, baby. I need to fuck you right now," Gabriel growls.

"Fuck her then, but I'm not done with her mouth yet. You were right, she is good."

I'm devouring Quentin's cock, trying to savor and memorize everything about it, noticing the way he tenses when I run my tongue under his head and how he groans every time I take him deep. And I learn quickly just how to make him come, but I'm not ready for that yet. I want to prolong this, so I stop twisting on the upstroke.

Then suddenly, I'm hoisted away from Quentin's cock, and I cry out in disappointment. I know Gabriel wants me for himself, and I'm not ready. But he's not taking me to the bedroom. Instead, he deposits me on the dining room table. He places me flat on my back and quickly tears off my sweats and panties.

"Get her shirt," he orders Quentin, who comes to where my head is and drags my shirt over my head, so I'm lying on the table completely naked.

Seriously, what is it with us and dining room tables?

Quentin is stroking his spit-covered dick and watching Gabriel, waiting for his cue for what to do next.

"You want to taste her pussy, cousin? You've never tasted a better cunt."

Gabriel leans down and swipes his tongue all the way up from my asshole to my clit, and I let out a high-pitched moan, squirming against the hardwood, desperate for more.

"Fuck yeah, I want a taste," Quentin replies, licking his lips as he watches Gabriel devour me.

Gabriel sucks on my clit for a moment, driving me crazy and taking me to the edge just before pulling away. Then, he wipes his mouth and moves away, letting Quentin take his place.

When Quentin's fingers touch me, my body lights up with the stored anticipation for this moment. How long have I truly wanted him? Longer than I thought, apparently.

He runs his fingers through my folds, admiring my pussy before spreading my lips and piercing me with his tongue. He moans low and loud against me, sucking hard on my clit, and nearly sends me flying off the table.

"Don't you fucking dare make her come," Gabriel

demands. He moves to my head and gazes down at me. My head is hanging off the edge so he cradles my neck as he leans down to kiss me. Just as his lips meet mine, Quentin dives two fingers inside me, and I cry out. His moans create the perfect vibration as he sucks hard on my clit and finger-fucks me to the point where I almost come.

"God, I want to fuck her," he says, pulling away from my body, but still playing with my pussy, watching his own fingers slide in and out of me.

"Not without her daddy's approval, but I'll let you come down her throat if you want."

"Fine, but I'm going to make her come then," Quentin replies, and without waiting for a response, he puts his mouth back on my clit and shoves three fingers inside me hard, pounding them in as he sucks hard.

"Oh fuck. Quentin, yes!" I yell, my trembling legs wrapping around his head as I ride out an orgasm so intense, I forget to breathe. Pleasure ripples through me, coming in waves, and the harder my legs clutch him, the harder he pounds his fingers inside me, so it feels like we're moving in unison.

I come down in a haze, disoriented with my eyes closed as I feel my body settle back to earth. Warm hands slide up my body, cupping my tits while someone's lips trail their way up my thighs. I have no clue where they are or who's who, but suddenly, there's a cock at my entrance, warm and hard, and then I feel another at my lips.

They slide in, in unison, and the room fills with their moans of pleasure. With my head hanging off the table and a cock down my throat, I can't see whose dick I'm sucking, but I know already by the feel of him and the way he's touching my cheek that it's Quentin.

And I recognize Gabriel's thrusts, the metal of his

piercing hitting my G-spot while he holds my legs, thrusting into me, sending me closer and closer to another climax.

"God, I'm going to come, Iris. Your mouth is fucking perfect," Quentin says, before pulling out and leaning down to kiss me. When he guides his dick back to my mouth, he thrusts all the way in, hitting the back of my throat easily at this angle.

"Come down her throat. I'm about to fill up her pussy now."

The sounds in this room are filthy as they fuck me from both ends, and just as Gabriel pounds harder and slower, a sign I know means he's coming, Quentin unloads in my mouth, salty jets of cum shooting down my throat.

"God, she is perfect, Gabe," Quentin says in between breathless pants. When his cock is spent, he pulls out and strokes my head. "I can see why you're willing to share. She likes it, don't you, Iris?"

I mumble a quiet, "Yes."

Gabriel's hands slide up my sides. I lift my head to look at him to make sure he's okay with this. His expression is soft, gazing at me lovingly. I hope he does see how much I do love it. I love being surrounded by these men, loved and treasured in a way I was never valued before. Before I found this family, I could never get attached to men because they were gone before I had a chance to know them.

Now, I am overwhelmed by their love and attention, and it's not just a matter of liking it—it's *who I am*.

Gabriel pulls me up to a sitting position and kisses me hard. I bury myself into his hug, letting him squeeze me so tight it almost hurts.

"I love you, baby," I whisper.

"I love you, Princess. I'm sorry for almost fucking everything up."

Behind us, I hear the sound of Quentin refastening his belt. "We should get some sleep. We have a busy day tomorrow."

My heart falls at his words. Tomorrow, we go home, but I can't seem to be as excited as I should be.

Thirty

Silas

"Basileus is leaving the compound at seven. He thinks he's meeting a client in Dallas, but once he arrives, he'll know it was a trap, and will head straight back. It only buys us four hours, tops."

"We got it," Carlisle replies.

"You sure your guys can get into the security system?" I ask, looking at the guys camped out in Carlisle's living room with eight computer screens.

"Whoever set up this security system is a real asshole," one of them mutters in frustration. They've been at it all day, and frankly, I'm running out of patience.

Ignoring them, Carlisle pulls out a map. "Okay, here is the compound." It's an aerial photo, showing a massive expanse of buildings sprawled over what must be fifty acres of land. "Based on the footage we've been able to procure before that damn firewall kicks us out, we believe your girl is being kept here."

He points to a single one-story building at the edge of the property. It's covered by an expanse of trees and a small dirt path that leads to the fence line on the southern border.

"Your boy has been spotted in the main building," he says, pointing to the large mansion in the center of the compound, like the beating heart of the property.

"Iris, first," I bark, quickly glancing around to make sure Baron didn't hear me. It's not that I'm only going in for her, but Gabriel has more defenses. We have to ensure her safety first, and while Baron would probably agree with me, I don't need my sons hearing that I would put my woman first.

"There's a loading gate at the back, only a few miles from her location. We take down the security system—alarms, electric fences, cameras, and we can buy you ten minutes tops. Someone will need to wait here," he says, pointing to the entrance. "We'll keep the team back here to avoid causing a scene."

"Baron can get in and out of there. He's a better shot than me."

"That's what I'm thinking too," he says before taking a drag of his cigarette.

"What about Gabriel?"

"That's going to take a little more work, but I think we get the girl out and reconvene after we have her in the car. She can give us some intel, too, that might help us get to him."

I let out a heavy sigh. Just the thought of having her back in my reach makes me breathe a little easier. I need to know what Iris has endured these past two weeks, and I hate to think about it. What if they've hurt her? Raped her? What condition is my little fighter going to be in when I see her tomorrow? I swear to God, I will make every single one of these assholes pay if they've laid a single finger on—

"I've got something!" one of the computer nerds yells, and I rush over to see what he's pulled up. It's a grainy black and white video.

There are two men, and I instantly recognize my son as one of them. They're facing each other with Iris between them.

"What is this?" I bark, leaning closer.

"I was able to hack into the security footage in the house they're keeping her at. I won't have long before it cuts out again. But it seems..."

He stops talking the second Iris drops to her knees between them. Chills skate down my spine as I watch the other guy, the one we've ID'd as Baxter's son, lean down and press his face close to hers.

She's...smiling.

The next thing I know, I'm watching him pull his cock out right in front of her and she eagerly wraps her lips around it with Gabriel watching from behind her.

"She seems to be doing just fine," the computer nerd chimes in, and I smack my fist against the table.

For fuck's sake, Iris. What the fuck have you gotten yourself into now?

I turn around before I can watch what they're about to do to her on the dining room table. "Just cut this shit off before my son walks back in, please," I bark in frustration. "And focus on getting that security system down for tomorrow."

As I'm storming out of the room, Baron meets me in the doorway.

"What's going on?" he asks.

"Nothing," I mutter. "But we saw Iris on the security

footage, and she looks safe. And with any luck, she'll be with Gabriel when we drop in to rescue her tomorrow."

"That's good news," he replies, glancing toward the computers, which have all gone dark.

"Yeah, great fucking news," I reply.

We all just need to get out of this place and go home. And once I get my hands on that girl, she's not going to like what I've got planned for her.

Thirty-One

Baron

What the fuck am I looking at right now? Iris is lying on a king-size bed between my brother and Basileus Junior. And she's...naked.

My Iris.

"What the fuck?" I bark, kicking the bed. Her eyes pop open, and she glances up at me quickly. It takes her a moment to register my presence before she screams.

"Baron!" She scrambles desperately, jumping into my arms and wrapping her beautiful legs around me. God, the feel of her body in my arms is so satisfying, I'm not even worried about the fact that she's naked and I have about a million questions to ask.

For now, we're in a hurry. It's a miracle we were even able to get in here when we did, but we only have ten minutes before the security system comes back up. Then, we're fucked.

She takes my face in her hands and kisses me hard, peppering my face.

"I missed you so fucking much," she cries, tears streaking down her cheeks. "Where's Silas?"

"Where are your clothes?" I reply, a little harsher than I mean to.

"My question first." When she pulls away to look at me, I brush her hair out of her face. She looks like a dream to me right now, even without makeup and her hair disheveled. I swear I never want to let her go again.

"He's not too happy with you," I say with a warning. I can forgive a lot, and I never want to lay a harsh hand on my girl. But when my dad is mad at her, that's between them, and I know he's not going to make this one easy on her. Not only did she lie to him, but she put herself in danger and made him worry.

"I figured, but I still want to see him. How did you get in here?"

"Talk later. Get the fuck out, now. He's waiting in the car, but we only have a few minutes before all hell breaks loose.

"Baron?" Gabriel mumbles, sitting up quickly when he notices I'm in the room. A second later, Gabriel's asshole cousin stumbles out of the bed, reaching for his gun. It's pointed at us before I can say a word. The hefty amount of research I've been doing on this family for the past week has given me names to all the faces I might see. Let's just hope they aren't all fucking my girl because I'll kill every one of them.

"Quentin, relax. It's Baron." Iris goes to step in front of the line of fire, but I grab her from behind.

"I know exactly who it is, Iris. I've been watching you

for months, remember? The question is, why the fuck is he in my bedroom?"

Shoving her back, I put myself between her and Quentin, aiming my own pistol at him.

"Why the fuck are you lying in bed with my naked girlfriend, asshole?"

"Both of you shut the fuck up," Gabriel snaps. "Where's Dad? We getting the fuck out of here?"

Gabriel climbs off the bed lazily, as if we aren't still pointing guns at each other.

"Wait! Tell me now," Quentin demands. "How the fuck did you get in here and why didn't my system pick up the intrusion?" He glances at his computers across the hall.

"Because we hacked your fucking system," I reply. "It wasn't easy, and it cost us a goddamn fortune."

"No, no, no, no," Quentin mutters to himself, lowering his gun and rushing past me.

"What's wrong?" Iris asks, following behind him. There's a panic in her tone that has me following behind her. Before we leave Quentin's room, I snatch her by the arm. "Put on some fucking clothes."

With a roll of her eyes, she grabs a pair of men's sweatpants off the floor and pulls them on, tying the drawstring tightly so they don't fall down. Then, she reaches into a dresser for a T-shirt, sliding it over her head before rushing to the computer room.

"What's wrong?" Iris says in a panic-induced state.

"Fuck, fuck, fuck!"

Iris walks to his side while Gabriel and I stand behind her. "Quentin! What?" she pleads for answers.

"I had a tripwire installed in the system in case anyone was able to hack through the security. Which means you were able to get through, but not without alerting the head of security of the breach."

"What the fuck does that mean?" Gabriel asks.

"It means you're fucked and hell is about to rain down on all of us."

"Silas," Iris gasps. "Where is your dad, Baron?" The terror in her eyes is apparent.

"He's fine. But we need to get out of here, *now.*"

Like, right fucking now!

Thirty-Two

Iris

I'm looking at Quentin when his face falls. "I can buy you some time, but you're going to have to go out through the back."

"Iris, now!" Baron barks, rushing toward the door, but I can't move. My feet are glued to the floor.

"Come with us," I beg, but I know it's useless. "Quentin, please."

He turns his chair toward me, pulling me between his knees. "I'm going to disarm the electric fence and I'll engage it once you're past the line, okay?"

"No," I reply, my voice breaking on a sob, "we can make it. Just come with us."

He doesn't respond, just grabs my face and pulls it down for a harsh kiss. But I don't want a kiss, because it feels like goodbye, and I know that once we leave, Basileus will be back, and he'll know Quentin helped us. I know exactly what will happen after that, and it makes me sick to think about it.

"Iris, *now!*" Baron snatches me by the waist and hauls me away. Quentin holds my gaze as I'm dragged toward the door.

We don't make it to the door, though. Windows crash around us and the room erupts in chaos as bullets fly in from outside. I scream as Baron throws me to the ground, covering my body with his.

"Stay down!" he shouts at me as he crawls toward the window.

I search frantically for Gabriel until I spot him, sitting near the door, peeking out before returning fire at whoever is shooting at us. Then, I find Quentin, scrambling for his own gun and aiming out the window, firing before ducking back down.

Fuck this. I don't fucking cower when things get hot. Crawling over to Baron, I seat myself next to him.

"Gimme a gun," I yell. He tosses me one from his holster, and I peer out the smashed window to see Hummer after Hummer parked around the perimeter of the house. Behind the open doors are probably at least twenty men, all armed and unloading hellfire on this house. We're fucked.

"We're never going to make it out of here," Baron calls, and my heart plummets. I just got him back. This can't happen now—all because I had to come after Gabriel on my own.

"Where's Silas?" Gabriel calls.

"Waiting at our rendezvous point. I've already called him on the radio, and he's bringing backup. I just hope it's enough."

"Tell him to meet you at the south entrance. There's a

service gate there. Use my truck. It's armored," Quentin calls from the other side of the room. He gets a little too close to the window to fire again, and I want to scream at him to take cover.

Then, I notice a growing red pool of blood near his feet. "Quentin!" I scream, crawling over to him. "You're hurt."

"I'm fine," he groans, but his left arm hangs tight at his side. Panic floods my senses as I inspect his body for any wounds. "It's just my arm. I'm fine. I promise."

Behind me, Baron shouts, and I know it's Silas on the other end of the line, connected to him through the earpiece in his ear. "It's a fucking ambush! I don't think Baxter made his flight to Dallas. I'm looking at him right now, standing by his Hummer."

Suddenly, the gunfire dies down, and a familiar voice calls over a loudspeaker out front.

"Hello in there," Baxter teases loudly. "Mijo, I know you've been keeping that little brunette as a pet in there. I hope you had your fun with her, but now playtime is over, and it's time to hand over your little toy."

"Fuck," I mutter, looking at Quentin. "I thought you said he was going out of town."

"Well, apparently he didn't take the bait," Baron says. "Dad was the one to set up that meeting."

"What? How?" I ask.

"We had Carlisle help us set it up."

"Oh fuck," Gabriel barks, "Carlisle?"

"Yeah, why?" his brother asks.

"Dammit!" Gabriel slams his head back against the wall. "The guy I interrogated for Baxter gave up the name Carlisle."

"Shit," we all mumble in unison.

"Well, that explains why our plan fell through."

I reach over and touch Gabriel's arm. He's wearing a

tense expression, clenched teeth and tight lips. I'm sure he must be beating himself up over this, but I mean, if we're about to die…we're all sort of to blame.

"Well, let's use him as a hostage," Baron barks, looking at Quentin, who immediately responds with an eye roll.

"He'd shoot me himself."

I catch the way Gabriel's expression changes as he looks at his cousin. Maybe it's pity or empathy, but he's definitely feeling something as Quentin utters that cold confession.

"Just take my truck," Quentin adds. "Straight over the hill and haul ass."

"I'm not leaving you," I say, cutting him off.

"Fuck no, *we're* not leaving you." Gabriel grabs Quentin by the collar and drags him toward the garage. I'm staring in shock as Baron takes me by the arm, pulling me along with them.

There's one Hummer parked in the garage, and Gabriel quickly shoves Quentin in the back. "What are you doing?" I ask Gabriel, a sense of panic setting in.

He doesn't respond as he shuts the doors, closing us in. Quentin winces in pain, sitting between us. I start looking around his arm, finding the wound near his shoulder. Blood is pulsing out, so I quickly apply pressure as Baron opens the garage door and starts the engine.

"Better hold on," he says as we speed out of the garage. Bullets fly against the window, but like Quentin promised, they don't penetrate the glass.

"Take that path," Q calls toward Baron, pointing at a dirt path through a few sparse trees. I notice the way Baron hesitates, glancing back at me. He doesn't know yet if he can trust this newcomer.

"Just go, Baron!" I yell. His jaw clenches, and he must realize he's out of options and he's better off trusting

Quentin than taking a risk driving back toward the army of cartel shooters at the front of the building.

As we fly over the rocky terrain, Quentin groans again, so I squeeze tighter.

"He's really hurt," I cry.

"He'll be fine," Gabe replies, and when I look into his eyes, he's giving me a reassuring expression. My heart clenches. There are too many emotions and not enough time to think. Fear, excitement, relief.

But I know reality is waiting around the corner. What are we going to do with Quentin after we reach the other side of this wall? Will El Basileus come after him? Silas and Baron may not consider him worth the risk and will easily eliminate him to avoid the trouble. To them, he is nothing but leverage against their enemy, and Silas could be easily tempted to exact revenge by taking his son the way Basileus took his.

And normally, I'd be on board, but now my heart is invested.

Not only do I have to break the news to them that Quentin means more to me now, but I also have to make them understand that he's not just a pawn anymore.

After all this is over, will I be able to truly let him go? Will *he* let *me* go?

"The fence is down, but I'm not going to be able to put it back up after we cross, so they're going to be hot on our ass all the way to the gate," Quentin grunts through the pain, as the Hummer bounces over rocks and ditches.

"Where's Silas?" I ask again.

"Waiting for us at the gate," Baron replies.

"Who hacked my system?" Quentin asks.

Baron rolls his eyes and glares at him. "Took a whole fucking team. They do not like you."

A sly smirk lifts at the corner of Quentin's mouth, but it's quickly replaced with a grimace.

"How much farther?" I ask.

"Just around this bend, you'll see the gate."

Bullets fly again, hitting the glass. A scream escapes my lips, and I quickly duck as if it would make any difference. Quentin grabs my hand, and I squeeze, burying my face against his chest. Baron glances back at us again, and a pang of guilt assaults my heart. What if I've fucked up? What if he can't forgive me?

As promised, we make the final turn and see the tall, steel gate in the distance. There's a wide opening, and I keep my eyes on it, praying we make it through before it closes. When I see the armada of black cars on the other side, I gasp.

Is Silas in one of those cars? My heart practically leaps out of my chest at the thought.

The mood in the car is tense as we race toward our freedom. How far will they chase us? They can't seriously follow us all the way, can they? El Basileus doesn't strike me as the kind of man to give up easily.

It seems to take forever before we finally cross through the steel barrier, and the second we do, I turn to look back, noticing the cars chasing us have stopped at the gate.

Could it be that easy? Did we really make it out?

"Don't get too excited," Quentin mutters as we speed down the dirt road toward town, "he won't give up that easily."

Thirty-Three

Iris

The black cars follow us all the way to a desolate location, where we pull up to the same private jet we flew here on. It's parked on a quiet runway, alone, and I couldn't be more excited to see it. I'm practically bouncing out of my seat to get to Silas. The second our car stops, I leap out of the car.

  The first black car stops in front of me, and I gaze into the driver's eyes. Those familiar brown eyes are glaring back at me. They certainly don't look as excited as I feel. In fact, he looks downright irate.

  My heart plummets.

  As Silas steps out of the car, his jaw clenches at the sight of me. Instead of greeting me, like I wish he would, he turns and talks to the man in the car behind him. Standing there, feeling frigid and alone, I watch as he shakes the man's hand, exchanges something, and turns to walk away.

  He's marching toward me, and it's not quite the warm

reunion I was hoping for. Instead, he glares down at me as he pauses.

"Are you hurt?"

"Silas," I whisper, pleading.

When Gabriel climbs out of the car, he shoots him the same icy glare. Then he notices Quentin, and I see his nostrils flare as Gabriel helps Q to stand. "What's this?"

"We couldn't leave him," I reply.

"Baron, take care of him."

"No!" I shout, and Silas's hot, angry glare lands on me. "You're *not* killing him, and I'm not leaving him here."

Silas steps up to me, toe-to-toe, and I keep my chin up, sending him the same fiery expression. "He's Gabriel's cousin, his *blood*. And he helped us escape. If he stays, I stay."

The air between us is tense as Silas examines me. God, I wish he would touch me. I missed his face, the warm comfort of his arms, and the safety I usually feel in his presence, but right now, he's staring at me like he hates me, and it's taking everything in me not to crumble.

"Everyone in the jet," he barks before walking away.

I share a quick remorseful glance with Gabriel, before helping Quentin toward the plane.

"I don't think your dad likes me," Quentin jokes, wincing as he walks.

"Stop it," I snap.

He's just trying to lighten the mood, but it's useless. I'm starting to feel the overbearing weight of my actions now. When I left to find Gabriel, I inadvertently put my relationship with Silas at risk. How can I be expected to make all of them happy, all the time?

Gabriel and I help Quentin into the plane, and Silas is already busy stewing and ignoring me by the time we reach the back seats. There's a lounge area at the rear of the plane that we lie Quentin in.

"I'm fine," he mutters.

"No, you're not, asshole. You're bleeding all over the fucking place," Gabriel mutters. Then he makes quick work, grabbing things from around the plane. They keep it well-supplied for emergencies like this one. I sit back and watch him as he opens the medical bag and cleans Quentin's wound.

"Bite on this," he says to Quentin, shoving a towel in his mouth. Quentin clamps his teeth around it as Gabriel pulls out the long, needle-nose tweezers. Quentin groans in pain, his cries muffled by the engine as we take off.

A moment later, Gabriel pulls the bullet out of his flesh and quickly discards it. Quentin looks like he might pass out, so I stroke his head, brushing the sweat-soaked hair off of his forehead. His warm honey eyes gaze up at me as he relaxes.

There were so many times when I was in my father's house that I watched his men clean and stitch their own wounds. They lived like they were invincible, reckless and wild, killing and dying for what? Money? Power?

My heart aches watching Quentin do his best to remain brave as Gabriel stitches his wound.

"Can't hurt as much as stitches in the ass," I say quietly, making him smile.

He could have died today. Any of them could have, and for what?

Me. They would have died for me, and that realization weighs heavy on my mind. I put myself in danger, therefore putting them in danger. I lied, betrayed the one person I swore to never betray.

My eyes travel up to find Silas watching me, and I catch

a vulnerable look in his eyes before it vanishes, replaced by indignation.

When we get home, I'll make him understand how sorry I am. I'll beg, plead, cry on my knees—do whatever he wants me to do, but he doesn't get to shut me out because I fucked up one time.

When Quentin falls asleep after his shoulder is cleaned, stitched, and bandaged, I find my way to the empty seat next to Baron. He's staring out the window in quiet contemplation. He's not quite as mad as Silas—I mean, he doesn't exactly have the right to be. He's caused this family just as much stress and anxiety as I have, so he has no place to judge. But he's not exactly rolling out the welcome mat for me either.

I loop my arm around his and rest my head on his shoulder. He squeezes me closer and presses his lips to my temple.

"I thought we were goners," I say.

"Yeah. Be sure to thank your new boyfriend for me." He's still resting his head on mine, but I feel the resentment in his tone.

"He's not—"

"I found you naked in his bed, Iris."

I lift my head and furrow my brow at him. "That's what you're upset about? We almost died, Baron."

"So, what are the rules when you have three boyfriends? I was never really clear on that. Can I have another girl-friend too, since you think it's fine to just fuck anyone you want."

Rage boils up in me. "I did *not* sleep with him," I whis-per. Silas is far enough away he can't hear us, but I still don't need him adding 'other man' drama to my already packed list of things Silas is mad at me about.

"Then let me go back there and put him out of his misery," he says so calmly, it sends a chill down my spine.

"No. Just because I'm not fucking him doesn't mean I'm okay with you killing him."

"Iris, I saw the way he looks at you. That guy is head over heels for you, and you just dragged him back to a house full of men who would rip off any man's arms just to have you."

I open up my mouth to reply, but nothing comes out. He's right, they would. But it doesn't make it *right*. "So you can share me with your brother and your dad, but anyone else is completely off-limits?"

"No, Iris," he argues back. We're getting so heated, I don't think we're keeping as quiet as we intended to be. "Just the enemy. Is it so much to ask that you don't fuck our enemies?"

I jump out of my seat and storm toward the back, but he's hot on my tail. I turn around and shove him in the chest. "Don't follow me!"

But he's too powerful as he shoves me into the lavatory and slams the door behind us.

"What are you doing?" I shriek, slapping him again. His strong hands snatch up my wrists and force me against the counter. The bathroom here is roomy for an airplane, but we're still pressed so close together, I can feel his breath on my cheek.

"Reminding you who you belong to," he says through clenched teeth. I'm still struggling to get my hands free, but he easily gathers up both of my wrists in one grip as he uses the other to tear my sweatpants down.

"Baron!" I yell, but he's relentless. And when his thick fingers run harshly through my folds, my yell turns soft into a moan of pleasure.

"That's right, scream my name, Iris. Remind them who this pussy wants." My next scream gets caught on my lips as he plunges a finger inside me. I'm already coating his hand as he pumps in and out of me.

As his mouth crashes against mine, I melt into the counter, my bound wrists relaxing and no longer struggling to be free. He nips at my bottom lip, growling into my mouth as he fingers me faster.

"Say it, Iris," he mumbles against my lips.

"Say what?" I reply between gasps for breath. My body is on fire, my hips thrusting to meet his fingers.

"Tell me who you belong to," he sneers against my mouth, and it's such a contradiction, his face so full of anger while his hands bring me so much pleasure. I'm chasing my climax, feeling it so close as his palm rubs harshly against my clit.

"I'm yours, Baron. I'll always be yours," I gasp.

Just before my orgasm sweeps me away, he tears his fingers out of me, and I cry out for them to return. While my mouth is open, he shoves his pussy-soaked fingers between my lips, almost making me gag. I close my mouth around them, sucking them with our eyes locked.

"Undo my belt," he commands harshly, dropping my wrists.

While his hand is still in my mouth, I quickly unfasten his button and pull down the zipper. Stepping out of my sweats, I climb onto the counter and draw him between my legs. He takes his cock out and drives it in hard, his hand still muffling the sound of my cries.

God, I missed this. The familiar feel of his cock as he fucks me. How my body knows each of them so well, reacting and melting for them so perfectly. How his hips are just a little narrower than Gabriel's and how Baron always thrusts hard and slow. How he likes to hold me closer as he fucks me, sometimes burying his face in my neck or tits as if he's trying to make our two bodies one.

Just as his thrusts pick up speed, he pulls his fingers out of my mouth and replaces them with his lips, kissing me so passionately it hurts. His tongue tangles with mine, and his fingers bruise my hips as he comes, his groans and grunts so sexy to me that I come right along with him, my hips still grinding against him to seek out that last bit of delicious friction.

We're left panting in our sex-laced silence. His body slumps against mine, and I never want him to pull out. Before he's fully caught his breath, he kisses me again. With one hand tightly around my throat, he explores my mouth, then my jaw and the spot below my ear.

"Don't ever fucking do that to me again," he growls, his deep voice quaking through me and sending goosebumps across every inch of my flesh.

"I won't," I promise in a small voice. And I don't know if he means let another man touch me or leave him, but I make this promise to him anyway because this is Baron, the man who commanded my heart when I swore I could only hate him. Our past is full of so much betrayal and animosity and every ounce of love we have for each other was forged in fire. There is nothing, *nothing*, I wouldn't promise him. If he asked me to dive off this plane with him, I would do it.

There are days I wish I could give each of my men one hundred percent of me, days I secretly regret making them share. I wish they understood that the only thing being divided is my time and attention. My heart beats for each of them the same. Even if they don't always see it that way.

When Baron and I slip out of the bathroom, Quentin

and Gabriel are awake, both of them avoiding me with their eyes. I quietly sink into my seat and let the day wash over me. We made it out, and I should be relieved, but I'm afraid I've only made things worse. This is far from over.

I have an injured Quentin to worry about and growing feelings that won't go away.

Silas still won't even look at me, and I'm a little nervous about what it's going to take to get him to forgive me.

And there's no way Basileus isn't coming after us. It's only a matter of time before this whole thing gets a whole lot worse.

Thirty-Four

Silas

I'm too fucking angry to be relieved. Or at least to show it. I am more than relieved. There aren't adequate words in the English language to portray how relieved I felt to see Iris, Baron, and Gabriel climb out of that car, not after the gunfire I heard coming from the grounds.

But after what these two have put me through, I'm not giving either of them the satisfaction of seeing my relief.

Gabriel and I can shout it out. He is more likely to understand the repercussions of his actions, and if he can't grasp the reality of what he's caused, then he'll face the consequences.

Iris is a little harder to express my frustration with. I find myself wanting to reprimand her, but she's my girl-friend, not my little girl. I want to yell at her, hurt her, hold her, and fuck her all at the same time.

My mix of emotions only has me feeling more frustrated.

When we reach the house, I try to let myself feel relief again, but it's not there. Instead, I have to face the fact that El Basileus will be busting down our door, and soon. We need a plan, especially with his kid, who is currently injured and under my roof.

I'm half-tempted to slice the little fucker's throat just out of spite, but I can't. And not because that would only piss Bax off even more, but because it would seem my *fucking girlfriend* has taken a liking to him. Which means hurting him would only drive her farther away.

These goddamn kids.

I don't stop when we pass the front door, heading straight for my office where the bourbon I was working on before we left is still sitting on my desk, waiting for me like a loyal girlfriend.

I close the door behind me, shutting out the shit I have to deal with. It can wait.

The warm amber liquid hits my tongue like gold, sliding down my throat and offering me a moment of quiet solitude.

Naturally, it doesn't last. A moment later, she comes bursting through my office door, stomping over to my desk with an adorable look of frustration on her face.

Fuck, she's cute when she's angry.

Instead of smiling at her or drawing her into my lap, so I can rub her against my aching cock like I want to, I keep my expression flat as I take another sip.

"Silas Black," she yells, "look at me."

My eyes slide upwards, landing on her face, but I don't show emotion. If I let even an ounce through, I'm afraid it will all come pouring out, breaking the dam and drowning us all. So I bite my cheek and keep quiet.

Tears well up in her eyes. "I'm sorry, okay!" Her hands

land hard against her sides, and it breaks my heart to see her look so sad. "I'm sorry I lied and I left and I almost got everyone killed, but I brought him back, didn't I? I know you're mad at me, but you need to get over it because I can't stand another second of this! This family is tearing me apart!"

Two lonely tears cascade over her cheeks as she cries, half-angry and half-desperately sad. Emotion builds painfully in my throat.

"Get over it?" I calmly reply.

"Please! Or just tell me you never want to see me again and put me out of my misery." More tears fall, but she doesn't move to wipe them away. She wears them like scars.

"Where will you go if I tell you I never want to see you again?" I'm being cruel. Harsh and unfeeling, and I don't know why I'm doing it. Because it's easier than breaking down and sobbing with her. Telling her how broken I was and how scared, the terror of losing her keeping me up almost every night we were gone. Maybe I want to scare her as badly as I was.

She lets out a small gasp and shakes her head. "I don't know."

"Why should I let you stay, Iris? You lied to me, betrayed my trust. Cost me millions to get you back."

"I did what I had to, Silas, and you know it. I told you I'm sorry. But Gabriel ran away too, and you won't kick him out of your life, will you?" She's trying so hard to argue. My tough little Iris, always resorting to anger before weakness. She's desperate to fall apart, but she refuses to let it happen.

Deep down, she must know I would rather die before turning her out.

"You're not one of my children, Iris. I can't exactly punish you."

Or can I?

The dark shadow that hangs over her expression seems to say she realized the same thing I just did. "Yes, you can." Her hands land hard against my desk as she peers at me. "Punish me, Silas. Do whatever you have to. Hurt me, yell at me, make me crawl on my knees and beg."

"I won't make it easy, Iris. I'm not playing around anymore."

"I can take it."

My cock twitches in my pants when she says that, filling up so fast it strains against the zipper. I can't let the image of her taking her punishment play too long in my mind or I'll lose it already.

"But then that's it," she adds, "I pay my punishment and you have to stop ignoring me."

"Okay."

Standing up, I brush past her and open my office door.

"Where are you going?" she asks.

"Stay here. I'll be right back."

After collecting what I need, I come back into my office and find her sitting in the overstuffed chair, nervously waiting for me.

"Pants down, baby girl. Bend over the desk." With one quick swing, I slap the paddle against my hand, and her eyes grow impossibly wide.

"What are you going to do with that?" she gasps.

"What do you think?"

"Why haven't I seen it before?"

"You never needed it before," I reply, before smacking my hand again. She turns a lighter shade of pale. "Pants. Off."

She swallows, lifts her chin and does as she's told. Fuck, I love her so much it hurts. No matter what she's faced with, Iris can take it. She walks into hellfire, without showing a shred of fear, even when I know she's scared. She can keep up with both of my boys in the field and goes out of her way to prove it. She is the best of both worlds, hard and soft. Tough and sexy. Sweet and terrifying.

With a brave face on, she shoves her sweatpants down, revealing that perfect round white ass I've missed so much. It won't be white for long, though. As she bends over the desk, I notice the healing wound on her right butt cheek.

"What's this?" I ask, touching it with the end of the paddle.

"I fell on a stick trying to escape."

I tsk with a devious smile. "That's too bad."

"What?" she replies, almost sounding hopeful, as if I won't give her what she deserves because she's already wounded.

"You'll be taking all your hits on one side. That's going to hurt twice as bad."

A small sound escapes her lips as she faces forward and grips the end of the desk in her hands. I love the way she looks right now, bent over my desk, waiting for her punishment, being such a brave girl. I'm going to enjoy every second of this, but I almost can't wait until the end when I can shove my fat cock in her and lick up her tears while I fuck her senseless.

"Ten for lying to me. Ten for running away. And ten for sucking that guy's dick last night."

She gasps again, peering back at me with an expression that begs for mercy, but I am all fucking out of mercy right now.

"Yeah, I know all about it, sweetheart. Had the privilege

of watching it on the security footage. Were you going to tell me about that?"

"Of course, I was," she cries.

"Hmm...too late now."

She responds with a scared sounding squeak.

Stroking her ass cheek with my hand, I admire how soft it is. Perfect and round and beautiful as I give it a gentle squeeze, watching the way her flesh shakes when I do. Leaning down, I kiss the surface, and she moans when I lick my way up to her spine. She should enjoy that now because she's not going to like me touching her there when I'm done with her.

While she's still wearing a peaceful look of pleasure on her face, I let the paddle fly, letting the sound echo through the room. She screams, shock and horror written all over her face.

"Silas!" she cries. "There's no way I can take that thirty times!"

"Guess you should have thought of that before," I reply, smacking it against her again. Her spine straightens, and she cries out. "That's two."

She's breathing heavily now, starting to panic. On the third smack, her screams turn to cries of anguish. I love to see the reaction in her body, the way it seizes up, the way her ribs look as she gasps for air. "Three, baby girl. Are you sure you can take it?"

The tears haven't started yet, but her face is bright red now, while she mentally prepares herself for the next one. "I can take it," she says, and my cock throbs in response.

I make the next three a little easier than the first three, but she's started crying anyway. Trying to hide her tears, she's white-knuckling the desk and yelling out so loud with each smack, I know it can be heard throughout the house.

The moment I reach ten, the office door bursts open and Gabriel and Baron stare wide-eyed at the scene before them. Iris's ass is blood red, and she's trembling, hunched over the desk and sobbing.

"Get out," I growl at them. They look at her before turning their attention back to me.

"Come on," Baron says, snatching a hesitant Gabriel by the collar and dragging him out of the room. I'm making this hurt for everyone. Her cries of pain are like torture for them, and they don't have the pleasure of being the one inflicting them. But I want everyone to suffer.

At least when this is done, I will pamper the fuck out of my girl. The boys are just going to have to fend for themselves for the rest of the night.

Between the first and second set, I stroke her red ass. The skin of her back is moist with sweat, but she's so tough. If she wants it to stop, we'll stop. She knows that, but I would bet my life that my girl will take her punishment without stopping.

I just hope she can do it without hating me when it's over.

"How are you doing, sweetheart? Ready to stop?"

"Keep going," she mutters against the wood of my desk.

By the end of the second set of ten, I'm more worried that I won't make it. Her pain is visceral, radiating into my body, so I feel it too. I'm starting to think I was too harsh, that my punishment wasn't fair and came from someplace more emotional than rational.

But with every swing of my paddle, I feel as if I'm beating down all of the pain I felt when I walked into this room. The fear of losing her and anger over the way she left me. It's driving the pain away while bringing me closer to her.

"That's enough," I say, trying to lift her off the desk. Her face is soaking wet, her hair matted against her skin, but she fights back.

"No! I can take the rest. Give it to me."

"No, Iris. That's enough."

She's hysterical as I gather her up in my arms. "Don't underestimate me, Silas!" she argues, pressing away from me. "That's what got us in this mess in the first place. You underestimated Gabriel, which is why he left. We can handle more than you think we can. You can't keep protecting us and trying to keep us safe from the world. We have to face the pain and get through the hard things on our own, so come on. Give me what I deserve."

Tearing herself away from me, she bends her trembling body over the desk and takes a deep breath. "Keep going."

My grip on the paddle falters, and I have to brace myself for the rest of these hits. I can't take it easy on her or she'll know. I know everything she said to be true, but I'm not ashamed of protecting my children. In this business, I already feel like a monster of a father for asking them to do what they do. Who could blame me for trying to keep them safe, even if it means denying them the independence they crave?

If anything, I make these last ten hits harder than the first twenty. She screams and thrashes and sobs with each one, and I bellow out the count as if I'm the one being hit too. My dick is throbbing in my pants, flinching with each hit. Her pain turns me on, and I don't feel bad for that. It means she's alive and wild and her body belongs to me. I doubt she'll sit down at all for the rest of the week.

There's a noisy scuffle going on, on the other side of the

closed office door, and I hear the distinct sound of that new guy yelling her name. Baron and Gabriel must be holding him back. I find his protective enthusiasm gratifying, but if he plans to stick around, he should probably learn I'm in charge. And at the end of the day, this girl is *mine*.

After the last smack of the paddle, I drop it quickly, and it hits the floor with a bounce. She doesn't move from her spot as I quickly unfasten my belt and pull out my aching cock. It's leaking already, weeping at the sight of her. She's arching her back and driving her hips backward because I know as bad as this hurt her, it turned her on as much as it turned me on.

As I thrust myself inside her, my shaft swallowed by her heat squeezing me so tight I could come already, she cries out again, but this time, it's sweet and salacious, like music to my ears.

"Fuck me, Silas." She hums. Still gripping the desk in her hands, she meets my thrusts, and we fill the room with the sounds of our bodies slapping together and the pleasure it brings us.

"God, I missed you." The words slip past my lips as I drive my cock home, feeling my release creeping closer. "You're mine tonight, Iris. I'm not done with you yet."

When she screams, her body locked in a spasm, I know she's coming, and I thrust two more times before yelling through my own orgasm. I haven't even touched myself since she left, and it shows. It's like my cock never stops.

Once we're both finally sated, she's in my arms, slumping against me as her muscles give out. I hold her up and kiss her with every ounce of emotion I was storing up over these past few weeks. It's heaven and hell, finally having her back but knowing how easily I lost her.

"You did so good, baby. I'm so proud of you," I whisper against her lips, trailing my mouth to her neck.

"I'm so sorry, Silas," she sobs.

"It's over now. It's okay."

Her weak arms latch around my neck, and I lift her off the floor.

"Take me to bed. Fuck me again."

"You're mine all night, sweetheart."

With her in my arms, I walk out of my office, barely noticing the boys waiting in the living room. Ignoring them, I take her to our bedroom and close the door. Right now, she and I are the only two people who exist in the world.

Thirty-Five

Iris

"Ugh," I whimper with each step to my bed. Silas really did a number on me. Not only the ache between my legs from the pounding I took, but the blows to my ass from his paddle. Thirty, to be exact. I've never been handled that way before and it was oddly satisfying. The pain mixed with pleasure was the perfect combination for a mind-blowing orgasm.

Baron comes up behind me, sweeping an arm around my waist. "Easy, babe."

"'I'm okay," I lie. The truth is, my insides feel as battered and bruised as my ass does. After my little ménage à trois with Quentin and Gabriel, my fuck sesh with Silas, and the bathroom on the plane with Baron, I'm pretty sure I need a pair of solid ice panties. Are those a thing? If not, they should be.

I'm officially delirious.

"You need sleep," Baron says, steering me to the bed.

I nod in response. "I most definitely do." Peering up, I look him in the eye. "Stay with me?"

A smile parts his lips. "You don't even have to ask."

My heart flutters with warmth and fullness as I drop my robe and slide into bed, wearing only a silk nightgown and nothing underneath.

Baron lifts the corner of the blanket and joins me. Stretching his arm, he turns off the light on my nightstand then curls his body against mine.

It feels so good to be back in my own bed.

It feels even better to be held in the safety of Baron's arms. Melding together, as if we're one body with two beating hearts.

When his warm breath hits the lobe of my ear, tickling its way down to my neck, I giggle and roll onto my side to face him. Finally saying the words weighing heavy on my mind. "Thank you for not being mad at me."

Baron bites his bottom lip, angling his eyes at the wall behind me. "I'm not mad *at* you. But I can't say I'm happy with the shit that went down."

I expected that. It'd be crazy for me to think he and Silas wouldn't be at least a little upset that I brought another guy home. Even though Quentin didn't come here for me. Gabriel and I brought him back to keep him safe. If we had left him with his psychotic father, I hate to think what he would have done to him. I won't pretend I'm not glad he's here, though. Quentin and I have an undeniable connection, and while it's apparent and it's real, it still doesn't alter my feelings for my guys. In some weird way, it makes me love and appreciate them all even more.

"There's something I have to tell you and you might be mad at me after you hear what I did."

Baron swallows hard and rolls to his back. His head

drops back, and his eyes close. "Let's hear it. What did you do?"

I draw in a deep and audible breath before spitting it all out on one exhale. "I may have fooled around with him a little bit in Gabriel's presence."

Fuck. That sounded so much worse than it did in my head. *In Gabriel's presence?* I should've left that out. Now he's going to be furious with Gabriel, too.

The veins in Baron's arms protrude as he clenches his fists at his sides. Bulging, blue and ready to rip through the skin. His chest heaves, so I place a calming hand over his heart. "I'm sorry, babe. We had been drinking and it was a heat of the moment sort of thing."

"Can't say I'm surprised," he finally says.

I watch as my hand rises and falls on his chest with each breath he takes. "I understand if you're mad."

Tension thickens, and I hate that I put this barrier between us on my first night home with him. Waiting until tomorrow would have been a much better idea, but the guilt was eating away at me.

Just as I open my mouth to speak, Baron lays his hand over mine. I prop myself up on my elbow to look at his face when he squeezes gently.

Peering over at me with open eyes, there's not an ounce of anger behind his blinking lashes. "As long as you're mine when we're together and you're safe about things, I don't care. I don't wanna hear about it. But I don't give a shit."

His hand slides down my arm to my stomach and shifts back onto his side. He parts my legs with his hand and slides a finger up my slit. "When you're with me, this is mine."

"Always." I lean over to kiss his lips, but he pulls back. My eyes widen in surprise.

"Say it. Tell me it's mine."

One finger slides inside me, compelling me to lift my leg. My hips roll into his hand, wanting more.

His hand pulls back, and I ache for his touch. My insides burn with desire.

"Say it, Iris. Tell me this is mine."

When his fingers find me again, I moan into the space between us. "It's yours."

"That's right it is, and I take care of what's mine. Now lie on your back so I can make my girl feel good."

I do as I'm told and fall onto my back, legs spread beneath the blanket. My nightgown bunches around my waist, and when Baron jerks the blanket off me, a brush of cold air rides up my parted legs.

With eyes locked on mine, Baron presses his hands on either side of me, then slides down until his face is between my legs.

"God, I've missed this." He hums before blowing a warm breath at my pussy. Chills skate up my entire body when he does it again.

I want to scream at him to touch me. Make me feel good like he just said he would. Instead, he's teasing me and loving every second of it.

My back arches off the bed, pussy in his face, hoping to grab his attention.

I'm in agony. Desperate for him to kiss my cunt. I push myself up on my elbows to look at him. "Please, Baron," I whimper through a bated breath.

Biting the corner of his bottom lip, he offers nothing but a sinister smirk before patting at my sex. "Did Quentin touch you here?"

My heart gallops in my chest, knowing that he's going to make me work for my pleasure.

"Yes," I spit the truth. "He touched me."

Baron grumbles before biting at my clit. My body jolts, though it doesn't hurt the way it should. Instead, it's a pleasurable pain that has my nails embedding into the skin of his shoulders.

He stops, but I want more. I *need* more. "Did you like it?"

"Yes," I say again, knowing I can't lie to him. I did like it and part of me wants him to touch me again. Not now, though. Right now, all I want is Baron. "Now, fuck me," I plead as my body cries out for him in anguish.

"Patience, baby. Let me play."

My hips flex upward, and I grab a fistful of his hair then slam his face into me. "Playtime's over. I've missed you too much for games. Now do what you promised and make me feel good, so I can return the favor."

A low rumble climbs up his throat, but he does as he's told and begins feasting on me. Sweeping his tongue between my folds, licking me like I'm his favorite dessert. Every once in a while, he stops and nibbles at my clit. Warmth rushes through my entire body when he slides two fingers inside of me. Digging and curling, pumping and prodding as he goes knuckle deep.

"Fuck, yes," I cry out, still fisting his hair while I ride his face.

My pussy throbs, walls clenched tightly around his digits as my body fills up with an insatiable urge for release. I take a deep breath and come undone.

"That's right, baby. Come for me. No one can get you off like I can."

He's right. No one can. Each guy gives me something different, but it's always satisfying.

My body relaxes, but not for long. Baron rips off his boxers, leans forward and removes my nightgown. When he slithers up my body, his cock slides inside me without resistance. It's like it knows where home is.

I gasp when Baron lunges so hard that my head ricochets off the headboard. He shows no mercy as he begins pounding into me at lightning speed.

Warm fingers trail up my breast, pinching and rolling his fingers around the bud of my nipple.

My hands find the back of his head, and I pull him in for a hard-pressed kiss. There is nothing gentle about this. But nothing about us has ever been gentle.

Our tongues tangle in a web of desire, teeth clanking, hearts racing.

Sweat drips from Baron's forehead, falling between us as his body slides against mine. I open my eyes and see him staring back at me. With our mouths still connected, he mutters, "Fuck, baby. I love you so damn much."

His admission sends me over the edge. I kiss him harder, using his mouth as a muzzle as I cry out. My nails drag up and down his back. "Oh, God," I moan into his mouth.

Baron plunges deeper, the head of cock swelling inside of me. He thrusts once more before taking a deep breath and dropping down on top of me.

With his head resting on my chest, I stroke his hair. "I love you, too."

We lie there for what feels like hours, silent and breathless, until we fall asleep naked.

When I peel my eyes open, it's still dark outside and the space in the bed next to me is empty. My ass hurts like hell, and the space between my thighs aches from all of these *reunions*, but I expected that. I knew they wouldn't take it

244 RACHEL LEIGH & SARA CATE

easy on me. I'm just glad they've all basically forgiven me, and everything feels as close to normal as it's going to be after everything that's happened.

Then my thoughts land on Quentin, and my anxiety is back. I know he has to go back, deal with Basileus, but every time I think about that, I want to be sick. There's nothing I can do about it, so I might as well get over it. I've dealt with worse, right? Lost my mother, my father, took down a major mafia kingpin who wanted to chain me to his bed for all of eternity. I mean...I can handle one measly goodbye. We've known each other for, what...two weeks? *God, get over it, Iris.*

I jump out of bed, grab my robe, and head toward the bathroom across the hall. The door is closed and the shower is running. When I peer down the hall toward the stairs, I hear Gabriel and Baron talking...which means there's only one person who could be occupying this shower right now.

Without a word, I quietly open the bathroom door and sneak in. The room is filled with steam, but I can still see his naked form through the frosted glass of the shower. He quickly snaps his head in my direction.

"What the fuck are you doing?" he whisper-shouts, covering his dick and glancing behind me like one of my murderous boyfriends is about to walk in and slice his throat for taking a shower in my presence.

"Relax. I've already seen you naked, remember?" I say, locking the door behind me.

"And I'm not dead yet, so that's a good sign."

I laugh. Walking toward him, I lean against the tile wall and watch him, keeping my eyes on his face as he leans back and tries to shampoo his hair with one hand. He's holding the other out of the stream to keep his bandages dry, but he's doing a terrible job.

Through a giggle, I say, "Let me help you."

Taking my robe off, I hang it on the hook and step into the giant tile and glass shower.

He lets out a groan, squeezing his eyes closed. "I'm a dead man." Then, he carefully peels one eye open and glances down at my naked body. "Totally worth it."

I laugh again. "Turn around, dummy." I fill my hands with shampoo and reach up, soaping up his hair and scrubbing through the dark locks. My eyes trail the bubbles as they slide down his tan neck and over his muscled shoulders. He hums as my nails scratch his scalp.

Then, I turn him again. He tilts his head back as I rinse the shampoo out. My body is pressed against his, and he really does look like he's in agony. But I savor the feeling of his hard pecs against my breasts.

Squirting body wash into my palm, I work up a lather with the soap and start at his shoulders, scrubbing in circular motions down his chest and over the curve of his ass. He doesn't take his eyes off of me as I work, but I can't look into his eyes.

Is this crossing a line? For sure. But this is all I'm going to get of Quentin, and we're not going to have sex, so I'm going to take what I can get. I know he'll be gone before the day is over, and it's bad enough I have to say goodbye, probably forever.

Naturally, his cock is hard, and I put some space between us, so it doesn't touch me, because as much as I want to, I can't let him think anything like that can happen between us. Not here and not now. Plus, I know if we did do it, it would make losing him that much harder.

Fuck, I'm so goddamn tired of losing people.

I'm so focused on what I'm doing, that I don't notice the hot tears building in my eyes. And once Quentin is clean and rinsed, he turns and shuts the water off, so we're standing together naked and wet, and I still refuse to look him in the eyes.

Suddenly paralyzed, I don't move, and he has to reach around me to grab two towels folded on the rack. He wraps one around me and then the other around himself. Once our bodies are covered, his arms pull me in, pressing my face against his chest. I feel his lips against my temple, and all I can think is that there must be some way to evade Basileus. Things are so good at this moment that it seems tempting to pretend there is no trouble waiting just outside our doors.

Before we get out of the shower, he mumbles against my forehead, "For what it's worth, having you at my place was probably the best two weeks of my life, and if I have to leave, I'm glad just knowing you're in good hands, and you're safe."

I nod, letting my tears fall.

Thirty-Six

Baron

When I woke up this morning, I was hoping the last couple weeks were just a bad dream. But, sure as shit, the leech we brought home is standing in the kitchen, clenching my fucking coffee mug in his hands.

"Good morning." He peers over the rim, blowing air into the steaming liquid.

"That's my mug."

He holds it up, inspecting it. "Didn't see your name on it." He takes another sip, smirking behind his slurp.

"I didn't feel it was necessary to write my name with a sharpie on *my* mug, in *my* house." I snatch it out of his hands and walk over to the sink to dump it out. My outburst is reciprocated with a low grumble.

Once I've got the water hot, I squirt half a bottle of dish soap in the cup and begin washing it. I don't know where his lips have been.

Wait. I do.

They've been kissing my girl.

My blood begins boiling again at the thought. I held my composure last night with Iris. I'm not mad at her. It's this asshole I'm furious with.

Scrubbing away at the cup, I push Quentin for answers. "How's it make you feel knowing you took advantage of Iris in a vulnerable state?"

Quentin grabs another mug from the cupboard and pours himself another cup of coffee. "I'd hardly call it that. What we have—"

"Nothing!" I shout, slamming my mug down on the counter. "You have nothing. She is not yours. She will never be yours."

After taking a sip of his coffee, he sets the cup on the counter, fingers still locked around the handle. "Look, man. I have no intention of taking your girl, but it doesn't change the fact that we connected in the time she was with me. There is most definitely something there."

The seriousness alone in his voice is enough for me to contemplate the many ways I could kill him.

Strangulation with my bare hands?

A knife straight to the celiac artery?

"Did you hear me, Baron?" he asks, snapping me out of my thoughts.

"Yeah. I heard you, and I call bullshit. The only reason you two *may have* connected is because you fucking kidnapped her and took advantage of her when she was in a fragile state."

His head shakes, tongue clicking on the roof of his mouth. "Nope. Not how it went down."

"All right then," I lean over the counter, fists clenched, knuckles grating against the granite surface, "tell me how it went down."

Quentin pulls out a barstool, making himself comfortable. "My security camera picked up a car parked outside the gate. I immediately drove halfway down, then finished the other half on foot, because I had no idea what to expect. When I saw her, I knew immediately who she was. My research was extensive. The beautiful, yet feisty, Iris Black."

The way his eyes light up when he says her name has my skin itching.

"She's lucky it was me that found her. Had it been my father, there's a good chance she would have ended up in the basement with the girls you freed."

"How the hell did you know about that?" I did free the girls down there. They were victims and were probably hours away from being sold to the highest bidder.

Quentin's shoulders rise with a grin on his face. "I'm a tech nerd. Cameras, computers, it's my thing. When your men disarmed the security system, the backup immediately kicked on. I watched the entire thing unfold."

Motherfucker. We thought we were one step ahead and it turns out we were two steps behind.

"Anyways, I snatched her up and had to knock her ass out because she wouldn't stop asking so many damn questions. She's a tough little shit. Nailed me square in the jaw."

That's my girl.

"Once I knew she was out, I got her the hell out of there. It wasn't easy keeping her stay a secret, but I managed, for a little bit."

I can appreciate him trying to keep Iris safe, but so much still doesn't make sense.

"And why the hell didn't you just give her to Gabriel. After all, he's her boyfriend."

Quentin takes a sip of his coffee, sets it back down and levels his eyes with mine. "It was too much of a risk. Gabriel was conflicted. Wasn't sure if he wanted to stay or go. Not to mention, he could have gotten them both killed if he tried to escape with her."

He's got a point. Regardless, I'm not going to just roll over and let him slither his way into my family just because his is fucked up. I am grateful that he kept Iris safe, though. She's home now and that's all that matters.

"It is what it is." My hand sweeps through the air before I grab my cup and fill it with coffee. "Just figure out your plan so you can get the hell out of our house." I take a sip, smirking over the rim of my mug. "After all, you are still the enemy."

Quentin snorts, completely downplaying my accusation of him being the enemy. He is, though. Is he not? The guy held Iris prisoner for weeks and somehow managed to worm his way into her pants.

Hell yes, he's the enemy.

With my cup in hand, I leave the kitchen before my thoughts get the best of me and I begin lashing out again. It's not that I care what this bastard thinks—I just prefer not to stick Iris in the middle of it and that's exactly where she'll end up.

Passing by my dad's office, I notice his door is cracked open, which is odd for him. For such a private man, he sure is making it easy for Quentin to invade the spaces of the house. "Baron," Silas barks out in a stern manner, "get your ass in here."

I backstep to his door, feeling the vein in my neck throb with annoyance. With my coffee in one hand, I push the door open with the other, not bothering to enter fully until it's deemed necessary. All I want to do is go back up to bed and curl my body around Iris until she wakes up.

Sitting like the king of his throne, Silas bites down on a

cigar hanging between his lips. He rarely smokes the things, but when he's stressed or overworked, he tempts himself. Pinching the brown roll of tobacco, he pulls it out of his mouth. "What are your thoughts on the Morales kid?"

"Quentin?" I say his name in question, though I know damn well who he's talking about.

"No. His fucking cousin," Silas spews sarcasm. "Yes, Quentin."

He makes no attempt to hide his frustration and it's looking like a tense day for all the members of this household. I make a mental note to distract Iris today, so she's able to avoid him. She's so emotional as it is lately, and I don't need him making her feel like shit for what happened.

"Well," I begin, deciding to step into the room, "he seems harmless. A little nerdy. Probably can't bench more than—"

"Would you quit fucking around? I'm serious! I heard you two shouting at each other out there. Do you think he's working against us? Here for intel?"

I step farther into the room, finally determining this won't be an in-and-out conversation. As I approach the empty chair in front of the desk, Silas snaps, "Shut the damn door."

With a huff, I do as I'm told. "I'm going to need you to calm down a bit if we're going to have a civil conversation." For fuck's sake, you'd think the damn stranger out there just ate his girlfriend's pussy or something.

Oh, wait. He did.

"You're right." He draws in a deep breath, exhaling slowly. "It's not like me to get worked up like this. I've been on edge lately, and it's showing."

"Uh, yeah, it is. Look. I know it seems like we're fucked.

That kid's father probably has an army ready to bust down every door in this house. But we're not amateurs. We've handled shit like this in the past. All we need is a plan."

Silas taps his fingers repeatedly against his oak desk, staring straight past me as he speaks. "What we need is to negotiate. I'm flying out in an hour to meet El Basileus with a surprise visit, and I'm bringing his kid with me."

"Whoa. Wait a damn minute. You're not doing this alone."

"Like hell I'm not. This is my family. It's my duty to keep you all safe. I'm going, and I'm going alone."

The door behind me flies open, causing me to whip around. "No, you're not," Gabriel says with a seriousness in his expression. "It's me he wants. I'll go."

I look at Silas, who is already shaking his head in disapproval. "You'll both stay here where it's safe, with Iris. I will handle this."

"No," Gabriel says again, slamming the door shut behind him. "Baron," he looks at me, "do you remember when you wanted to leave and go work for Maretti, because he promised you you'd be in control of your own fate? He was willing to give you the freedom of choice. I was so angry with you. But I get it now." He walks closer, solemn in his steps. "My uncle promised me the same thing. For a sliver of a second, I was ready to take his offer and leave you all behind. Then I realized, I couldn't do that. *This* is my family. You two and Iris are my family. We stick together. I made a promise to myself when I made the choice to come home; I won't settle for anything less than the utmost respect. Baron and I are adults. We shouldn't have to consider leaving just to live our lives the way we see fit."

Silas holds up a hand, halting Gabriel, but he doesn't stop.

"I'm not finished. It is not your responsibility to keep us safe. It is the responsibility of all of us to work together —to keep *each other* safe. And it's about time you trust me to handle shit on my own. That's why Quentin and I are going back, and we're settling the score. You and Baron can stay here and protect Iris."

Gabriel looks at me, waiting for acknowledgement that I understand. For the first time in a while, I completely agree with him. It's time we stop living in Silas's shadow. He won't be here forever, and we need to make our choices and learn to stand on our own two feet.

Then, I look at my father sitting across the desk from me, and I see the conflict on his face. The fear etched into his features, maybe from losing David or from almost losing me, then Gabriel. And I know it takes everything in him to finally nod at my brother.

"Fine," Silas finally says, teeth clenched and brow furrowed. Gabriel and I both snap our attention to him.

"Fine?" Gabriel questions his response.

Silas nods. "You're right. It's time I let you two live to your fullest potential. You're smart men—strong-willed men. I'm very proud of you both." His chair slides back, and he stands. His expression drops, and he presses his palms to the desk, leaning in. "I believe in you, Gabriel. Unfortunately, the only way you'll ever be free is by ending him."

My jaw drops, but not nearly as far as Gabriel's.

"You want me to kill my uncle? My own blood?"

Silas steels his spine, shoulders drawn back. It's apparent he's dead serious. "Is that a problem? You chose your side. Now prove it."

"I, I umm...I'm gonna have to think about this. I think

we can find another way. Besides, it's Quentin's father. Regardless of how much he hates his dad, it's still his dad."

Silas does have a point, though. The only way Gabriel will be free from that family is to end the leader. However, that would make him the next El Basileus. Is that really a position Gabriel wants? He's only twenty-years-old and that's a lot of power for a man of that age.

"Think about it. Let me know what you've decided by this afternoon. Otherwise, I'll end him myself."

Gabriel steps back slowly before turning around and opening the door with a shaky hand. It's obvious this decision won't be easy for him.

I look at Silas, trying to get a read on him. "You're just planning to let him go alone and take on that guy?"

"Hell no," Silas sputters, "pack a bag. We're going out of town."

"But you just told us you believed in us. That we were strong and all that shit. Was it all for show?"

"No. I meant every word I said. It doesn't change the fact that everyone needs backup. Gabriel is just too hot-headed to accept it. Gabriel will kill his uncle. As soon as he finds out that he murdered his parents, the present El Basileus is as good as dead."

Fuck. This is not good. "You're planning to tell him? That's a pretty harsh way of getting him to end the guy, isn't it?"

"Gabriel deserves to know the truth. However," he strokes his cheek, "it might be best to have Iris break the news to him. She has a way of calming him down when he gets...the way he gets."

"Lemme guess, you want me to be the one to break this to her?"

"Unless you prefer I do it."

"No," I spit out on an exhale, "I've got this. You just make the call for a jet. We can't let Gabriel and Quentin get too far ahead of us."

Now we just need to hope Gabriel doesn't find out we're going. There's no saying how he'll react if he thinks Silas is still fathering us during work hours.

Thirty-Seven

Iris

"Babe, wake up."

It's Baron's voice. He sounds anxious, but it's too early for that.

His hands rock my body back and forth, and I crack a smile. "Good morning to you, too."

"I need you to get up. We have to talk."

Four words no one likes to hear. *We need to talk*. In this family, it can mean many things. Someone's about to die, someone needs to die, someone is taking a trip—or something as little as I'm horny or I'm hungry for your famous Belgian waffles.

"Babe," he says again. I take a deep breath, still smiling, and roll onto my back. Baron is sitting beside me with an anxious look on his face.

This must be serious.

My entire body shoots up to a sitting position, bringing

the sheet with me since I slept completely naked last night. "What is it?"

"I had a talk with Silas and Gabriel. Gabriel and his cousin are going back this afternoon."

"What?" I huff out a breath, "like hell they are!" When I begin ripping the sheet off me, Baron grabs my arm, stopping me.

"It's done. Well," his head wavers, "assuming Gabriel is keen on turning his back on his blood family."

"Oh my God." I continue to free myself of the linen covering my body and get to my feet, ass and tits hanging out. "What does he plan to do? He can't stop that guy unless he kills him."

"On second thought," Baron says, biting his bottom lip with a seductive grin. "Let 'em all die." He grabs me by the waist and pulls me down on top of him as his back sinks into the mattress.

"Baron, this is serious. Gabriel and Quentin can't take on El Basileus alone. We need to help them."

"Mmm," he hums, nuzzling his face between my breasts. "That's the plan." His mouth finds my puckered nipple and my back arches on impulse. Head dropping back, I follow the path of pleasure he's taking me on.

No! We can't. Not now.

I pull his head back, hands cupping his face. "How do we help them?"

Baron exhales a pent-up breath, hopefully understanding that we need to stay focused. "We're taking a private jet and trailing quietly behind. Gabriel can't know, though. He'll be pissed if he thinks we're all babysitting him."

He's right. Gabriel would be more than pissed, and

Baron won't admit it, but he'd feel the exact same way if the roles were reversed.

The more thought I put into this, the more nervous I become. It's a last-minute plan thrown together and it's careless. Silas, of all people, knows how dangerous a spontaneous plan is. I can't believe he's agreed to this. "And when he gets there, he'll just let him down gently and tell him he's not staying? His uncle will never go for that. This is a terrible idea."

Baron breaks eye contact and I can feel his body tense up. "I don't think there will be much talking."

"Baron," I enunciate slowly, "what is Gabriel planning to do?"

When he doesn't respond, I've pretty much answered my own question in my head. "He's planning to kill him, isn't he?"

He finally looks at me and nods. "If he can do it. It's a lot to ask of him, considering it is his uncle. But I don't think it'll be a problem once he knows his uncle killed his parents, just so he could take the role as El Basileus." Warm fingers pinch at the bud of my nipple, sending a wave of heat through my body. When Baron's eyes bore into mine, I want nothing more than to devour his mouth before milking his cock.

Stop being a whore, Iris. There's no time for that.

Snapping out of my trance, I pull his face back up again. "You're too much of a distraction." I giggle through my smile.

Only we could sit here like this, getting turned on while plotting a murder.

Scooping me in his arms, Baron flips me over so that he's lying over me like a warm blanket. His fingers ride up my ass and clench at the skin as he growls, "I can't help it.

You walk around here looking sexy as hell and I lose all train of thought."

My head tilts instinctively when his mouth sucks at the delicate skin of my neck. "This is important."

"Ugh," Baron growls, lifting his head to look at me, "you're right. As much as I'd love to make a home between these thighs, you're right."

Trailing my fingers featherlike down his shoulder blades, I probe for information. "Have you all considered how Quentin is going to feel about this? It's his dad. And what makes you think Gabriel will even go through with it?"

"Well," Baron drawls, "Quentin probably won't know until it happens. As far as Gabriel going through with it, that's where you come in."

My head drops back on the pillow, eyes rolling. "What do I have to do?"

"Gabriel needs to know the truth about his parents. It's the only way he'll ever be fully free from his uncle. It's the only way we can ensure that he'll go through with it. There's no way in hell he'll let that man live once he knows what he did."

There's a pang in my chest at the thought of breaking Gabriel's heart. While he does deserve to know the truth, it's going to hurt him. He might not have a relationship with his uncle and he made the choice to come home, but it doesn't change the fact that he considered staying because part of him probably did want to get to know his biological family.

I blow out a breath. "So I have to be the bearer of bad news?"

"He'll react differently if it comes from you. You can comfort him in a way that Silas and I can't."

He's got that right.

"Fine. I'll do it. Only because I hate that he's in the dark about this. I'm not going to pressure him into killing a member of his family, though. That decision will be his and his alone."

One way or another, this will all be over soon and we can go back to our normal lives. I just hate that Quentin might not be a part of it.

If only I could find a way to get him to stay.

My knuckles knock against the wood door, nervous energy pooling in my stomach. "Gabriel, it's me," I announce before turning the handle and cracking the door open.

He spins around in his chair at his desk. His wide eyes soften when they land on me. "Hey, baby. How'd you sleep?"

I tug the straps of my robe tighter as I walk in, closing the door gently behind me. "A little sore, but I'm okay."

He sucks his teeth, glancing down at my ass. He lifts the robe to inspect my bruised ass cheek. "God damn..." he mumbles.

"I'm fine," I reply, pulling my robe down. "Do you have a minute to talk?"

"I've always got a minute for you." He pulls me between his legs, a smirk parting his lips.

I force a smile. Knowing what I'm about to tell him, it's hard to feel as happy as he looks.

Gabriel pulls me down on his lap, resting his chin on my shoulder. "What's wrong?"

I swallow hard before beginning. "There's something I

have to tell you. Something I should have told you when you found me at Quentin's place."

His head lifts and his arms tense around my waist. "What did he do to you? I swear to God if he—"

"No. It's nothing like that, babe. I promise." When he relaxes, I go on, "It's about your parents. Your real parents."

"What about them?"

"After you left, Silas met with a man to try and get some information on your uncle. It was the man he thought hired him to kill your mom and dad. It turns out, he wasn't the one who hired him."

"So what? Doesn't matter. I know my parents were stealing from the old cartel leader."

I turn on his lap, legs dangling off the side. My arms drape around his neck and I look him in the eye, my sadness likely showing. "The man who put the hit on them did it for his own selfish reasons. Yes, your father was planning to kill El Basileus and take his spot. Your uncle found out and..." I take another deep breath, my heart thundering in my chest. "He had them killed because he wanted the title of El Basileus for himself."

"No," he chuckles. "No. That's not possible. He'd never do that. My dad was his brother. They were close."

"It's true, babe. Quentin confirmed it."

Gabriel goes to stand, letting me slide off his lap, but I catch myself with my own two feet. He turns away, raking his fingers through his hair. "It doesn't make any sense. He killed my parents for power?"

As suspected, my heart hurts for Gabriel. This poor guy has been through so much betrayal. He's had to make choices that no one should have to make, especially at such a young age.

I walk up behind him, placing a hand on his shoulder and turning him to face me. "I'm here for you."

"I'm fine," he deadpans with dark orbs of fury.

He's most certainly *not* fine.

"What are you going to do?"

Looking straight past me as he talks, his fists clench at his sides. "I'm going to do what I should've done while I was at that house. I'm gonna fucking kill him. An eye for an eye. A tooth for a tooth."

My heart drops into my stomach. This is exactly what Baron predicted, and I feel like I manipulated the entire situation. The thing is, it doesn't matter when or how Gabriel found out, once he did, he'd kill his uncle one way or another.

"You know what this means, don't you? If you kill him—"

"I'll take his place. A position that should have been my father's before he stole it from him. Yeah. I know what it means. I won't accept it, though. There's not a chance in hell I'd ever walk in that man's footsteps."

Thirty-Eight

GABRIEL

With my duffel bag thrown over my shoulder, I go into the kitchen where Silas and Baron seem to be having an in-depth conversation about smoked salmon.

I swing my bag around and toss it on the counter between them. "Are you two serious, right now? I'm getting ready to go kill my uncle and you two are arguing over smoked salmon versus grilled salmon?"

"It's Iris's first full night home and we wanted to make something special for her."

"Well, I'm glad you'll all be enjoying a nice dinner with our girl while I'm dragging my cousin's ass back to his father, so I can end his life for killing my parents."

Both of them look at me like I'm on the verge of combustion. "She told you?" Baron asks.

"Yeah. She did. Because you two made her. Do you think that was easy for her?"

Am I a little sour right now? Yes. A couple days ago, I was practically eating out of my uncle's hand as he fed me lies. All the while, he knew that he was only in the position he's in because he stole it from my dad by ending his life.

"We figured it would be easier for you to take the news from her," Silas adds.

It was. Iris knows how to comfort me in a way that no one else can. "Look. I'm not angry at you guys. I just wanna get this shit done, so I can come back home and be with her."

Silas and Baron both look over my shoulder when the sound of footsteps come near. I glance over my shoulder and see Quentin, dressed in a pair of my torn, black jeans with a destroyed black T-shirt.

He takes one look at the clothes I tossed at him an hour ago and snarls, "You couldn't give me something without so many holes?"

Baron busts out laughing, while Silas holds a straight face.

Snatching my backpack off the counter, I lock an arm around Quentin's neck and rub my knuckles to his head. "Let's go, cous."

He winces. "Watch the arm, asshole."

Quentin doesn't know my plan, and he will not know what I'm doing until it happens. It's best this way.

As we walk out of the kitchen through the corridor, I stop. My arm drops from around Quentin's neck and I gaze up at the beauty standing in the middle of the staircase. Her cream-colored silk robe wrapped tightly around her, and tears soaking her cheeks.

My bag drops at my feet, and I hurry up the stairs to meet her. "Baby, what's wrong?" I cup her cheeks in my hands and kiss away her tears.

"Please be safe," she whispers, splintering my heart in two. I wish I didn't have to leave her again. Fuck! I wish there was another way.

"Always," I say the promise to her and to myself.

I drop my hands and grab her fingers, grazing my thumb over her knuckles. "Don't do anything stupid while I'm gone. I know how you like to try and fix things. I'll be back as soon as I can, and we will continue our lives together."

She nods, though I'm not certain she's not plotting something behind those emerald eyes.

"I love you," I say, pressing my lips to hers.

"I love you, too."

I turn to walk down the stairs, and she follows behind me. As soon as we reach the bottom, she's throwing herself into Quentin's arms. Then the tears really start to fall. "Will I ever see you again?" She sobs into his shoulder.

Quentin looks at me over his hold on her. He wants me to give her some sort of answer, but I've got nothing. The truth is, I don't know what will become of him when this is all over.

"Yes," he finally says, "you'll see me again." His lips press to her forehead and I'm waiting for Baron or Silas to come in here and pry them apart, but when I look over, they're both just standing there, allowing them to have this moment.

"We gotta go," I say, hurrying this along. Not because I care that he's touching her. Or because I'm worried the feelings between them have sprouted into something more than a forced friendship. But because our jet is waiting, and time is of the essence.

Quentin takes a step back, and I kiss Iris one more time before we head out.

~

Once we're in the air, I go over the details of our plan with Quentin. "You said your dad comes back at six o'clock?"

"On the dot." He nods. "He's very precise. I know his schedule like the back of my hand. He's had the same routine for years now."

"Remember to stick to what we discussed. You're going to play victim. I forced you out of the house at gunpoint as my hostage."

Quentin grimaces. "Or I can just kick the old man in the balls and tell him to fuck off, then go live my life the way I want."

"That works, too." I chuckle. "So, what would you do if you could live your life the way you want?"

Quentin focuses his gaze out the window of the jet. He seems unsure of the answer.

Seconds later, he responds, "Anything?"

I humor him. "Sure. Why not."

"I'd go back and be with her."

"Iris?"

"Yup," he says, peering down at his hands in his lap. "She's pretty fucking amazing." He bites back a smile as if the thought of her alone gives him life.

I know that feeling. She does the same thing to me.

"That she is." I nod in agreement. "You do realize she has three boyfriends already?"

His shoulder shrugs. "Doesn't bother me. I've never lived a conventional lifestyle."

"Well," I drawl, "Iris has a big enough heart for all of us. Last year I would have probably strangled you at the mention of such a thing, but she's proven that her love for others doesn't take away from her love for me.

However, I'm not so sure Daddy Silas would feel the same way."

Quentin laughs. "Yeah. It's a ridiculous thought. But," he slaps his hands to his legs. "Doesn't matter because I'll likely go back there and do twice the amount of work for my own father to make up for your absence. He's had your stay planned out for a while. He's not going to be happy about your decision to work for him from your own home."

"He can take it or he can leave it, but I'm not changing my mind. I won't stay."

Quentin is under the assumption that I'm going to make an offer to work for his dad from out of state, with an occasional pop-in for serious matters. I really hate lying to him. The guy ain't so bad. He actually reminds me a lot of Iris. They've lived similar lives, and soon, they'll both be without a mother or a father.

An hour later, we're touching down in Tijuana. The car is already waiting for us with the driver situated outside the back passenger door.

Once we're at the car, I tip my head to the driver and he pulls open the door. "Motherfucker," I spit out when I see that the back seat is already occupied.

"One step ahead of ya, *mijo*. Now get sorry asses in here so we can go home."

I look over my shoulder at Quentin who's just as surprised as I am.

Surveying the area, I notice at least six different cars, likely holding his goons. It's not like me to let my guard down like this. I should have fucking known.

"Well," Baxter says, "we ain't got all day."

Giving my bag a toss right into Uncle Bax's lap, I slide in, and Quentin follows suit.

"Seems we have a lot to talk about," Baxter says, looking from me to his son.

"That we do," I reply smugly, clutching the pocket of my pants that holds my knife.

Thirty–Nine

Iris

I've paced the length of this hotel room at least a dozen times, chewed my thumbnail down to the skin, and asked Silas at least ten times if there was an update.

"We can't get a track on his location. He must've shut his phone off," Silas says, slamming his phone down on the bed. "Dammit!"

He's tense. I'm tense. Baron is tense. There is so much fucking tension in this room that I'm surprised the windows haven't shattered.

Stopping in my tracks, my palms plant on my hips. "Well, what are we going to do? They are obviously somewhere."

Baron snatches up his jacket and begins putting it on.

"What are you doing?" I ask, sucking the blood off the tip of my thumb.

"We have to go to the house. Gabriel said he and Quentin were planning to arrive before Basileus at six o'clock. It's after six. They have to be there."

My heart begins racing, nausea swimming in my stomach. Something is wrong. I can feel it in my bones.

"Okay. Let's go." I grab my holster off the bed, holding my gun, and wrap it around my waist.

Silas's eyes sweep over me with uncertainty.

"What is it?" I ask him, clicking the belt in place and tugging my shirt down.

"We can't. They'll see us coming from a mile away. Chances are, they've already made our presence known. Security is on high alert. We have to lay low until Gabriel reaches out."

"He won't reach out because he doesn't know we're here." My voice rises, panic-induced, and I don't mean to be so loud, but I am really fucking scared right now. "We have to go help him."

Silas stands up. Slow steps bring him in front of me. His hands cradle my face, and he looks knowingly into my eyes. "He's going to be fine. We will all be just fine."

I swallow hard, trying to believe the words he's saying. The same words we've all said countless times, but at some point, things will not be fine. What if that time is now? What if El Basileus turned the tables on Gabriel, and he's...dead.

"No! We can't stand idly by and wait for an SOS call from him, because if we wait too long, he may not even be well enough to make a call."

"Iris is right," Baron chimes in. "I know you're doing this because you want to keep me and her safe, but we need to go to Gabriel. Even if it's just for backup. You told us how strong we are. How proud you are. Let us all prove it and give you an actual reason to be proud."

Silas is silent for a moment, still looking deep into my

eyes as if they hold all the answers. I blink back my tears when he finally says, "Okay. Let's go."

I exhale the pent-up air in my lungs, and we waste no time hauling ass out the door.

Wherever Gabriel is, I just hope it's not too late.

We arrive at the property in record time. Silas was able to make a call for backup from the same men who apparently helped him last time. They weren't able to disarm all forms of security, but the cameras at the main gate have been shut down. It should give us enough time to get in, camouflage ourselves and wait until we're needed—if we're needed at all.

Gabriel will use his skills to overpower his uncle—I know he will. From what Silas said, he's a weak man who hides behind his paid army of men. He achieved his title from being conniving and using money to gain power.

"Iris," Baron says, a glint of seriousness in his tone, "stay back, please." His hands find my waist and he squeezes. "I'd die if anything happened to you."

My first thought is to spit out the word 'no,' but I can see that my safety is heavy on his mind, so I reason with him. "I'll stick close to you and Silas. I have my gun and the skills I acquired from you all. This is no different than any other job I go on."

With his eyes closed, Baron takes in a deep breath, and on the exhale says, "Okay. But if shots start firing you need to get your ass to safety."

I nod in agreement, hopeful it won't come to that.

Baron takes my hand in his. Silas comes up on the other side of me, expressionless and unbending, per usual.

Dressed in all black, we walk through the gate like we own the damn place. A sense of empowerment washes over me. Most men would force their woman to take the back seat in situations like this. They'd internally belittle them and never see their worth. My guys build me up and give me a voice.

I look to my left at Baron, then to my right at Silas, and I smile. My family is truly a circle of strength, and when someone fucks with a member of our family or tries to take them from us, we fight back.

With heavy steps pounding against the cement, we make our way down the outskirts of the paved driveway. There are a half-dozen men behind us with semi-automatic weapons clutched under their arms. Camouflaged, prepared, and willing to go to war for us. We lead them and they follow—for the right amount of money.

Five minutes later, the house is in sight. Just as I remember it from my view in Quentin's condo. Ornamental trees overtop the freshly cut lawn. Birds chirping as if this is their own personal heaven. Little do they know that behind the scenes, mass destruction is plotted, lives are put at risk, and deals are made with the devils of the world.

It all ends today. The title of El Basileus will no longer belong to Baxter Morales. That damnation should cease to exist, but I know better than to think that's a possibility. Someone will continue to lead the Mandola Cartel. I just hope Gabriel doesn't decide he wants that power.

"Search the perimeter," Silas barks out the order.

The men scatter like mice as we stand by idly watching them.

A minute later, one of the men chirps through the walkie-talkie, "Perimeter is clear."

We continue to walk side by side, making our way up to

the house. The view is the same, but the vibe is different. There are no dancing, naked chicks. No open bar by the pool. It almost feels dreary. Like the life has been sucked out of this place since Quentin and Gabriel left. Perhaps it was just for show. Baxter's way of enticing Gabriel to stay.

The sound of gunshots ring through the air, and Silas throws an arm out, stopping me.

Our movements freeze, feet rooted to the ground where we stand. More gunshots sound in the distance. Glass shatters from the far end of the first floor.

Baron drops my hand and tips his head toward a shed off to the left. I follow his lead, but stop when I notice Silas walking toward the house. "Silas," I whisper-yell, "wait."

He doesn't listen. Being stubborn like he always is, he walks right up to the house with drawn shoulders, and his gun still tucked in his holster.

"What the hell is he doing?" I ask in a panic-induced state. "It hasn't been cleared yet."

"He'll do what he wants to do. No sense in trying to stop him."

Baron is right. In this environment, emotions have to be set aside. No matter how much I love these guys, and no matter how much they love me, we have to think like assassins. No feelings, no animosity toward each other for making a move we don't agree with. We are here for one thing and one thing only—to support Gabriel and kill anyone who gets in his way.

All the calmness I was wearing like a warm winter coat has dissipated. Each passing second has my heart galloping faster, thunderous in my chest.

Who am I kidding? I can't put my emotions aside when it comes to these guys. This isn't a job. This is my family we're talking about.

I step out into the wide-open space. "Babe, no," Baron says, grabbing me by the arm and pulling my back to his chest. Strong arms wrap around me, and while I feel safe at his side, I don't need comfort right now. I need to go in that house and make sure Silas and Gabriel are okay.

"Please. We can't just stand here and do nothing." I know damn well if I wasn't here, Baron would be in that house right now with his father.

The pop-pop sound of a gun startles me. It's not the same as the shots fired minutes ago, which leads me to believe it was a small caliber gun.

Silas.

"Let me go." I squirm, trying to free myself from his hold. I wanna cry and break down, lash out like a child until I get my way. "Please. I have to make sure they're okay."

Baron only strengthens his hold on me. His lips press softly to my ear. "Going in there right now would be reckless. Wait until we're given the all-clear."

I take in a jerky breath. *Wait. Okay. I can do that.*

Finally resting my body against his, I embrace his touch and remind myself that soon this will all be over.

We'll be home. Me, Silas, Baron, Gabriel. My family. My everything. Only, the pang in my chest reminds me that Quentin will still be here. I've always considered our family to be complete. Never wanted any other man and never had any interest in pursuing other men. Then I met Quentin. There wasn't an instant connection, but he breathed life into me when no one else could. He made me laugh in a way that no one else does. I felt alive and free, even as a prisoner.

Baron's walkie-talkie chirps. "They're not here," Silas says through the speaker.

"What?" I gasp.

Baron looks at me as he responds, "What do you mean, they're not there?"

"We've scoured the entire place. Roped a man to get some info and in one breath, he said that his boss was headed to welcome home his son and nephew at a private airfield outside of the city."

"Fuck!" Baron shouts, slamming the walkie-talkie to the ground.

"Baron," Silas says through the speaker lying at my feet, "they were expecting us."

El Basileus knows we're here?

I look around, wondering how many eyes are on me at this very moment. Even if Silas and the men were able to take out the ones in their way just now, it doesn't mean there aren't more here.

Forty

GABRIEL

"Tell the driver to pull over," I cough out the demand, eyes held straight in front of me on the thin layer of plexiglass separating the front seat from the back.

"Now why the hell would I do that?" Baxter grumbles with his hands locked on his knees.

Our bodies are scrunched together in this one-row seat and the empowering scent of his designer cologne might choke me before I have a chance to confront him about his lies and scheming.

I know what's waiting back at his house. An army of men who have his back. Him arriving at the airfield, actually works in my favor. This way, I can kill him off his property when he has no protection.

"It was a long flight. I need to take a piss."

"Pinch it for twenty more minutes, *mijo*. We've got people waiting on us."

"Oh yeah," my attention snaps to him like Velcro, "like who?"

"Let's just call it your own personal welcome committee."

Baxter looks past me, noticing Quentin's quiet demeanor. "What's with you, boy? You haven't said a damn word since you got in this car. Aren't you happy to see your old man?" Baxter chuckles, answering the question himself. "Of course you're not. After all, you ran away on your own free will. Helped your cousin and his whore, didn't ya?"

My jaw clenches, fists knotting so tight my knuckles protrude. "What the fuck did you just say?"

Baxter laughs menacingly, pissing me off to the core. I squeeze my hands tighter, grinding my teeth as I shout, "Pull over the fucking car!"

He sits there, calm and collected, while his son on the other side of me stares out the passenger window, likely out of fear of his own father.

Quentin might be angry for a while, but one day, he'll thank me for changing his fate.

Baxter leans forward, taps a finger to the glass window before it comes rolling down. "Pull over," he tells the driver.

The tension in this back seat thickens as we come to a rolling stop. I bump my leg to Quentin's, gesturing for him to move, so I can get out of the car.

He immediately opens the door and steps out while I do the same. "Get back in the car and stay there," I whisper the demand.

His curved eyebrows wrinkle his forehead.

"Just do it."

With slouched shoulders, he drops back into the seat and closes the door.

I'm well aware that there are cars behind us, waiting and willing to protect this asshole the second he gives them the signal. Regardless, I round the car and waste no time grabbing the handle of the door where Baxter sits.

In one swift pull, I jerk it open then grab him by the collar of his neatly pressed jacket. His arm swings around like he's ready to knock me on my ass, but his aim is terrible.

Continuing to pull, I drag him out of the car while keeping him on his feet.

"You're asking for trouble, *mijo*." His voice is unruffled as if he holds not an ounce of terror. Foolish man.

"You scared, Baxter?"

He blows out an airy chuckle. "Not in the least bit."

"You should be. Might wanna call on your men for backup." Walking my body into his, I force his steps backward. I don't stop, taking him off the road, nearly falling into the cotton field, likely owned by the farmhouse that sits on a hill to the east.

He won't ask for help because he won't admit defeat. This man puts on this tough guy façade, but we all know he hides behind the title he stole.

Knowing that I don't have much time, I get straight to the point by shoving him hard against his chest until he stumbles back even farther, his feet disappearing into the cotton. "Why'd you do it?" I ask, knowing that he has no fucking clue what I'm talking about.

When his hand reaches down to his ankle, I quickly kick it away, knowing that he was going for a gun. I'm not the idiot he takes me for.

Car doors open, but being the stubborn ass Baxter is, he waves them off. "I've got this. Get everyone out of here."

His confidence is soaring, and it's almost comical. He seems pretty sure of himself that he will either overpower me, or break me before he has to.

Once the cars begin to pull away and it's just us left—no backup, no help for this poor old man—I continue with my own personal interrogation, one I will thoroughly enjoy.

"Did you think I wouldn't find out?" I ask the unknowing question.

For a brief moment, I take him to be nervous. Just a sliver of a second when his eyes look into mine, already begging for his life. That is until he looks over my shoulder and smiles.

I don't dare turn around to see who's there. For one, I'm sure it's Quentin. Two, I will not give him the chance to gain the upper hand because I carelessly turned my attention elsewhere.

He might have hope at this moment. Probably thinks his son is here to save him. And he very well could be. For all I know, Quentin's a snake. Regardless, he's about to watch his father pay for his sins in the same way this rat bastard ended the life of my parents.

I reach into my pocket and pull out my knife, giving it a swift jerk and slinging the blade free.

Now I've got his attention.

One step has me behind him with my arm locked around his neck, and the knife pressed to his throat, then I give him my own piece of knowledge. "I know you put the hit on my parents."

"Someone's feeding you lies, son."

I laugh. That same menacing tone he tossed at me earlier in an attempt to intimidate me.

This fucker doesn't know me at all.

"Don't call me son. In fact, don't even call me nephew. From here on out, until I slice your throat, you can call me your worst nightmare."

He chuckles nervously. "Come on now. You wouldn't really kill a man who shares your blood? We're family."

My lip curls, snarling in disgust at his empty words. "Family? Isn't that what my father was to you? Your own fucking brother. You killed him for what? Power? Jealousy?"

"I was never jealous," he spits out. "He knew of my plans to overthrow the former leader." His anger grows as if he's forgotten who's holding the knife here. "He's the one who got in my way!"

"So you admit it. You're the one who hired Silas Black to take them out after feeding him some bullshit story about stolen drugs and a deadly addiction to your product?"

My finger grips the knife tighter, ready to slit his throat if he so much as takes a breath that pisses me off further.

The car door opens, and Quentin steps out. It seems it's time for him to prove where his loyalties lie.

"All right," he holds his hands up in surrender, "I hired Silas Black. He's the best in the business and he got the job done. Doesn't change anything. You still won't kill me."

I raise a brow. "Pretty cocky for a guy who's got a knife to his throat."

"You call it cocky. I call it confident." There's an arrogant self-assurance in his tone that unnerves me.

"All right then, humor me. What makes you so sure I won't kill you?" My arm's getting tired. I've got a nice bed at home I'm anxious to return to with my girl. This guy is dragging this out far more than I should allow.

"You scold me for killing my brother and his bitch, yet you have no problem killing your own father."

"What did you just say?" I'm not sure what I'm questioning here: the fact that he called my mother a strumpet or mentioned killing my father as if I had something to do with his death.

"Well, if you do what you say you're gonna do, it's the truth, *mijo*. You'd be killing your own father."

My heart races, sweat protruding around my hairline as I struggle to understand his words. "You're delusional."

His head tilts to the side as if he truly believes that I'm going to believe this bullshit. "Am I?"

"Don't listen to him," Quentin finally says, proving that he is, in fact, on my side in this. "He's a master manipulator. He'll say just about anything to stop you from slicing his throat."

"I'm sorry I lied to you, son. Quentin here isn't your cousin. He's your brother."

My hand begins shaking forcibly with my fingers clenched around the knife. "Quit lying," I scream. "Just shut the fuck up."

Unaffected by my outburst or the fact that I have a knife to his throat, he continues, "It's true. Your mother and I had a lengthy affair that resulted in pregnancy. She knew you were mine and kept it from your father. I agreed to keep her secret so long as she stopped him from making the huge mistake of going after El Basileus. When I caught wind of his plan, a few days before their deaths, I went to take you from her. You were my son," his voice rises, "you were always mine. Not his."

This is unreal. No part of me believes a word he says. Yet, I keep listening, regardless.

"I tried everything I could do to get you, so I could bring you home where you belonged, but I lost. I knew that if he took the role as the next El Basileus, I'd lose you forever. So I stopped him."

"You're lying," I spit out. "Save your last breath for some honesty."

"It's all true. I'll take a DNA test. You're my son, *mijo*. And if Silas Black hadn't taken you away and made the world believe you had died, you would have been mine that day. I spent years looking for you before I finally came to believe the rumors that you were killed or sold. Part of me always knew you were out there."

No. This can't be true.

"Stop lying!" I scream even louder.

Instead of listening, he keeps on trying to sway my decision to kill him. "Part of me wished that it was Quentin taken that day. He's never been good for much when it comes to this business. Just a techy with too much time on his hands. Nothing to contribute and really just a pain in the ass."

Quentin stands tall with a scorned look on his face.

"Shut up," I tell Baxter.

"Quentin never took to this life the way you have. You're strong, like me. We can be a great team. Let him go back and take your place. Give him that whore of yours. You'll be better off without her. The bitch wants to spread her legs for everyone, might as well—"

Pressing the tip of the knife into the first layer of skin on his throat, I shut him up. Now it's time for him to get some of my cold, hard truth. "I'd die before I ever worked for a man like you. You're nothing but scum. Murderous scum. The world will thank me when you're gone."

Just as I go to slice his throat, Quentin pulls out a gun, aiming it at his father.

"Move," he shouts, gesturing me to the side, but I stay put.

"No! I have to do this. Put the damn gun away."

Instead of listening, he holds the gun straight out, trembling as if it's painful, yet necessary. "You know what, Dad," he enunciates the title, "I wish Silas Black would have taken me, too. Sure as hell would have saved me from a life of abuse at your hands."

"You were weak," Baxter spits out. "Weak and pathetic. Someone needed to toughen you up. All you wanted to do day in and day out was play on that damn computer. The one and only thing you've been good for is finding me Gabriel, my beloved son."

Hearing him talk about Quentin like that just triggers something in me, and I can't stop myself. In one swift movement, I dig the blade deep enough to slice through his carotid artery. Baxter crumples to the ground between two rows of cotton.

"What did you do that for?" Quentin yells, lowering his gun. "It should have been me. You don't know the hell that man has put me through."

"No, it shouldn't have. You don't want this shit on your conscience."

"And you do?" he asks.

Even if Baxter is my biological father, I had no connection with him. There will not be any love loss or regret. Quentin grew up with him as his dad. He might feel like he could do this now, but years down the road, he'd question himself. I couldn't let the weight of that burden rest on his shoulders.

It doesn't faze me in the least to watch this guy lie here and bleed out. A few jerks and grumbles, then his body stills and he's gone.

"Didn't you hear him? You just killed your father, Gabriel." Quentin asks with a subtle shake in his voice.

I look down at the man I don't recognize, bleeding out

into the white cotton he's lying on. I kick him before wiping my blade across his pants to clean off the blood.

"No, I didn't. I already have a father."

It's over.

A minute or so passes before I hear Quentin vomiting profusely behind me. It's obvious he's not used to this, which surprises me given his dad's business. Either that, or he's got a really weak stomach. Makes me wonder how he will survive if he did come back to live with us.

"You all right?" I ask with my eyes still on Baxter.

Quentin coughs a few times, spitting out the excess in his mouth. "Yeah. I'm good."

"That was fucking disgusting."

"You just slit a man's throat and drooled in ecstasy like you were slicing a Thanksgiving turkey and me throwing up is what grossed you out?"

Kid's got a point.

What can I say, I live to kill and torture those who deserve it.

I look over my shoulder and he's just standing there, staring at his dad's body. "Think you can help me out here? If you can't do it—"

"I can help. I'm fine now."

When I lift Baxter by the arm, Quentin comes over and grabs his other arm, and together, we pull him to the car.

"Tell the driver to open the trunk," I instruct Quentin.

While Quentin gets the driver's attention, I pull Baxter the rest of the way until he's on the pavement behind the car. Blood streams from his neck downward, leaving a trail of fresh blood behind.

The trunk slowly rises and Quentin joins us at the back of the car. "Whose side is that fucker on?" I ask, assuming he knows I mean the driver.

"Whoever isn't against him. Staff don't take sides when it comes to El Basileus. Their loyalty follows the title."

We share an awkward silence at the mention of that title. I know what he's thinking—it will be me.

"Let's get this shit over with," he finally says.

Quentin and I lift Baxter and drop his lifeless body into the trunk then I slam it shut, giving it a couple knocks before rounding the car and resting my arms on the driver's open window.

"Where to?" the driver asks.

"The Mandola headquarters."

He nods in response. "You got it."

We could dump his body, hide it from the public and let him be deemed a missing person for years to come, but I prefer the news of his death to be widespread so the entire world knows that this son of a bitch is no longer in control.

I slide in the back seat beside Quentin. His bloody hands are shaking, legs bobbing up and down.

"Chill out, man. It'll all be over soon." I reach into my pocket and pull out a handkerchief and begin wiping as much blood off my hands as I can.

I offer it to Quentin, but he shakes his head, declining before rubbing his hands up and down the holey jeans I lent him.

I didn't expect Quentin to be so receptive to his dad dying today. Thought maybe he'd put up a fight for him. I also didn't realize their relationship was so toxic. Seems like it's really done a number on Quentin emotionally, which really sucks because he seems like a decent guy with a good head on his shoulders.

"I should have done it a long time ago. Almost did when I found out he was trafficking underage girls. Pulled a gun on him, but I cowered, just like he knew I would.

That's when he kicked me out of the main house, and I had to go stay in the condo."

"Wait. He kicked you out? I thought you wanted to live there?"

Quentin shrugs. "Little of both. I just want out of this fucking city altogether. I hate it here."

"Ya know," I say, ready to get this elephant out of the car, "I don't want that title. I'll deny the murder and when no one comes forward with proof, it'll be overturned by The Commission and given to his heir."

The Commission is like the cartel's fucked-up board of members who make final calls when it comes to decisions for the organization as a whole. It makes me wonder how many next of kin have been declared the leader over the hundred years the organization has been in business.

"Well, it seems I'm not his only son, so that'll be up for debate."

"Nah." I sweep the air with my hand. "No one needs to know that. In fact, I don't even want to know. Maybe he was lying, maybe he wasn't. I've got a father and he's the only one I need. It's yours if you want it."

Quentin offers a blank stare over my shoulder. "I'm not sure I want any part of that business, unless some big changes are made."

Quentin might have a soft exterior, but I can tell he's tough. The thing is, I don't think he's tough enough to live the lifestyle his dad did. Maybe some changes in the business wouldn't be a bad idea. He's book smart and knowledgeable when it comes to security. Someone good to have on the inside. Then again, him coming back to the house might not be such a bad idea. After all, there's a chance he's my brother. Might be nice to have a blood family member of my own nearby.

Fuck! My brother—my father. Iris.

I reach into my pocket and pull out my phone, forgetting that I shut it off. They're probably sick with worry right now, wondering what's going on.

Once my phone is powered on, I skip all the messages and call Iris right away.

She picks up on the first ring. "Dammit, Gabriel. Where the hell are you?"

Quentin chuckles, hearing her voice from his seat beside me. I look at him and smirk. "It's over. He's gone."

"Oh, thank God!" There's some shuffling on the other end of the phone before I hear her fill the guys in. "It's done," she tells them.

"We're going to get rid of the package. I'll be on the first flight out tomorrow morning."

"Baby," Iris says in that tone that means I'm not going to like what's coming, "there's something I need to tell you."

"For fuck's sake, what did you do, Iris?"

"We might be in Tijuana."

My head drops back against the headrest, and I close my eyes. "Might be or are?"

"We are. Please don't be mad. We were only here for backup, but everything went to hell, and it seems you really didn't need us at all."

I should be mad. I should be furious at their lack of trust in my abilities. But I'm not.

"I'm not mad. I'm just glad this is over with and we can get back to our normal, but fucked-up, lives." Iris laughs, and fuck if I haven't missed that sound. "Text me the address of where you're at and I'll see you soon, baby."

The call ends, and I look at Quentin, noticing he's been abnormally quiet. Usually the kid can't shut up. I suppose his father's death could have more of an impact on him than I imagined.

"Hey," I say, grabbing his attention, "why don't you pack a bag and come back to our house for a while until this mess with Baxter is sorted out."

His eyes widen, surprised by my offer. "You think the others will care?"

"Nah, they don't give a shit. Besides, I think it'll make Iris happy."

I don't usually give two shits about other human beings, aside from Iris, but Quentin is blood, and he's proven his loyalty.

As long as he doesn't interfere on my time with my girl, I'm cool with him coming back for a bit.

Forty-One

Iris

"I'm so glad you're okay," I screech as I run down the hall of the hotel and into Gabriel's arms. "I was so worried about you."

My face burrows into the crease of his neck, legs wrapping around his waist. His tired arms hold me up and I never want to let him go.

He smells like trash and something metallic, likely blood, but I don't even care right now. "Don't you ever scare me like that again."

I know it won't be the last time. This is Gabriel we're talking about. Right now, though, all that matters is he's safe and we're all back together again.

Wait. I look over his shoulder and notice Quentin isn't there. My head lifts, and I look into Gabe's sleepy eyes. "Where's Quentin?"

Gabriel drops his hold on me and my feet hit the floor. "After we dumped the body in the driveway at the headquarters, where The Commission holds their meetings, he had to go back home and settle some scores with the organization."

"You're not thinking about—"

"No. Definitely not," he responds, knowing my question. "I want no part of that shit. Quentin doesn't either, but it's not as easy as just walking away for him. Someone will be appointed the next El Basileus, but it's up to The Commission to make that decision." Gabriel takes my hand and we walk the rest of the way down the hall to the room we're staying in.

I'm thankful Gabriel is safe and that this mess is behind us, but I can't help but wonder if it truly is. "Do you think anyone knows it was you?"

"Probably. Baxter had some men following us that he sent off. I'm sure once word gets out that he's missing, fingers will be pointed at me and Quentin, but it doesn't matter. The Mandola Cartel is their own government. Their leader is dead; therefore, his position has dissolved. The second he took his last breath, he became a nobody."

I don't understand much about that business and I really don't want to.

We get to the room and Gabriel gets a welcome from Silas and Baron in their typical male fashion of, 'hey, good work, son,' and 'glad to see you didn't get yourself killed.'

Gabriel goes into detail about his day, filling the guys in, and I just stand back and watch them all interact as if this is a totally normal conversation.

This life we live is totally abnormal, but I wouldn't change a single thing about it—aside from adding Quentin, of course.

"Well, I need to shower," Gabriel says. He closes the space between us, places a hand on my hip, and whispers, "And I need you to join me."

Not much fazes any of us, but I'll be the first to admit that sharing a suite with all three of them is slightly awkward.

Silas and Baron have distracted themselves, likely on purpose, so I take Gabriel's hand and lead him into the bathroom.

Before I can even close the door, Gabriel grabs me and hoists me up around his waist, using my body to close it for us. "All I could think about the entire ride here was stripping your clothes off and fucking you in a hot shower."

Even soaked in blood, Gabriel turns me on. His body pressed against mine, my pussy throbbing for his touch.

Our mouths connect in a tantalizing kiss. My head tilts when his tongue sweeps into my mouth, and I greet it with my own.

We tear at each other, ridding ourselves of every article of clothing. With our mouths still connected, Gabriel carries me over to the shower, holding me up with one hand under my ass. Stretching his free hand out, he turns on the shower.

The mirror begins to fog, but it's not due to the heat rolling out of the shower, it's the heavy breaths shared between us. I suck in Gabriel's exhale, filling my lungs as his finger slides into my pussy from underneath where he's palming my ass.

My back arches, rolling my hips into him as he steps inside the shower. I pull the shower curtain closed, inhaling the thick cloud of steam.

Gabriel's finger slides out of my pussy and I whimper, already missing it. Desperation burns inside of me like hot lava. I'm in need of more and not above begging at this point.

"Gabriel," I groan into his ear, nibbling and sucking on

his lobe. My mouth moves to his neck, bruising his skin as the need for him climbs through every inch of my body.

Gabriel raises me up so that my breasts are flush with his mouth.

When his teeth graze the skin of my nipple, I whimper in pleasure, wrapping my arms around his head and arching my back.

His fingers find me again, and this time, he pushes two inside me. Hot water spills down us, causing our bodies to slide together. I move up and down meeting each thrust of his fingers.

Another finger slides in, spreading my pussy apart while his thumb circles my asshole. I hold on to him tightly, fearful that I'll slip right out of his arms. His face nuzzles between my breasts, his hot breath mixing with the steam filling the shower.

"God, I was so scared I would lose you." I exhale a raggedy breath. "Fuck me, Gabriel." The need to feel him inside me is indescribable. Nothing else in the world matters right now. Silas and Baron could bust through the door and I'd still let Gabriel fuck me while they watch.

"Patience, baby. I just got you back. Let me savor this while my fingers dig into your swollen pussy."

His words alone set my soul on fire.

"Put your feet down," he demands in an authoritative tone.

Doing as I'm told, my feet hit the ceramic tub. Gabriel gets on his knees, watching me with wondrous eyes as he lifts one of my legs and rests it on the edge of the bathtub. His fingers find me again. He slides in one, two, then three, filling me up.

Getting a firm grip on his soaking wet hair, I slam his face into my pussy. The piercing in his tongue sweeps up and down my folds, smoothing over my clit. He removes his fingers then flexes his tongue inside me, swirling and licking before sliding it back up again.

My hips roll as he fingerfucks me, stopping every few seconds to lick up my arousal that's mixing with the dripping water.

When my body fills up with an insatiable need for release, I grip his hair tighter, tangling it around my fingers while I ride his face to my climax.

"Fuck, Gabriel," I cry out as his fingers dig deep inside of me, curling and hitting just the right spot to send me over the edge. My sounds cannot be muffled. I moan out in pleasure when he begins rubbing feverishly at my clit.

Holding my breath, I come undone.

In one swift motion, Gabriel gets to his feet, swoops his arm around my waist, spins me around so that my back is to him, then he pushes me forward. My hands find the back edge of the tub, using it to brace myself.

Wasting no time, he rams his cock inside me. The bar of his piercing hits my G-spot, and it's a feeling I've missed just as much as I've missed him.

Gabriel's hands slap to my hips, fingers pinching the skin as he slides his dick in and out of me. In a matter of seconds, his pace quickens until he's full-on pounding me from behind.

Locking his fingers in my long hair, he pulls back while one hand presses firmly to my hip. "Damn, baby, I've missed being inside of you." His voice is gruff and lust-filled. "Turn your head and look at me. I wanna watch your face while I come inside you."

I turn my head, eyes locked on his. Gabriel bites his bottom lip, and I find myself doing the same. Water rolls freely down his body, over the artwork on his chest and down to his cock, getting it nice and wet. Gabriel pulls out just enough for me to feel the piercing on his head at my entrance, then he slams back in, filling me up and repeating the process.

Electricity shoots through my entire body, zapping every cell as I clench my walls around his cock, squeezing him tightly until I come again.

Gabriel leans forward, his chest blanketing my back. One hand comes up, squeezing my breast as he fucks me at lightning speed until he stills inside me. Taking a deep breath, he releases a low, husky groan.

We stay in this position for a moment before I hear Gabriel take in a couple more deep breaths. His hand slaps my ass. "That was a nice welcome home."

I laugh before leaning forward and letting his cock slide out of me. "It sure was."

Once we're both steady on our feet, I press my lips to his. "Don't you ever leave me like that again."

"Never." He kisses me back.

We clean ourselves up in the shower. Me helping Gabriel scrub off the remnants from his hard day's work and him just savoring every second of rubbing his sudsy hands up and down my body.

Once we've finished, I go back into the room where Baron is passed out and Silas is sitting with his back to the headboard and his ankles crossed, still wearing his suit, but with the top three buttons undone on his white dress shirt. He's got his phone in hand and looks deep in thought.

How the hell did I get so damn lucky to find these guys? I'm so undeserving of their love, but I couldn't survive without it.

Silas takes note of my presence and sets his phone

down. He takes off his glasses, then pats at the mattress beside him.

In just a plush robe with my hair still damp, I go over to him. Before I sit, I lean forward and press my lips to his. "Everything okay?" I ask.

"Everything is perfect now. Lie down beside me and get some rest. You've had a busy day."

So I do. I curl up beside Silas, resting my head on his lap while Baron sleeps peacefully in the bed beside us and Gabriel takes the pull-out couch. Chances are, I'll wake in the night and join one of the other guys before moving to the next when I wake in the morning.

That's the beauty of what we have; I've never felt more loved in my life and I've never felt like I have so much love to give.

It doesn't change the fact that it feels like a part of my puzzle is missing. An empty space that yearns to be filled, and there is only one other person who can fill it.

Forty—Two

Iris

Waking up this morning felt like a dream. We're not home, yet, but all three of my guys are safe and we're together, and that's what matters. I just wish this nagging feeling that something is missing would go away. But I know it won't and I have no fucking clue how to bring this up or how I'm going to ask the guys for what I really want. I can't just pretend these feelings don't exist.

"Thanks for delaying the flight," I tell Silas in a warm hug. He's fresh out of the shower in a neatly pressed suit and smells frickin' amazing.

"Anything for you. I would like to know why you were so persistent on the delay."

I look into his eyes, trying to get a read on his mood. He's been so sweet and attentive since I've returned, and even right now, there is nothing but softness in his eyes.

"Come on." I pull his hand, leading him over to the bed where we slept last night. Once my eyes closed on Silas's chest, they didn't open until the sun peeked through the blinds. It was the best sleep I'd had in weeks.

Gabriel is tying the laces of his black boots, while Baron is reading the news online and taking it very seriously, I must add.

This is nice.

This feels normal.

I sit down on the bed, facing where Gabriel is leaning over. Silas opts to stand, and I'm wondering if he thinks I'm about to break some devastating news. I suppose it could go either way, and it could potentially be devastating to one, if not all, of them.

Clearing my throat, I grab everyone's attention— everyone but Baron's. Gabriel's head shoots up, and he straightens his back. "What's wrong?" he asks with worry in his tone.

"Baron," I say. When he still doesn't lift his head from his iPad, I say it again, "Baron."

Must be a damn good article he's reading.

Gabriel smacks one of his legs where they're kicked out in front of him on the bed.

His eyes lift. "Huh?"

"Iris wants to talk," Gabriel tells him.

"Holy shit! Did you all see this?" Baron holds up his iPad, showing us what he's reading, but he's too far away for me to see any of it. "There was an ambush at El Basileus's private home last night."

"What?" I spring to my feet, flying across the bed and snatching the tablet from Baron. The headline immediately catches my eye as my heart jumps into my throat.

Home of the infamous Baxter Morales, also known as, El Basileus ambushed—dozens dead.

My hand claps over my mouth, and I re-read the last words at least five times. *Dozens dead.*

"Oh no," I say out loud. At least, I think I said it out loud. I don't know. I can't think straight.

Rolling off the bed, I get to my feet, though I feel wobbly and off-balance. "I have to go to him."

Silas is already on his phone, likely getting the scoop on the attack. Someone puts an arm around me. I'm not sure who it is as I walk away from it.

"I have to go to him," I repeat. "He has to be okay."

Please let him be okay.

"It's not safe, babe. There's no telling what you could be walking in on if you go to that house."

Regardless, I step into my slip-on Chucks and grab my phone off the end of the bed. Two arms wrap around me again as my thoughts elude me. "No! I have to go."

He squeezes me tighter. That's when I look up and realize it's Baron. I can feel Gabriel behind me, resting a hand on my shoulder.

Burying my face into Baron's shoulder, I begin sobbing uncontrollably. "This was all supposed to be over."

"In this business, it's never over, babe." Gabriel rubs my shoulders, trying to comfort me.

I don't need comfort, though. What I need is to make sure Quentin is alive. He's the missing piece. If anything happened to him...

All I see in my mind is his smile. I hear his lame jokes and playful banter. That moment in the shower plays on repeat in my mind as if I just had him in my arms a second ago, and I let him go.

Silas comes to my side, stuffing his phone in his pants pocket. We all look at him, waiting for something. "It was the Grim brothers. Sante Grim intended to assassinate the leader and take his position. Little did he know, the title isn't absolute until The Commission appoints Quentin as the next in line."

I gasp. "He wanted to kill Quentin?"

"No," Silas shakes his head, "he probably didn't realize Baxter was dead. Chances are, he went there looking for him. It seems the security system has been out since we were there yesterday. Sante must've been watching him for a while. Working to stay under the radar and use this opportunity to attack."

"In the absence of a leader, all hell is going to break loose." Baron runs his fingers over his chin. "It's going to be a bloodbath for control."

My head shakes continuously as I try to call Quentin, but it goes straight to voicemail. "No. Not with Quentin there. We have to get him the hell out and bring him somewhere safe."

Unless he doesn't want to be found. He doesn't want to stay here, does he? He hates it here. But what if the craving for power takes over him like it almost took Gabriel? Maybe that's why he didn't stop Gabriel from killing Baxter. All I know is I need to talk to him, see where his head is at with all of this. Most importantly, I need to make sure he's okay.

"Take me to him," I demand of anyone who will listen. When no one responds and the tears keep falling, I raise my voice. "Please. Someone just take me there."

Silent glances are exchanged before Silas finally agrees. "Okay. We all go. If I get the slightest inkling that something is off, we leave."

"Yes. I promise. It won't take long."

As we're driving to the same property Gabriel and I were held at, my phone rings with a call from an unknown number.

Gabriel leans over my shoulder to get a look at the screen. "Who is it?"

"I don't know. Maybe it's Camilla. There could be a problem with the boutique." I decide to answer it, just in case. "Hello."

"Iris. It's me."

"Oh, thank God, Quentin." I look around at the guys who are all looking at me. "Where are you?"

Hearing his voice is like music to my ears.

"I'm at my condo packing a bag. I'm gonna be leaving town for a bit until things are settled here."

"Wait," I spit out, "come back with us."

Baron's eyebrows hit his forehead while Silas and Gabriel seem unaffected. I'm actually surprised. I figured Silas would be the one to deny my offer to Quentin.

"I appreciate the offer, but I don't want to put you or your family in danger, Iris."

"You are family. Meet us at the gate. We're already on our way there now."

A few seconds pass before he agrees, "Okay. I'll be there."

I end the call and look at Baron first. "He needs our help."

He stays silent, his nostrils flaring as he reaches across to grip my hand tightly in his. What am I putting my family through, asking them to share like this?

"This is actually what I wanted to talk about before we heard about the attack," I continue. "I want him to come home with us."

Baron sneers and glances at the window beside him,

avoiding eye contact with me. "Why?" His voice is laced with anger and I'm worried he isn't going to make this easy.

"Because I care about him...a lot."

His head slowly turns and I reach across Silas's lap, placing a hand on his leg. "It's important to me. I know you don't understand, but—"

"But you want to be with him? In the same way that you are with us?"

It sounds so much worse when he says the words out loud, but that's exactly what I want. "Yes," I say, not willing to lie.

These past couple years I have learned so much about myself and what I want. For so long, I was not given a choice and I was forced to live my life to please others, now I don't have to do that anymore. Baron, Silas, and Gabriel love me for me, in the same way that I love them for who they are.

This is us. This is who we are. A screwed-up family of trained assassins who found love in the unlikeliest of places. Without these guys, I have no purpose—that goes for all four of them.

"Whatever," Baron grumbles, "but if he thinks he's cutting in on my time then he's got another thing coming."

Biting back a smile, I also refrain from jumping over Silas's lap to hug him.

"Are you guys okay with this?" I ask both Silas and Gabriel.

Gabriel places a hand on my leg. "You know I'm okay with him coming back. He is family."

After my drunken night with Gabriel and Quentin, I assumed Gabriel would be okay with it.

"Silas?" I say his name in question.

He glances down at me, a softness in his eyes that I don't often see there. There's a tremor under my skin as I wait for his answer. He's the one we have to get the real approval from. If Silas says no, then it means no. And as he strokes my cheek, I wait for his answer.

"Whatever makes you happy."

I swear my heart actually cracks in my chest. My lips press to his cheek. "Thank you."

Gabriel squeezes my leg. "Well, I guess since we're sharing news..." he says with a sarcastic smile on his face. "I suppose there's no better time than now to tell you all a bit of information I found out. Could be a lie. Could be the truth. Either way, I don't really give a damn."

He has all of our attention as we look at him, waiting to hear what he has to say.

"That fuckwad Baxter claims to be my biological father. Apparently he was fucking my mom and I was their bastard love child."

The car falls into a very long, awkward silence.

"What?" I drawl, while Silas and Baron offer the same response.

"Yeah, so it turns out my cousin is actually my brother." Then he looks at Baron. "I guess in some way that makes him your brother too."

Baron responds with a roll of his eyes.

"We'll get a DNA test before they bury his body," Silas tells him.

"Nope," Gabriel retorts. "Don't want one because it doesn't matter. I've got the only father I need."

"Touching," Baron replies, making a face at Gabriel who flips him off, and I can't help but bite back my smile.

My heart squeezes because, even without showing it, I know Gabriel's words touched Silas.

"Your choice," Silas says point-blankly. A man of few words, but he doesn't need many. I can read him like a book and the way his shoulders tensed at the announcement then relaxed when Gabriel refused a DNA test tells me all I need to know—he loves his sons more than anything in this world.

We pull up to the gate and, as promised, Quentin is waiting there. His leg kicked up on the driver's side of his black Bugatti.

Gabriel gets out first and I slide out after him. Baron and Silas stay in the car while Gabriel and I go to talk to him.

The first thing I do is throw myself into his arms. He wraps his hands around my waist and pulls me close. Everything about this moment is perfect. Being close to him, having him hold me this way, it feels so natural and right.

I pull back, look him in the eyes and plead with him. "Please come back with us. I promise you'll be safe and we'll be safe, too. We have top-notch security."

Quentin looks at Gabriel. "How do you feel about this?"

Gabriel shrugs. "We're blood. Mi casa, su casa."

Taking a few seconds to think on it, Quentin finally opens the driver's side door. "All right then. Give me the address and I'll meet you all there."

"Hold on," I put a hand on Quentin's shoulder, stopping him from getting in before I turn to Gabriel. "Can we ride with him? Just to make sure he's not being followed?"

"Sure. Why not?" He steps away and goes to the car we came here in.

A minute later, he returns. "Silas insists they follow behind us."

I nod in response, and we all get in Quentin's car.

On the ride, he fills us in on the ambush by the Grim brothers. Apparently they got away unscathed, which could be dangerous for Quentin if they are determined to assassinate the leader.

Quentin goes on to tell us his plans to erase all evidence of our encounters. Without proof, no one would ever suspect he'd be staying at our house. We have very little connections to the Mandola Cartel or the Morales family.

It's actually pretty genius—which I'm starting to realize is Quentin's nature. His skills could come in handy for our family business as well.

It's a win-win. I have the four of them, and while Quentin's stay might be temporary, something tells me he's with us for the long haul.

Iris

Quentin is all settled in two rooms down from me. It's nice having him so close. I've realized there's something about him that reminds me of my dad and feels like home. Could be the way he always makes me laugh when I'm feeling like shit, the way my father did.

I'm changing into some clean clothes when there's a knock at my bedroom door. "It's open," I holler, picking up my dirty sweatshirt and dropping it into the laundry basket.

Gabriel pokes his head in the room with Punk in his arms. "Breakfast is ready."

I walk over to him, petting the stray cat that is apparently no longer a stray. Punk's eyes lock with mine before she hisses. My hand flies back, and I screech, "Why doesn't she like me?"

Gabriel laughs. "Well, when you first arrived here did you like anyone?"

He's got a point—sort of. "No, but I'm not a cat."

"Give her some time. We're scary people. She'll cozy up to you soon. Just like I did." Gabriel winks before pressing his lips to my forehead in a chaste kiss.

"Thanks, babe. I'll be down in a few."

He looks good with a cat in his arms. Makes me wonder how he'd look with a baby.

No, Iris. Don't you dare go there! The last thing any of us needs is a baby—not in this sort of environment.

Gabriel leaves, and I walk back over to my vanity, running my brush through my hair a few times. It's our first morning together, and it should be interesting. Hopefully, there isn't too much awkward silence between the guys and Quentin.

Speaking of, I should probably check on him and see how he's doing. I mean, the guy just lost his father, and even if he wasn't too fond of him, that shit will likely still haunt him for years to come.

I set my brush down and slide on a black cardigan sweater over my white V-neck.

I can hear Gabriel's voice down the hall, and it sounds like he's on the phone. Appears to be business as usual, and it's music to my ears.

As I draw closer to the sound of his voice, I realize he's not on the phone—he's talking to someone. I stop, with my back pressed to the hallway wall, and listen, being the nosey little shit that I am.

"I just want you to know that I'd never purposely allow you to put yourself in danger. If I'd known—"

"Stop. Don't carry any guilt over this. It was my fault. Had to learn for myself, and, of course, I was a dumbass, once again."

It's Baron and Gabriel. And I know I shouldn't be

eavesdropping like this, but I can't help it. After two damn years in this house, this is the first heart-to-heart conversation I've heard them have.

"You're good at what you do," Baron says. "I don't doubt your skills, and believe it or not, Dad doesn't either."

He called him Dad. Not Silas. Oh my heart.

It's always up in the air with these guys and Silas. Sometimes they call him Silas, when they're trying to act tough or if they're mad. When they have warm moments such as this, they call him Dad, and I absolutely love it.

"Thanks, man. Same goes for you."

My guys might not be perfect, but they are perfect for me. I'm not sure I could love them any more than I already do.

Baron and Gabriel leave the hall, so I backtrack toward Quentin's room. The door is ajar, so I poke my head inside.

"Quentin?"

His room is empty. Biting the inside of my cheek, still smiling from the moment I just witnessed between Gabriel and Baron, I sit down on the bed and wait for him to come back.

God, is this really happening? Am I bringing *another* man into the mix? Am I ready for this? Three is a lot to handle as it is, but I guess if Gabriel can bring in a stray cat, I can bring home another boyfriend.

A minute later, Quentin steps into the room, wearing just a towel around his waist. The sight in front of me does strange things to my insides. God, he's so sexy.

As he shuffles around in his bag on the floor, he clearly doesn't notice I'm sitting in his room. So, I just watch him. Leaning back, I sink my elbows into the mattress, legs crossed in front of me. The corner of my lip tugs up when he begins getting annoyed, tossing clothes over his shoulder.

Finally, he stops, and it seems all he was in search of was a black polo shirt.

"Good choice," I say, catching him off guard.

He spins around, wide-eyed, surprised to see me. I chuckle at his obliviousness. "Iris. Hey. I didn't even know you were here."

"Ya know," I stand and close the space between us, "there are hundreds of men out there who want nothing more than to see you dead before you claim your father's former title. You should be more careful." My fingers rim the towel at his waist and in one fell swoop, I loosen it and watch it fall to the floor.

"Is that so?" he says, examining my body as if he's reading what's beneath my clothes. "Well, it's a good thing no one knows I'm here. It'd be a shame to die when I just found you." Warm, water-logged fingers sweep my hair off my shoulder as we gaze into each other's eyes.

I look down, noticing his cock is greeting me with excitement. "That would be a shame."

Trailing his fingers down the V of my shirt, he watches his own movements. My nipples pucker against the fabric as my body fills with a greedy need to make the men wait for breakfast.

I know they won't start eating without me, but the selfish whore inside of me says a few minutes won't starve any of us.

My hand wraps around Quentin's girthy, long cock, and he flinches as if he wasn't expecting it. It has me wondering if he's reserved in the bedroom. This is our first time alone like this together, so I have no idea what to expect from him.

Regardless, the sexual tension between us is undeniable. Quentin and I connect on so many different levels and I'm anxious to explore this relationship further. We fooled around with Gabriel in our presence, and it was hot as hell, but right now, it's just us.

I keep stroking his cock, without a word said between us.

Quentin pinches my chin with his thumb and forefinger, looking knowingly into my eyes. "Do you see what you do to me? Just being in the same room with you drives me wild."

If he only knew what he's doing to me right now. I swear my thighs are sticking together from the dampness pooling in my panties.

As if he read my mind, Quentin shoves his hands down my leggings and wastes no time cupping my crotch and shoving his fingers inside of me.

Our mouths collide in an inviting kiss. My hand rests on the back of his head, the wetness of his hair seeping into my skin.

My heart pounds in my chest and we walk backward, our lips never parting.

Once my legs hit the bed frame, it's like a new man has grabbed hold of me. His hands grip my waist as he spins me around and pushes me down on the bed onto my stomach. My lungs deflate and before I know it, Quentin is jerking my leggings off, taking my soaked panties with them.

He settles his weight on my back, kissing his way down my spine. As his face reaches my ass, he takes a bite of one cheek, making me squeal.

"Better keep quiet, sweetheart. Don't want one of your boyfriends hearing you scream."

With a quick lift of my hips, he plants my knees down on the mattress, and my eyes widen as his tongue sweeps across my sex, up to the tight ring of muscle.

Holy shit, Quentin.

I bury my face in his pillow and let out a muffled cry of pleasure as he laps his tongue down the center again, and my body is bathed in warmth and pleasure. His heady groan is so fucking sexy, and it turns out that the funny, nerdy guy I fell for in Tijuana is actually a dirty little freak.

And with what he's doing to me right now, I love him for it.

"God, that feels so good," I moan loudly into the pillow, thrusting my hips back into his face.

"I can't wait to fuck you here, but not today, baby."

His hand sweeps up my thighs, separating them, and I can feel the head of his cock sliding between my legs. "Because I've been wanting this pussy since the second I laid eyes on you. It's my turn now, baby." His voice is gruff and filled with a confidence that I find sexy as hell.

I'm seeing a different side to Quentin, and it has me in agony.

My fingers clench the satin sheets, back arching, hoping he does something soon because I need him like I need air.

"Take it. Take all of me." My words are nothing but a desperate plea.

"Oh, I will." His palm slaps my ass and I flinch at the beautiful pain. "Tell me you're mine now."

"I'm yours," I whimper through a heady breath.

I am his. I am theirs. I belong to all of them.

Right now, though, I just want Quentin. I want this unification. I want him to fuck me like he owns me and no one else does—just like my other guys do.

"Damn straight you are."

My entire body jolts when Quentin shoves his cock inside me. He fills me completely, stretching me and moving rapidly. Our moans of pleasure mingle together as they echo between these four walls.

"Yes!" I cry out, gripping the sheets tighter, bridging my back and relishing in the heat flowing through me.

"Your pussy feels so good around my dick."

If I were questioning his reservations in the bedroom before, I certainly *am not now*. Quentin is taking full control. In doing so, he has me on the brink of explosion.

One hand comes around my side—while the other cinches my hip—reaching down as he begins rubbing my clit erratically. It's like nothing I've ever felt before. I've had it rough, I've had it hard, and I've had mind-blowing orgasms, but something about the way he's touching me while filling me up with his dick has my whole body sweltering from the inside out.

"Quentin," I cry out, "holy shit." I'm full-on panting, rocking my hips to his movements, meeting his dick thrust for thrust while making sure those magical fingers keep massaging my clit.

With my breath held, I clench my walls around him and release with a drawn-out exhale.

The next thing I know, Quentin is pulling his dick out of me.

I glance over my shoulder to see his glossed-over eyes looking back at me, mouth agape as he comes all over his own hand, massaging it all over so that his fist is coated.

"What are you—"

"Shh," he presses, before shoving his cum filled fingers in my pussy—all of them at once.

My head turns before dropping down onto the mattress. "Oh my—"

There's a twinge of pain, but as it subsides, it's replaced

by rapture. Quentin goes knuckle deep, stuffing me so full with half his hand.

"That hurt, baby?"

I shake my head no, out of fear that if I tell him it hurts a little, he'll stop. I do not want him to stop. In fact, I want more.

All his fingers hit my back wall, curling, poking and sending a rush of electricity through every nerve ending in my body.

For a moment, my eyes roll into the back of my head.

I gasp, mouth open and breaths labored. "Holy shit. Oh my God."

His entire fist is inside me.

It's a first for me, but with the way my body is reacting to him, essentially punching my vagina, I want more.

With his fist still inside me, I'm flipped over onto my back, his hand turning like a key in a hole. He stands there watching his hand slide in and out with lust in his eyes. His chest rises and falls as rapidly as mine does.

When the pads of his fingers on his free hand begin rubbing violent circles at my clit, I lose all control.

"I'm coming," I cry out, feeling my pussy squeeze his hand that's still plunging inside me.

My arousal squirts out, hitting my stomach, his arm and the sheets beneath me. Quentin doesn't stop pulsing his fingers against my clit, sending me to a new high that I never want to come down from.

I watch his eyes while he stares back at me, drinking up every moan I make, knowing he did this to me. God, he did this. He made me feel so fucking good and showed me a side of him that I didn't know existed.

When I come down, Quentin slowly slides his hand

out, still watching me as he licks each of his fingers one by one.

Who would have guessed that my nerdy boyfriend had such a freaky side?

Quentin smirks, leaning over me and pressing his lips to mine. I can taste myself on him, bitter, yet sweet. "How do you feel?" he asks through breaths of kisses on my lips.

"Umm," I clear my throat, searching for the words, "alleviated." I can't help the giggle that slips out.

Smiling against our melded lips, he says, "Good," before dropping down beside me.

"I didn't scare you, did I?"

I love that he's comfortable to be as crazy and dirty as he wants with me.

"Not at all," I reply. "Well...maybe a little, but in a good way."

The bed is a mess, sheets are stained with cum, but we just lie there silently taking in this moment.

Quentin pushes his arm under my head and curls me against his chest. "I'm glad I came here." His lips press to my forehead.

I push myself up on my elbow so that I can see his face. "Me, too. I wish you'd stay for good."

He shrugs a shoulder. "I'm not sure I could ever leave you, Iris. I'd be a fool to walk away from this."

A smile tugs at the corner of my lips. "Then it's settled. You're staying."

Grabbing me by the waist, he pulls me on top of him, squeezing my body against his. "Not even an army of three assassins could force me away."

We both laugh, and I love this moment between us. It's real, it's raw, and it's so us.

Quentin is going to bring so much life to this family—

to me. His quick-witted personality and quirky ways are exactly what we didn't know we needed.

"Good, because I don't think I'd ever let you go. Especially since I'm falling for you."

He draws back, looking me in the eyes. "I'm falling for you, too. You were so unexpected, Iris Black, but it's the unexpected that changes our lives."

I kiss him again, and again, before a pounding on the door separates us.

"Are you two about done in there? We'd like to eat our damn breakfast."

Oh no! Breakfast! I completely forgot they were waiting on me.

"Coming," I holler over my shoulder before busting out laughing again.

This is going to take everyone some getting used to, but we always seem to settle into new routines pretty easily. This time will be no different.

Forty-Four

Iris

"Your cat still hates me!" I yell at Gabriel as I barge in on him in the garage, holding out the freshly bleeding scratch on my forearm.

"I'm working, Princess," he mumbles, holding a knife between his teeth as he proceeds to torture the current victim in his chair. The man is howling through whatever is gagging him at the moment.

"Well, I'm bleeding again, and she attacked me for no reason!"

Finally, he looks up and sees the drops of blood hitting the epoxy floor. "Babe…" he replies, driving the blade into the man's thigh. "Hold this for me."

Then he walks over to inspect my fresh cat scratch. Holding my arm in his hand, he licks across the wound with a sympathetic look on his face. "I'm sorry."

"I'm going to kill that fucking cat."

"She's just jealous. She doesn't like to share me," he

replies, taking me to the counter, where he pulls out some gauze and a bottle of peroxide from the cabinet. The screaming man has passed out, so at least it's quiet.

"That's why you two love each other so much," I reply, hissing as he pours peroxide over the scratch. "Two stubborn assholes."

He laughs.

"How much longer until you're done?" I ask, nodding to the man in the chair. "It's Friday. I was promised a movie and pizza tonight."

I don't miss the subtle roll of his eyes. Ever since we came home from Mexico three months ago, I have insisted that we spend at least one night a week together *as a family*. Before everything went down in Tijuana, I lived with three boyfriends who barely lived together, and that's what drove us apart in the first place. I recognize my place as the glue in this family, but I can't possibly hold all of that responsibility on my own. Those three, I mean four, need to learn to get along and be a family, even without me in the picture.

"Yeah, I'll have the guys clean up this mess in a little bit."

"You got what you needed?"

"Yep. With all of these new toys I've inherited from the compound, my job has gotten so much easier." He has a wicked grin on his face, and I decide I don't really want to see what he's got going on over there, so I'll leave him to his dirty work.

"Well, don't be late. It's my turn to pick the movie."

"I won't." He pulls me in for a quick kiss. "Please don't kill my cat."

"No promises."

Just as I head out of the garage, I hear the man in the

chair wake up. "Good morning, Mr. Yarros," Gabriel chimes with a sinister smile as the door closes behind me.

Upstairs, Silas is still working away in his office, and I peek my head in to point at my wrist where a watch would be. He's on the phone, so he quickly nods at me and sends me a wink. I blow him a kiss before closing the door.

There are voices in the kitchen where I find Baron and Quentin arguing, as these two often do.

"You're fucking high," Quentin barks, holding his hands up.

"I'm not the delusional asshole who can't see how fucking obvious this is," Baron replies in a cooler, more irritable tone.

"What the hell are you two arguing about?" I ask.

"Iris, tell him there's no way his Lambo could beat my Bugatti in a street race," Quentin replies, sliding his hand across my waist and pulling me into his side.

"You wanna test this right now?" Baron challenges him. "Let's go."

I quickly put a hand up. "No one is racing anything."

Footsteps carry from the office as Silas walks right into the conversation. "My car could smoke both of yours," he says nonchalantly, leaning down to kiss the top of my head and muttering a near silent, "Hi, baby."

Baron and Quentin both erupt in protests as I glare up at Silas. "Don't encourage this."

He grins and shrugs his shoulders before pressing the button on the espresso machine, letting it buzz to life.

"You guys are ridiculous, arguing about whose car is faster. You might as well be fighting over whose dick is bigger."

The room falls silent as they all look my way. With a laugh, I march right out of the room, leaving them waiting for that answer, though I would never tell them that. It's not like I've measured or would even compare, but it's fun to watch them squirm.

An hour later, we're in the living room. Gabriel and I share one side of the couch, him in a pair of gray sweatpants and me in one of his T-shirts that I wear as a nightgown. Baron takes the other end and Quentin reclines on the floor with a large pillow. Silas is the last to arrive, and he takes his leather chair in the corner.

"All right, Green Eyes," Quentin asks, scrolling through movies on the screen. "It's your pick tonight. What's it going to be?"

"Hmmm..." I say, looking through the options. I don't even bother trying to please all of them. They all pick something different on their nights. Silas always picks a Bond film. Baron likes *John Wick* and mobster movies. Quentin goes for the super hero flicks, and Gabriel makes me sit through super gory horror movies. I've suffered enough, which means they can sit through...

"The vampire movie!" I yell, and they all groan in unison. Not just any vampire movie, a campy high school b-rated vampire movie.

Are they going to sit through it for me? Yes.

Will they hate every minute? Yep.

"I need liquor for this," Silas complains, getting out of his chair and heading to the kitchen.

"You better bring enough for everyone," Quentin calls. A minute later, Silas passes out cold beers to everyone just as the movie starts. And they sit through most of it without a word. I kick Baron for scrolling through his phone, and have to stop Gabriel when he tries to sneak into my pants.

But just before the movie ends, I look around at them and wonder how the fuck I ended up here. A girl is lucky enough to have one loving boyfriend, who would die for her, and I got four. Do I even deserve this? Probably not, but I don't fucking care. If anyone tried to take any of these guys away, I would fight like hell for them. I would gladly murder for them, so I guess in that way, I do deserve them all.

"Please don't make us sit through that again," Baron whines as the credits start rolling.

"It wasn't that bad," Quentin says from the floor, and I smile at him.

"Too bad she has to choose between the werewolf and the vampire. Doesn't the dumb bitch realize she can just have them both?" I laugh as I climb off the seat to take the popcorn bowls and empty beer bottles that have been collecting all over the living room to the kitchen. When I get back, the guys are all sitting there, staring at me.

"Well, wait a minute..." Gabriel says, leaning forward. "What if we made you choose right now?"

"Gabriel!" I yell. "That's not funny."

Quentin, still lying on the floor, tackles me by the back of the legs and pulls me down to straddle his chest. "Pretty obvious, I think. The novelty of you old fuckers has worn off. She'd obviously want the new guy." He pulls me down for a kiss, and I can't help but smile. Maybe it's the beer or maybe because of just how happy I am, but I let him kiss the grin right off my face.

He drives his quickly thickening cock against me, and I let out a groan, knowing the guys are watching.

"Fuck that," Baron says, tearing me off Quentin and dragging me into his arms. "I know exactly who she'd choose." He digs his hand into my hair and kisses me hard, taking a bite of my lower lip as he does. I let out a helpless whimper, feeling like melting wax in his hands.

Then, there's another hand on the back of my neck and I'm pulled away from Baron's kiss and into another familiar pair of lips. My tongue glides against Gabriel's lip piercing as he tangles his tongue with mine. I'm still on Baron's lap as Gabriel's mouth devours me, and I know this situation is escalating quickly.

And if someone doesn't stop it soon, this family night could turn into a much different type of family night.

"Iris," a deep voice commands from across the room, and I pull away from the kiss, feeling hazy as my head swims with lust. Looking over at Silas, he gently pats his lap. "Come here."

Without hesitation, I slip to the floor and crawl over to the man in the leather chair. Climbing into his lap, I bite my lip, giving him a coy smile. For a second, I think he's putting an end to this little game, but then he pulls my face closer and presses his lips to my ear.

"Be a good girl, and show these boys who you really belong to."

When I pull back, I look into his eyes, searching for confirmation that he's saying what I think he's saying. With a shift of his hips, he grinds my ass against his erection, and the signal is crystal fucking clear.

Is this really happening? Excitement and anticipation swim down my spine, accumulating in my lower belly.

"Yes, Daddy," I whisper as I lower to the floor on my knees in front of him. His eyes are on me as I pull down the zipper of his pants, eager to feel his warm, hard cock in my hands. As soon as I touch it, he groans, letting his eyes close. When I reach my tongue out, licking him from the base to the head, he opens his eyes and watches me, gathering up my hair in one hand and guiding my open mouth to swallow him down.

"Good girl," he murmurs as I lower my lips as far down as I can, gagging as the tip reaches the back of my throat. But God, I love the sounds he makes as I do. "Fuck, yes," he groans.

I don't stop, bobbing up and down on his wet shaft, keeping my gaze locked with his.

From behind me, I hear, "Well, that's not fucking fair." And I'm not quite sure which one of them it was, but Silas continues to pet my head as I suck his cock, feeling the head swell and tighten against my tongue.

"Iris doesn't want to choose, do you, baby girl?"

I shake my head.

"She likes being fucked by all of us. One man just isn't enough for you, is it?"

Again, I shake my head.

"You're a filthy little whore, aren't you?" he says almost sweetly, grasping my hair tighter, and I almost tense at his words. Silas would never be so cruel to me. But as he pulls my head away from his cock, he smiles lovingly at me. "But you're our filthy little whore, Iris Black."

"Yes," I yelp as he attacks my mouth with his. We are lost in a feverish kiss, our mouths fighting for each other's, biting, gnashing and licking. Arousal swims through my body. I don't think Silas's words have ever affected me so much, but the way he talks to me turns me on like flipping a switch. I would gladly be Silas Black's filthy little whore for the rest of my life.

I feel warm hands lifting my oversized shirt and soft lips peppering my lower back. I let out a hum, thrusting my hips backward, not even knowing who it is that's touching me.

But a second after my panties are pulled down, I feel his tongue dance hungrily across my back entrance. *Hello, Quentin.* While he licks at my ass, he plunges his fingers in my cunt, collecting my arousal and slicking up the tight ring of muscle.

My face is guided back to Silas's cock, and I suck eagerly, lost in this whirlwind of need and hunger. I'm too focused on his pleasure to notice what Quentin is doing, only knowing that everything just feels like heaven right now.

"Oh, Iris," Silas groans. "God, you're so good, baby. I'm gonna come down that pretty throat of yours."

A second later, the salty warm jets hit the back of my tongue and I quickly swallow, taking all of him in. It makes me feel like I own him, like I've claimed this man and he's claimed me.

When I finally pull my mouth off of his cock, he strokes my chin and smiles down at me. I rest my face against his thigh as he pets my head, making me feel downright euphoric. My eyes are locked with Silas's as Quentin slowly works his cock in, but he's not plunging into my pussy as I expected him to. As he presses his slick shaft into my ass, I let out a gasp, clutching onto Silas through the sting.

"Oh my God!"

"You can take it," Silas whispers, stroking my head.

My body is on fire, scared and yet eager for more. Quentin inches in the head of his cock, and I feel myself opening for him. It's a mix of pain and pleasure. I'm so desperate for someone to touch my clit, that I finally reach down and circle the sensitive nub myself. Crying out from the sensation, I lean back into Quentin's slow thrusts.

"I told you I was gonna fuck you here," he grunts as he

slides all the way in. "You should see how beautiful this is. You're doing so good, Green Eyes."

My moans are so loud, they vibrate through my body. The way he fills me up feels so wrong and so right at the same time. Intense and terrifying.

"The other boys are waiting," Silas mutters into my ear, and I look back and see Gabriel and Baron on the couch, like Silas said, eagerly waiting for my attention. Gabriel already has his cock out, stroking slowly with hooded eyes and dilated pupils. The look on his face says he's about one second away from fucking me senseless, and I wish he would.

With Quentin behind me, still working me slowly, I rotate, shifting toward Gabriel. He drops to his knees in front of me, and I waste no time wrapping my lips around his swollen cock. And he's not gentle either, thrusting his hips forward and shoving himself down my throat.

"Oh, Princess," he growls. His hands are on my head as he fucks my mouth, so I reach my other hand out, grasping for Baron.

When he finally kneels next to his brother, I hear the rustle of his belt, and a second later, I have his cock in my hand, stroking his hard length.

My body feels tightly wound, ready to explode. The sensation of Quentin driving slowly into my tight ass is only making my need more intense. If someone doesn't fuck me soon, I might scream.

Both Baron and Gabriel stroke my head, giving me all of their attention, all four of them murmuring words of praise as they use my body relentlessly, taking me to new heights of pleasure.

I pop off of Gabriel's cock and bring Baron to my lips next, letting them both take turns with my mouth. It's a filthy sound in this dim living room with all of us moaning and our bodies slapping together.

"Look at you, Iris," Baron says with his cock down my throat. "Taking all of us at the same time."

"I think she needs someone in that pretty pussy," Gabriel replies, and I answer him with a desperate look and a nod of my head.

"Stand up, Q," Baron commands. And suddenly, I'm weightless, still impaled on his cock as Quentin stands up, holding me tight to his body. And Gabriel is there, letting me wrap my legs around his waist as the two men hold me sandwiched between them.

When Gabriel slides his cock in, I let out a scream. The pressure is intense and just what I needed. I clutch tightly to his neck as they pick up speed, all of us panting in a frenzy, chasing our orgasms together. Quentin's lips are on the back of my neck, whispering to me as he fucks my ass.

"I'll never leave you, Iris. I swear to God, I'll never leave you as long as I'm alive."

Using one hand, I reach back and dig my nails into his arm letting him know I feel him. I'm with him.

Gabriel is kissing my mouth, his lips peppering mine and trailing down to my earlobe and neck.

I feel so close to both of them, as if they make up my whole world and my body only sings for them. When it feels as if I can't take another second, I let out another wailing cry, and I come so hard I see stars, my body trembling and shaking through the climax. I'm only hazily aware of Gabriel and Quentin coming too because the next thing I know, I feel warm cum dripping down my thighs as I'm lowered into Baron's lap.

Clutching my arms around his neck, I stare into his eyes

as I lower myself on his cock. I ride him hard and fast, kissing him hungrily as his fingers dig into my hips.

"You're all ours, Iris. You know that, right?"

"Yes," I gasp.

"I would kill anyone who tried to hurt you. You belong to us forever now."

"I love you," I cry out as my body explodes in pleasure again. When my legs tense, Baron takes over, driving his hips upward rapidly, pounding into me as he lets out a roar of his own.

Then, I barely have a chance to recover as I'm pulled from his body again and forced onto all fours as someone drives into me from behind.

"We're going to fill you up so much, you'll be leaking cum for days, Iris."

"Silas!" I shriek as he pounds into me.

"You want that, don't you, baby?"

"Yes," I cry out. "Just don't stop."

He holds me by the neck, pulling me up until his mouth is next to my ear as he growls, "Never."

At some point, I lose track of where I end and they begin. After Silas comes, Gabriel pins me to the floor and whispers delicately how much he loves me as he kisses every inch of my body while I stroke Quentin until he's unloading on my chest. Then, Baron is there, Silas again, and soon, I know them only by their touch, their mouths, and their dicks. Their pleasure becomes mine as I'm passed around, fucked until I'm so sore and exhausted, that I collapse onto the carpet of the living room, all of their hands on me at the same time.

We are a sweaty, cum-covered mess, all of us catching our breaths and happy. There's not an ounce of shame in the room, and while I'm sure a lot of people would judge us for this, we don't care. This is who we are. A fucked-up family of killers. And while Silas called me his dirty whore, at least here, I'm not judged for how much I like to be treated like this. There isn't a safer place on this earth for me or anyone else who could possibly love me as much as they do.

Before I drift off to sleep, someone lays a blanket over my naked body and I use someone else's warm, soft arms as a pillow. It's the most content and relaxed I've ever been in my entire life. My body is sated, and while I'm sure I'm going to need at least a week off from sex to recover, I'm already dreaming about our next family night and how I can talk my guys into doing this again.

Epilogue

Quentin

One year later

"You're not supposed to be working..." Soft hands wrap around my waist from behind.

"I know, I know. I'm sorry." I snap my laptop closed and push it away.

"Everything okay?"

"Yeah. Just checking the cameras again." I spin her around, putting her in my arms. My fingers immediately start fiddling with the knot of her bikini.

"The cameras are fine. They always are," she reminds me.

Ever since I passed on the position as head of the Mandola Cartel, Iris has been my biggest supporter. That wasn't an easy decision to make. Well, deciding to stay with her was easy as fuck. But walking away from the life I lived in Mexico, the system I built there, and the power I was accumulating, that wasn't hard.

Waking up to this face nearly every day makes it all worth it.

Finally, I get the knot undone, and the fabric covering her breasts falls away easily.

Scooping her up by the backs of her thighs, I wrap her legs around my waist and carry her to the bed.

"Thanks for the vote of confidence, Green Eyes," I mumble, dropping her onto the mattress and covering her body with mine.

"I'm serious, Quentin. Do you think we could even be on this vacation if you hadn't set up the company with the best security on the planet?"

I smile up at her, trailing my lips down her body, stopping at her perfectly round tits to circle my tongue around her nipple.

She hums in response, digging her fingers in my hair.

"I mean, do you even know how hard it was to convince Silas that he *needed* a vacation. He would never have agreed to this without you."

"Keep talking," I reply, kissing my way down her sun-kissed belly.

When my lips reach her belly button, she wraps her legs around my ears.

"You found this private beach and this beautiful property," she says with a sigh, as I pull her bikini bottoms down. Burying my face between her legs, I take my time savoring her pleasure on my tongue.

"Tell me again how much you like having me around." I hum against her beautiful cunt.

She grinds herself against my face, moaning and writhing on the bed. I guess that's a good enough answer. After she climaxes in my mouth, I don't stop.

"Quentin, come on. We're on vacation. We can't spend it all in our room."

"I don't know what you're talking about. This is paradise right here," I reply.

She laughs, pulling me up until my face is inches from hers. She kisses her own taste right off my lips and I let my weight settle on her frame.

When her fingers drift down my bare chest, they pause over the black anatomical heart tattoo on my chest, the one matching hers—and theirs.

"You know I'm more than just glad you're here," she whispers softly, looking at the black ink. "You're a Black now, Quentin. You make us whole."

When I find her lips this time, I kiss her softly, trying to absorb those words and everything they mean to me, to be a part of a family that actually cares about me. To have a father that puts us first. To stand next to my brothers who would take a bullet for me the same way I would take one for them. And to be able to live out the rest of my days with the love of my life.

I thought being in this type of relationship would be weird as fuck, and I'll admit, at first, I held on to hope that I could someday make Iris just mine, but as the past year has gone by, I realize that it's so much more than that. I'm not sharing her. Our love is not divided—it's multiplied. And in some weird fucking way, watching her with them only makes me want her more.

And considering how much we like having her at the same time, I'd say that feeling is mutual.

"Thanks, Green Eyes," I whisper, kissing her again. "But you know what would really make this family whole..." I tease.

She rolls her eyes. "Not again."

"Oh, come on...you know you want one."

"You know babies cry all the time and grow into toddlers and then bratty little kids, right?"

"Yes, but not our baby. Our baby would be the cutest baby ever," I argue, unable to keep the grin off my face. I've been pushing the issue for the past few months now, and I think I even got Gabe and Baron on my side. I mean, Baron won't admit it, but I see the way he's stopped arguing against it lately.

"We're literally killers, Quentin."

"Imagine our cool-ass killer baby."

She pushes me off of her and I can tell by the way she's biting back her smile that she doesn't want me to see how much she's starting to like the idea. As she climbs off the bed, I pull her back, holding her between my open legs. Imagining her with a swollen belly just does shit to me.

"How would that even work?" she argues. "You all just pump me full and we don't bother to question which little sperm made it to the egg?"

"Yep."

Her head tilts as she glares at me with a suspicious look on her face. Maybe it's because I grew up in a family obsessed with legacies and bloodline, but I've always wanted to have kids of my own, and by the look on her face right now, I'm actually starting to think I could get what I want.

Finally, with a heavy sigh, she holds up a hand. "Maybe," she says boldly. A wide grin spreads across my cheeks. "Maybe...if you can set up our house like Fort fucking Knox, Quentin. It would have to be the safest place in the world for me to even consider this."

"Yes, done. I'll do it."

"And everyone—*everyone*," she enunciates, "would have to be on board."

"Convince Silas. Got it."

She laughs, and I pull her face to mine to plant a kiss on her lips. As she wraps her arms around my neck, I pull her into my arms.

"I love you," she whispers against my lips.

"I love you, too."

After our kiss, she pulls me toward the door. "Now, come on. We didn't rent this place for nothing."

"You're just going to walk out there naked?" I ask, following her out to the patio area where the other guys are waiting. They glance up at us from their phones. Well, Baron and Silas are on their phones. Gabriel is carving boobs into a coconut with his knife.

"What's the point of a private beach if you can't have sex on it?" Iris says as she waltzes right past them and down the sand toward the water.

"You're asking for trouble, Princess," Gabriel calls as he jumps up from his chair and chases her into the crystal blue water.

"I think I finally convinced her," I announce. Gabriel pumps his fist in the air, tackling her against the gentle waves. Baron tries to hide his smile, but I still catch the subtle smirk. Silas lets out a heavy sigh and rolls his eyes.

I'll take it one day at a time. For now, it's enough. I'm doing the job I love and living the life I didn't even know I needed. I couldn't be fucking happier than I am now. My life is complete... Well, almost.

Acknowledgments

Thanks for coming along with us on this ride back to the Black family. When we decided to revisit Iris and the boys we didn't quite know where their story would lead, but as always, it was a blast and we hope you had as much fun reading it as we had writing it. As always, we couldn't have done this without our amazing team.

A big thanks goes out to...

Editor: Rebecca's Fairest Reviews

Proofreader: Rumi Khan

Amanda Anderson with Wildfire Marketing Solutions

Our PAs, Lori Alexander and Carolina Leon

Amanda Kay Anderson, our beautiful beta reader

Our graphics designer, Claudia Lymari

Cover Designer: Cassie Chapman of Opulent Swag & Designs

The readers and members of Rachel's Ramblers and Sara's Sweets

Our amazing ARC and Street teams

All the wonderful bloggers who have supported and shared for us. We couldn't do this without you.

And last but certainly not least...

The Shameless sisters to whom this book is dedicated: Katie, Gail, Ashton, Lori, and Amanda. We can't wait for -3. It's going to be amazing. Shucky darn!

Love always,

Sara & Rachel

Also by Rachel Leigh

Standalones

Guarded

Devil Heir

Claim your FREE copy of Whiskey Lies

Find me on Facebook

@rachelleighauthor

Reader's Group: Rachel's Ramblers

Or visit

www.rachelleighauthor.com

About Rachel Leigh

Rachel Leigh writes Contemporary and New Adult Romance with twists and turns, suspense and steam. She resides in West Michigan with her husband, three kids, and a couple fur babies.

Rachel lives in leggings, overuses emojis, and survives on books and coffee. Writing is her passion. Her goal is to take readers on an adventure with her words, while showing them that even on the darkest days, love conquers all.

Bookbub bookbub.com/profile/rachel-leigh
 Readers Group http://bit.ly/rl_ramblers
 Goodreads goodreads.com/rachelleigh
 Instagram instagram.com/rachelleighauthor
 Facebook facebook.com/rachelleighauthor
 Amazon amazon.com/author/rachelleighauthor
 Newsletter https://bit.ly/rl_news
 TikTok http://bit.ly/rl_tiktok

About Sara Cate

Sara Cate writes forbidden romance with lots of angst, a little age gap, and heaps of steam. Living in Arizona with her husband and kids, Sara spends most of her time reading, writing, or baking.

You can find more information about her at
www.saracatebooks.com

Printed in Great Britain
by Amazon

20218221R00196